A Murmuration of Humans

T.L. Hulsey

STAGIRITE  PRESS

Published by Stagirite Press, Fort Worth, Texas, United States.

ISBN-10: 1-883853-05-2
ISBN-13: 978-1-883853-05-1

Murmuration: The ability to maintain cohesion as a group in highly uncertain environments and with limited, noisy information.

George F. Young

Muhammad Nigredo

1

"Man, tell me about it," Lagarius mused aloud to himself as he watched the lizard on the rail.

Carmine Lagarius had just spoken to the lizard panting in terror on the patio rail before him. Beyond the low hummocks with their beach grass and picket and wire fences stretched the blazing blue and gold of Virginia Beach.

The small bright green lizard raced across the top of the iron rail toward him. Lagarius watched it stop and do five girl's pushups - forward limbs only - and when it raised on the last one, an orange goitrous flange flashed beneath its chin. It repeated the movements as it approached him: Racing, stopping, pushing up, flashing the orange semaphore. Lagarius smiled, leaned forward, and the terrified lizard leapt to a vertical rail, its tiny rib cage palpitating. It cocked its head, evaluating the danger.

"Don't worry, my little limbic friend," Lagarius said aloud.

He admired the creature's green skin, knobbly like a football, and he exchanged glances with its intelligent eyes. He imagined the animal at the base of his own brain, its tiny fearful heart pounding deep inside his own head, a live packet of chemically driven logic.

Lagarius looked down the sand-dusted decking to the corner where the sun would eventually sweep out black shadows. At that corner were a few panels shielding part of the outdoor shower, although any viewers in the highest floors of the hotels much farther south would need a telescope to see even the jalousies of the upper floor of this house, snug in the dunes. Although this October had been unseasonably hot, the shade that would come in the next few hours would make it cool, especially when the land breeze came in.

Lagarius stretched his big frame back almost flat in the canvas chair, letting the sun warm his bare skin, covered by swim trunks and, now, by the rolled-up towel that he placed across his eyes. He looked at the red curtain of his closed eyelids and the motes that seemed to dance there when he moved his eyes. There was much for him to consider. He had already set the pieces in motion - there was no going back - but as always he must consider what he thought of as Plan Z: The moves that must be taken if all the wheels fell off, the moves that might save him from prison, or worse. But he did not think of that now. He meditated on the sun warming the tops of his feet, his legs, his torso and face. Emptying his mind, he meditated on the faint chopping and the occasional sound of water running in the kitchen, where Ana was preparing supper. The thought of her eventual presence out-doors made him smile. The Lebanese princess would likely be naked, as she most certainly had been when he last saw her inside working.

A quarter hour later the glass door opened, breaking the bubble of his thoughts, breathing a wave of air conditioning across him that carried a touch of her fruity Nectar des Îles perfume. The door closed. She must have been standing there, arms akimbo, wondering whether he was sleeping. Lagarius refused to move, but he smiled.

"Ah ha," Ana said softly, as if to acknowledge assent in the wordless game. She walked, her feet sifting along the sandy decking, her hands osten-tatiously slapping her naked thighs and buttocks. Lagarius heard the creak of the rail where she must be leaning now, looking out to sea. Then she must have straightened up.

"Fauk theam," she said in a self-conscious foreign lilt, still looking out to sea. Hearing the words from her lovely plump lips seemed to Lagarius that he was hearing them for the first time, at the beginning of creation. Yes, this was how it must have sounded when god said of the gentiles, Fuck them: The stilted diction, the self-conscious emphasis. He kept his eyes closed in mellow ataraxis, as if he had just drained his first negroni, slightly aroused, floating in the thoughtless Nirvana of musing on her mouth, her eyes, on the subcutaneous jiggle of her hard, deeply-cleft, perfect rump with the corkscrewed tail of a dragon inked on her sacrum.

She turned, bounded back to Lagarius, snatched the towel from his eyes, and stepped back.

The vision that was Ana stood before him, dividing the blue sky with her firm, tanned figure. She had heavy brows, a prominent nose, and square chin. With her hands on her hips, the firm perfect hemispheres of her breasts pointed up and away with the nipples at ten and two o'clock. Below the muscled belly and its deep navel, below the bikini line, on her delta was the tattoo of an authentic Chinese dragon, head down, with flaming scales and bulging eyes, its head tilted so that its snarling mouth opened vertically with her shaved mound of Venus.

"You don't even know if you saving anybody!" she said, her dark eyes flashing. "You hack into the gold mine, now it's time to run away. So what if you find out something - that's their problem. What you gonna say? '*Pardon*, monsieur officer, I steal millions, but don't send me to jail because I also find out *une attaque terroriste* for you!' And what if *patron* Nigredo find out? He think you go to police to turn on him, Larry. *Ya habibi*, he fucking kill you."

Lagarius was of course familiar with Ana's use of "Larry" when she was mad, and with "*habibi*," implying lovingly mad.

"I've taken steps to protect us," he said simply. He put his hands behind his head.

"Yeah, you the coolest cucumber, *n'est-ce pas?* You the *compartiment* maestro – left hand and right hand don't know each other." She gave a deep sigh.

She straddled his pelvis as he lay stretched on the lounge chair. She began to rock back and forth slowly, with each approach to his face softly slapping her palms on his chest and breathing close to him without kissing, continuing the movement. He could see and feel her breasts growing firmer each time they pressed against him, her perfect skin a dark cream made firm as living flesh. When she came near he could smell the fruity perfume, mixed with sunscreen. He thought he could also smell the salty beads of sweat that were gathering in the little well between her clavicles. He looked into the dark pools of her eyes and tried hard to suppress a smile as he felt his passion awakening.

"So, you want I give 'maximum pleasure'?" she whispered as she came close. Then, raspingly at his ear: "I can party hardly."

Here Lagarius laughed out loud. It was their joke – her recitation of one of her first remarks to him, part of her continuing effort at American vernacular. It was over a year ago, at the opening of the Ricce gallery. After a short conversation she had said the words hurriedly, so he sensed, to keep him from excusing himself and walking away. Her visa was about to expire, and she was looking to latch on to someone who could keep her in America. She had seemed so innocently silly saying "I can party hardly," but simultaneously seemed timorous and almost pleading. Her speaking the words had opened his heart to her. At the same time, he had wondered whether she would have said the same thing to someone else, to someone with "Green Card" written more boldly on his forehead. She had, after all, then married one of his friends only to divorce him after nine months. Did it matter? She was here. She wanted the adventure and danger he offered, and at times he believed that she loved him.

"You gonna see Lucas tomorrow?" she asked. "I think the little faggot want to jump your bone."

Lagarius had to turn his head to keep his plosion of laughter from her face.

"That's 'jump your *bones*,' Ana," he said, hissing the "s."

"What, you got another one I don't know about?"

Laughing, he planted his feet alongside the chair and stood up with her, she wrapping her long powerful legs around his waist and kissing him.

"Let's go for a swim," he said. "Or you can jog. Perfect time for your supper when we get back."

A few moments later she returned from the house wearing bright red
spandex shorts and bra, carrying her sneakers and two big white bathrobes.
She was thinking of the chill that would come after their workout. Lagarius
took the robes. They trudged through the loose sand path between the
palings, then after reaching the packed sand, walked a bit south. They
stopped, and Ana put on her socklets and shoes, leaning on him. There was
no one near. Over a mile away there were a few dots of people on the beach
in front of the hotels. Seeing them, Lagarius had a curious vision. He
imagined them disappearing at random, the victims of the terror attack that
he was convinced was coming.

"Why so serious?" Ana asked. "You gonna swim? Back here in thirty
minutes?"

He nodded, and she pushed up on her toes to give him a quick kiss. He
watched the heart-lifting ripple of her thighs and legs as she jogged away, her
hair swinging in a pony tail.

Lagarius waded into the cold water and without second thoughts dived
into the first low wave. The chill was off him after a few strokes. Though he
was a good swimmer, he did not want to go twenty yards beyond the break
in the surf, so he turned south, stroking slowly, parallel to the shore. Soon
he turned over to backstroke, then relaxed into an occasional whip kick.
The sun was low on his left. He opened his eyes and looked up at the cloudless blue. He began to think.

His hacking into the defense contractor's site had been successful, and
he had gained access to the Promised Land: The files of the contractor's pro-
posal to automate the messaging network used by governments and the
largest banks and financial institutions on the planet. A few years previously,
in an exploit entirely different from the current one, he had been fabulously
successful in redirecting such messages from an Ecuadorian bank so that
twelve million dollars was transferred to secret accounts instead of to the
intended recipients in Hong Kong and Dubai. Although he would not allow
himself to trade on stolen personal information, these current exploits, in
his mind, were quite different, and he felt not the slightest compunction in
taking money from governments and their hangers-on among the big banks.
For him these were the biggest thieves of all, calling money into being out of
thin air, extending credit to the giant casino that Wall Street had become,
spending on their cronies and institutional parasites at every level, down to
the grant-milking artists who studied the sexual behavior of the Japanese
quail and the alcoholic preferences of sun fish. No, he would spend his
share of the money on his Antonio Meccariello bespoke shoes, on his Jaeger-

LeCoultre Memovox watch, his MV Agusta motorcycle and beach house – money not wasted!

This success would have been much more dangerous without the involvement of Muhammad Nigredo, who had supplied the safe banking accounts, the IRS-proof cover clients in Mexico who were supposedly paying him fabulous consulting fees, and all the other resources that amounted to what Lagarius called "insulation." Considering that those services permitted him the enjoyment of his money outside prison, he considered Nigredo's take of fifty percent well worth it.

Now, threatening this wealth, threatening him and Ana, threatening the very dangerous Mr. Nigredo, was the accidental discovery by Lagarius of the files at the defense contractor that had to be revealed – without the revelation of himself as the finder. It would have been easy to accept Ana's rationalization that the evidence was small while the risk was very great, but the evidence was not small. He had decided to follow the principle of compartmentalization so assiduously followed by Nigredo. He had enlisted the services of his friend Lucas Meeth, a fellow student who had come into Stevens Institute of Technology in Hoboken three years after him. Lucas had volunteered to get someone in government or the media interested enough to act on the threatening discovery, although Lagarius did not want his friend implicated as having made the discovery himself. And despite being given the information only a few days earlier, he had apparently delivered. He had indeed gotten journalists interested – "a handful" as he put it – and he and Lagarius were to meet one of them tomorrow in Hoboken.

Lagarius felt a very cold current pass beneath him over his back, and he turned over, looking landward.

Good god! – Well over fifty yards out to sea! he thought with alarm. The images flickered across his imagination in a second: The discovery of his bloated corpse on some Cornish beach by horrified children; its more likely fate of being crushed beneath tons of water, to finally provide a meal for the monstrously-toothed creatures of the sightless deep. He calmed himself. Should he go straight in, or take the angle back to where he started? The current should favor the angle, he thought, so he spotted the bright white dot of the bathrobes on the beach and began his measured but determined crawl, concentrating on maximizing each scoop of water that he passed underneath and close to his body, the Weissmuller stroke.

After about fifty strokes he pulled up to re-sight the dot of bathrobes. Halfway home. He was pleased with himself. He went back to "turning 'em over," as he called his long swimming rhythm.

After ten minutes Lagarius was into the low breaking waves. He waded in, thoroughly but pleasantly exhausted. Ana was wearing her robe and holding his open for his arms as he approached. He savored the clean deep nap of the robe warming his arms and shoulders. She pulled out her earbuds and he heard the wailing of Fairuz, the only Lebanese artist of hers that he could reliably identify.

"Good swim?" she asked.

"Yes."

She took his hand as they turned to walk home, caressingly raking her fingernails inside his palm. They walked for a long while in silence.

"I showed my uncle your picture of you and me," she said.

Lagarius groaned.

"Ya, I know, 'Don't share the images,' but I had to let him see you. You know what he says? He ask me, 'You dating George Best? I don't know he's still around.'"

"Who the devil is George Best?"

"Irish footballer – oh, *mille pardons* – *real* football, a soccer player." She playfully poked his chin. "He had the big... *fossette?*"

"Dimple?"

"Dimples, yeah, and at the cheeks with the big smile, like you."

She pulled his arm close, then after a few steps, pulled him around to face her. She held him very tightly, nuzzling under his arm. He rested his chin on the top of her head. Then she looked up at him, the slanting light of autumn golden on the right side of her face. Lagarius looked carefully at her – at Ana's big longing eyes with the black spoke at five o'clock in the hazel iris of her right eye, at the several tiny blond hairs above the full lips of her wide, parted mouth. She rose on her toes and slowly gave him not a sensual kiss but a kiss of love.

They walked the rest of the way arm in arm without talking. At the turn onto the loose sand Lagarius saw the shadows stretching blackly from the outdoor shower across half the lower deck, and saw the upper deck still in the full, fading sunlight.

They undressed and rinsed together at the outdoor shower, kissing but saying little. They dried with their bathrobes, putting them on again. After Lagarius made his habitual check of perimeter alarms, at Ana's instruction he went to the upstairs deck, and soon she reappeared there with a tray of the previously prepared supper, which had been simmering in their absence.

On the small French café table she placed a bowl of moghrabieh, with its distinctive big round couscous, chunks of chicken, and small onions. Lagarius breathed deeply the aroma of caraway, cinnamon, and other spices. Ana placed bowls of eggplant baba ganouj and tabouli alongside, and Lagarius swallowed at the scent of their tahini and lemon. There was just room for a basket stacked with hot khubz, the typical flat bread, under a towel. Lagarius poured out the cold Côte de Beaune Grand Cru for them and they ate wolfishly in the last warmth of the sun.

They took liqueurs indoors – arak for her, Jägermeister for him – and went to bed early, in the downstairs bedroom where in one of the lamps Ana had placed a bulb activated by clapping.

Among the cooling leaves and twigs outside the bedroom window, several lizards drowsed in nocturnal torpor. With each slap of flesh and corresponding wink of the lamp, they roused and twitched in alarm. At last one of them plunged into the leaves, spawning a ripple of myriad scurryings through the dark underbrush.

The clock on the bedroom nightstand showed Sunday, October 27, 2024.

2

Lagarius had thought about making the run from Virginia Beach to Hoboken on his new MV Agusta F4 1000 motorcycle, but knowing that it would be a firm ride of six hours, decided against it. He had eased the beautiful machine designed by Massimo Tamburini from the beach house garage into the sunlight and admired it before mounting. It was a sleek red and silver beast with Brembo clutch and brakes, an Öhlins steering damper and suspension, and all the electronic bling to make for a thrilling ride. Ah, well. At least he had the twenty minute zip to the airport at Norfolk.

Ana had watched him mount, her arms crossed. She could think of other ways to spend thirty-five thousand dollars, and found his attraction to the toy inexplicable.

"You like the power between the legs, yes, Carmine?"

"And the need to stay erect," he had rejoined, smiling, pulling the big casque over his head.

His phone had clicked, and he had checked the Telegram reply from Lucas stating that everything was still set for the three o'clock meeting with the journalist at his Hoboken apartment. He had then closed the phone and removed its battery, placing both in a small RF bag inside his black Tagliatore lambskin jacket. In the other inside pocket was the key fob to enter Lucas' apartment, which Lucas had given him at their last meeting.

Comfortable now on the plane to LaGuardia, Lagarius took a deep relaxing breath before mentally rehearsing several scenarios for the meeting.

He considered how lucky he had been that Lucas wanted to help him. Dear tousled-headed Lucas Meeth was something of a mess for his flighty nervousness and his unwanted nonprofessional interest in Lagarius, but he was discretion itself: He was deaf, and he was gay, with an unenlightened anxiety about his predilection. He was also a born coder and network administrator, who had quickly become head of the computer lab at the Stevens Institute and remained there, now two years after his graduation. He could have made more money elsewhere, but it was a safe, familiar environment where he was daily immersed in the latest technology, and where there were ample, and transient, romantic opportunities. In spite of everyone's affection for him and his excessive helpfulness, he could never relax in company. His nails were chewed to the quick, with grime underneath what remained.

Lucas and Lagarius never exchanged email messages, instead using encrypted chat in Telegram, Signal for voice, and Tor over VPN for files and typed longer conversations. Anyone finding files from Lagarius on Lucas' computer would have to conclude that Lucas had created them. Most importantly, there would be no trace that the files had been acquired illegally. Such were the files that Lagarius had stolen from the defense contractor.

Key among these files was a .jpg image that was updated every day with a new version of an embedded message – in this case steganography not to launch malware but to conceal a message that Lagarius was convinced pointed to a very sophisticated terrorist operation. The first and most obvious question he expected from the journalist was: Why should terrorists use such a convoluted way to communicate when they could have used encrypted chat? The fact that they didn't indicated that they needed a much more robust way of coordinating a great number of operatives involved in a single complex attack. He also anticipated the question of how was it that this supposedly sophisticated system relied on a simple image file. Then there was the obvious question: Why was this thing on a defense contractor's server in the first place?

For those first two questions, Lagarius would have to explain to the journalist how he believed this communication system was constructed, and why a simple image was the elegant key to its operation. As for the third question, it seemed evident to him that there was someone deep within the bowels of the defense establishment directing the show.

Everything he said could be doubted: There was no detailed message in the clear, spelling out any such attack. The proof would come in getting someone with much more computing power than he could possibly have to decrypt the message – more exactly, the variable messages, which should be more easily decrypted by comparing them all. It would take a certain amount of salesmanship, which Lucas, for all his value in concealing the crime of acquisition, simply did not have. If Lagarius could convince the journalist, the latter could bring the influence of his media organization to bear in bringing this information to the attention of the government.

Lucas had been oddly cagey about this third person. He had not shared his name, nor the name of the media group he worked for. This suggested to Lagarius that whatever organization it was, it had not energetically responded to the information nor decided upon whom to send. Then too, it was not unlike Lucas, ever eager to please, to set up a meeting with principals who were less than committed to attend. Well, thought Lagarius, we would just have to see; Lucas had done well to find someone just days after getting the information; it was a start.

The previous week Lagarius had met Lucas in person with the files in order to better explain, and to emphasize their importance. Lucas had been visiting in Washington, DC, saving Lagarius the long trip to New Jersey. They had met at Hill Country Barbecue on Seventh Street, silly Lucas dressing the part in cowboy boots, a pearl snap shirt, and blue jeans. They sat down at the big Texas star mounted on the brick wall, their metal trays heaped with sliced brisket, Kreuz sausage, bacon and greens, and corn pudding casserole.

Toward the end of their meal, a curious incident took place.

Though he could make himself understood at signing, Lagarius was never very good at it, relying instead on sketching and writing out on paper. Fortunately for him, Lucas was good at lip reading and vocalizing, though he did not like vocalizing in public. While chatting about how Lucas was doing at work, Lagarius easily signed "Everybody loves you": The pinkie, index finger, and thumb of one hand all extended, shaking the hand in big sweeping circle, and finally pointing to him. To this Lucas replied "Bullshit": Pinkie and index finger raised (the bull), with the other hand wiggling its fingers at the elbow end of the bull.

At that point a Hispanic who was seated at the street window angrily stood up, overturning his chair on the wooden floor. The room fell silent. He strode to their table, followed by a short Hispanic woman wearing a tank top and a black and blue bandana. The man glowered at Lucas as he stood squeezing his left fist with his right hand, whose knuckles were tattooed with the letters "EWMN," and whose pinkie nail was longer than the rest. He was wearing a red plaid shirt buttoned all the way. The neck above the buttoned collar was heavily tattooed, with "MS-13" barely discernable in gothic letters. Though not inked around his moustache and soul patch, at the corner of his left eye was a black teardrop.

"What you throwin' up, mothafokka?" he demanded, eyes ablaze with anger.

Lagarius raised his arm between them, as Lucas vocalized, "Wha?"

"Yeah, who you claim, who you down with? You think I don't see you dissin' *la clica*?"

Lagarius had stood up.

"Hey, hey, brother, my friend is deaf. He's not making any gang signs."

A wildly astonished look passed across Lucas' face as he looked toward the street window. He began pointing excitedly at several men just entering the restaurant wearing dark blue nylon jackets.

"Migra! Migra!" Lucas shouted in a cry lost somewhere in his nose.

The Hispanic man shoved Lucas down to his chair with his left hand, and from his right let fall a steak knife – evidently previously folded under his fist and forearm – which rattled onto the wooden floor. He ran wildly toward the kitchen, shoving a server to the floor in the direction of the men in jackets. The woman followed him, and a clatter of pots and pans came from the kitchen as they charged through amid a welter of yelled Spanish, evidently exiting at the back door.

The men in jackets stood looking at each other in confusion, and the room buzzed with the astonished patrons talking again, some of them laughing, having understood what had transpired. Lucas was having a fit of laughter, slapping his blue jeans, gasping for air.

"Migra!" he said, leaning on Lagarius. "Immigration! They thought the men were Customs and Immigration!"

Lagarius laughed. He wanted to sign "you are something else," but stopped thinking how to put it together and just hugged his friend.

The restaurant manager came over, angry but at the same time suppressing a smile.

"OK, which one of you jackasses just closed my restaurant? All my Mexican help just ran out the back door!"

Lucas and the manager laughed, but Lagarius was mute and serious. Lucas was hugging him, but he was looking over his friend's shoulder, staring at the dropped steak knife under a patron's chair, gleaming on the wooden floor.

Lagarius arrived an hour early to his three-thirty appointment with Lucas and the journalist. He wore a hoodie over his black jacket, carrying his tablet in the joined front pockets. In the coffee shop on the corner of Tenth Street, he ordered a mocha and set up his tablet, facing the window so as to look down Bloomfield Street and the nearby front door of the four-storey apartment where Lucas lived. Looking over the top of his computer screen, he saw nondescript traffic at various times. Going in were several women with two-wheeled grocery carts and a woman with an Indian headscarf; going out were an elderly black man with a cane and a young man in a business suit – all of them moving with purpose, not lounging or looking about, and none of them looking particularly like a journalist. At ten after three he left the coffee shop and walked away from his destination, going east on Tenth Street. He walked down a basement stoop to remove the hoodie, folded it beneath his jacket, and returned to the street. After three left turns to circle the block, he was walking up the steps to the apartment entrance. He swiped the key fob and bounded up to the third floor, taking every other step.

At apartment 314 Lagarius found the door ajar. He pressed the doorbell that flashed a light inside the apartment.

He pushed the door open and took a step inside. He froze.

Interrupting the path of light along the hallway toward the street window on the dark, highly polished walnut floor was a pair of feet with socks but no shoes.

"No," Lagarius murmured softly to himself. He walked down the hallway, past the kitchen into the larger room.

There on the rug before the sofa was the body of Lucas, lying on its side. He was wearing dress slacks and a white shirt, but the front of the shirt was red with blood. Approaching, Lagarius could see the steel handle of a knife protruding from his left side at his heart. His eyes were closed. His right arm was outstretched, and just beyond the rug's wet circle of blood - bright red and uncongealed - lay his phone near his hand. There seemed to be no scratches or marks on the visible side of his face, and none on the visible hand. The dirty, bitten fingernails would indicate little in any case.

Lagarius knelt down but could not force himself to place two fingers on Lucas' neck. He touched his blond tousled curls instead, and he sobbed once.

"My fault. I'm sorry," he whispered. He rubbed the back of his wrist at his eyes. He focused his mind. He must call 911 immediately. No! but not on his own phone... - on the phone before him. He picked up the phone at Lucas' hand. It was unlocked.

What? The last number dialed was 911. Lagarius pushed up his own jacket sleeve to reveal the splendid jewel on his wrist, and compared the time: Six minutes ago - god, he must leave this room immediately! Think!

Angry that he had to do it, he took out his own phone from his jacket and inserted the battery. While it booted up, he looked for Lucas' laptop. On the small desk by the window were a charger and mouse, with a vacant space between them. He looked around for anything out of place. Why was Lucas not wearing shoes? Then, with his own phone in service, he photographed the list of recent calls and texts on Lucas' phone. Hurry! He took a tissue from the desk, wiped down Lucas' phone, and replaced it on the carpet. He took the key fob from his jacket, wiped that, then eased it into the slacks pocket of the prostrate body. He stuffed the tissue into his own pocket. Nothing more could be done; he must leave. He put on his hoodie, placed his tablet inside, and hurried toward the door. Closing it, he took out the tissue and wiped the handle. He flew down the stairs.

As he placed his hand on the door to leave the apartment building, he heard the siren of the ambulance loudly oscillating at an intersection. Ducking his head, he briskly walked down the steps, turned away from the corner coffee shop, and forced himself to slow his pace as he looked down from his hoodie at the tops of his shoes. He walked to Hudson Street and got on the 89 bus south to Hoboken Terminal.

Seated at the back of the bus, he launched Signal to call Ana. No answer. He left a text message without expiration.

"Ana, leave the beach house at once. Take nothing. You have the card, you can buy new things. Go to your girl friends. Do not go anywhere alone. The more friends you're with, the better. Don't call; text the OK sign when you're safe."

Then angrily, willfully heedless of the danger of the impulse, he called one of the throwaway numbers available to him in an emergency, and at the beep left a message.

"I need to move up my quarterly interview as soon as possible."

He would be going south to Miami, to speak face-to-face with Mr. Muhammad Nigredo.

3

"28.16180339"

The seemingly cryptic text from an unknown number had come back to Lagarius even before he had arrived at LaGuardia from Hoboken. It simply meant that tomorrow, the 28th, at any time after 4:18 pm, there would be a car waiting to pick him up at Level 3, Section 3R at Miami International Airport. The rubric was familiar to him as part of the protocol of his work reports given in person every three months at Nigredo's compound.

After flying from LaGuardia to Norfolk, Lagarius had arrived just before midnight at the beach house, which showed no illumination other than the dim landscaping lights. Before bringing his motorcycle into the garage, a check of his phone showed the house alarms set and undisturbed. It also showed the familiar emoji from Ana that she was OK: A happy face surrounded by three red hearts.

Ana had not heeded his instruction to leave at once. Downstairs most of her bathroom articles were gone, as were clothes and a suitcase from the bedroom. Fine. Looking at the rumpled bed, he knew that he would not be able to sleep unless completely exhausted, so he changed into running shoes and shorts, and tied a sweatshirt's sleeves around his waist.

The beach was an abandoned, dim luminescence in the moonless night, with a silent explosion of stars in the clear sky above it. He ran south, with the somehow reassuring noise of the waves on his left, breathing deeply the air heavy with salt and the evanescent scents of dry grass, of seaweed, and of the detritus of the shore. He tried not to think. He focused his attention on the phosphorescent line of low waves, the vanishing veil of foam tirelessly cast before him, the clumps of beach grass nodding slightly in a current of land breeze. After about a mile he reversed course and kept up the pace until he returned. With his fists on his hips in exhaustion, he walked through the soft sand up to the house, showered outdoors, and dried his body and feet with the sweatshirt that he had not put on.

He put on sweat pants and top in the bedroom, mixed a negroni in the kitchen, and went to the upper deck where he had taken supper with Ana the day before. After a deep sip of the bittersweet drink, he exhaled with gratification and settled back against the cushions. Then, looking out to the black horizon, he commanded his welter of thoughts to present themselves in order.

Why would anyone want to murder Lucas? His murder would make sense if terrorists believed him to be the sole possessor of files that would expose their operations – and if so, Lagarius was guilty of placing his friend in mortal danger. His "compartmentalization" in that case had indeed worked, he thought bitterly. Assuming that was the motive, either his messages to the journalist had been intercepted by his killers, or the journalist had relayed the messages to them – whether knowingly or not. Lagarius could not know how they might have been intercepted since he did not know the details of how Lucas was working. The laptop that might have told him had been taken. Nor could he know the involvement of the journalist since he did not know his name or the company he worked for. Nor could he even assume that he was a journalist at all, instead of merely posing as one. Lagarius thought of the original possibility as a "digital" interception, and the alternative as a "human" interception. The first would suggest a sophisticated operation, though the second would not exclude it.

Apparently Lucas knew his attacker, since he let him enter his apartment all the way to the far window without a struggle. What person did he know, who was entering at just the appointed hour, who committed the murder just minutes before Lagarius entered? Unless some fourth party backed him into his room at the point of a gun, it could not be anyone other than the journalist. But in either case, *where was the journalist?* Had he been early for his appointment, Lagarius, seated at the coffee shop, would have seen him enter the building. Had he been late or had never arrived, then of course the involvement of some fourth party would seem plausible. But that person had not been seen entering, either. Yes, there was that window of opportunity when Lagarius had to circle the block to change from his hoodie, but that was fifteen to twenty minutes at the very most. Good god, could someone have rented in the building just days before the killing, removing the need to enter and exit? No, impossible, there was no time for that: Lucas had started working the files only last week.

There was of course the mystery of Lucas missing his shoes, but Lagarius put this out of his mind as insignificant – and unfathomable in any case.

Then there was that other alternative: The thought of this alternative had come to Lagarius on the bus ride to Hoboken Terminal, kindling his anger. It was the possibility that Nigredo had learned of his approach to the authorities and had coldly ordered the murder of Lucas as a caution to him, preserving his life for its lucrative usefulness. Certainly Nigredo was capable of such a deed. – And Lagarius with his impulsive phone call was in effect calling him out!

Impulsive though it was, Lagarius would not have made the call without an unconscious trust in himself that he could succeed in learning what he had to know. Suppose Nigredo had indeed ordered the murder and were forced to reveal as much? Lagarius would have to obediently pretend that he "got the message," at least until the media announced that he had averted a spectacular attack, or if he failed, until they had broadcast that event. At that time, Lagarius could demonstrate to Nigredo that his approach to the authorities was in no way an exposure of him, but instead was a moral obligation to act, with no reference to him, and he could then without danger part ways with him. On the other hand, what if Nigredo had nothing to do with the murder? That would mean that he furthermore knew nothing of the discovery of the terrorists by Lagarius, and nothing of his approach to the authorities to avert their attack. To simply and honestly explain his moral impulse to Nigredo would be met with incomprehension: Much like Ana, he would say that any such attack, if it really existed, was their problem, fuck them. Thus here was the extreme place of danger for Lagarius: In his sounding of Nigredo, he must not drop the slightest hint that he had found these files and had taken them to the authorities. One mistake would mean that he had written his own death warrant.

As Lagarius lay on his back in the ocean, Lucas danced on his chest, drumming the heels of his cowboy boots, dressed in the blue jeans and pearl snap shirt of his lunch visit in Washington. He was juggling steak knives – first a few, then seemingly dozens – throwing them incredibly high into the blue sky as they sparkled brilliantly in the sun. But each thump of his heels forced Lagarius under water, and he gasped, shaking his head for him to stop. He craned his neck to look for land, but there was only water, in every direction. Distracted, Lucas lost track of the knives, and each fell from its sparkling point in the sky, growing in size, buzzing more and more loudly on approach, to finally zip into the water around Lagarius' head and chest.

Lagarius sat up in bed with terror from the dream, his heart pounding in his chest. The clock showed 5:11 am. He rubbed his face and sat for a long while on the bedside, trying to shake the terrible realness of his unconscious witness. He got up to shower.

His first task was to research the history of phone calls and texts on Lucas' phone that he had photographed. The 911 call was most likely dialed by Lucas, who would have been able to vocalize something before dying, and who in any case would have known the 911 silent dialing protocol. Why would anyone else have dialed that number on his phone? After over two hours online, he found not one of the remaining numbers significant: Two outbound calls to pizza delivery, a help desk call from the Stevens Institute computer lab, a call from a dentist's office, a number of robocalls. He had hoped to find a call either to or from the journalist, but there was nothing. He closed his laptop and prepared for his flight.

At 4:30 pm Lagarius touched down at Miami International Airport. With no baggage to claim, he was soon standing in the north parking lot, at the nearest entrance to Section 3R. He waited as the few fellow travelers went past him to find their cars and drive away. When no one was near, a plain sedan with tinted windows pulled up at the curb where Lagarius stood. He got in at the right rear door and placed himself in sight of the driver's rear view mirror.

The driver turned his head to him, and wordlessly they made the familiar exchange: Lagarius giving his phone, the driver giving a pair of black goggles that made vision impossible. The driver removed the phone battery; Lagarius put on the goggles. In them he saw himself saying what he would soon need to say, and how he would say it.

Although the sun had only just set by the time the car had arrived at the Nigredo compound, sunset had been smothered in the black clouds gathering in the west. Lagarius put the goggles into his suit coat pocket and stepped out onto the gravel drive before the majestic home before him. The car pulled away, its headlights piercing the mist. He was assailed by the incessant cheep of katydids and the soft police whistle of tree crickets, punctuated by the occasional croaking of frogs. – Assailed too by the autumnal mist heavy with the scent of impending rain and of delved earth. The remembrance of the wake of a nameless uncle came to him – the remembrance of a dim parlor in wavering candlelight, of respectfully murmuring elders, of the cloying rot of lilies.

Before him a colonnade swept up a man-made outcropping supporting a balcony at its top edge. On the height behind the balcony was a veranda with terracotta roof tiles skirting a low house, its rock walls punctuated by glowing windows. The colonnade supported an arched trellis of vines all along its ascending length. In daylight the eminence would provide an excellent view of anything approaching from the coastal plain around it. Lagarius could well guess that what appeared to be a Spanish bungalow on a natural outcropping – nonexistent in South Florida – in fact concealed several floors of Nigredo's operations, warehouses, and escape tunnels.

At the nearest arch stood an enormous Hispanic man, familiar to Lagarius, whom he approached. His close-cropped black hair did not conceal numerous scars on his left scalp, nor the nick in the top of his left ear. His impassive eyes evaluated Lagarius a moment, then he stepped alongside to remove the visitor's lambskin jacket, which he folded and placed on a concrete bench. He patted down Lagarius swiftly and professionally, then produced a detector wand from his own jacket, plying it carefully at the pockets of his Savile Row slacks and his Meccariello shoes. He then took up the jacket and walked up the gravel path beneath the trellis, sounding a crunch with each weighty step, just out of conversational range as Lagarius followed. Neither man had spoken.

As Lagarius tread up the gravel path, his irrepressible anticipation of pleasure inspired a curious wistfulness in him, as if it might never be his to enjoy again. He noticed the vine's flecks of white and blue at the mouths of the furled morning glories, closed for business for the night. He thought of Nigredo's slow ritual: The splendid supper in the dining room with a view over the plain below, the business review giving way to casual talk with brandy and cigars on the veranda. He sometimes wondered, as he did now, how Nigredo might have been not a criminal but a great man, and how he might have been turned aside from being so by his rumored terrible injury.

On the veranda Lagarius' guide walked past the corner where the table could be seen through the window, bright and already set with linen, crystal, and silver, and he opened the French door to the center of the room, remaining outside. Lagarius smiled as he entered the big room with sand-colored walls, black carved ceiling beams, and dark hewn wood floors. A leather Spanish colonial sofa stood on an enormous Persian rug, azure with bright colored arabesque patterns, and he imagined how gloomy the room would have been without its ornate blue relief. He inhaled the room's aroma of saffron, mint, and sautéed onions and garlic and closed his eyes.

"Carmine, Carmine!" boomed Muhammad Nigredo, striding into the room through a side door, followed by a Puerto Rican boy in a starched linen jacket. He held up his two enormous hands as if displaying a pair of crabs, then made Lagarius' extended right hand vanish in their grip.

"You look healthy!" he said in his peculiar Spanish accent, sounding the 'h' with a harsh guttural. "¡Albricias! You have good news, sí?"

Lagarius nodded.

The man who now looked at Lagarius with the eagerness of a partner in gaining twelve million dollars had dark rings under his black, deep-set eyes, which were surrounded by a nest of faint wrinkles. In his thick black beard the lower lip was very full, which made it always seem as if he were about to smile or laugh, yet incongruously failing to relieve the brooding melancholy of the face. His oiled black hair fell to his shoulders in tightly coiled, hyacinthine ringlets. The nose in his long face was prominent, Middle Eastern.

"Can I get you an aperitif? I've got a new one for you."

"Of course, thank you."

Nigredo nodded slightly to the boy behind him, who bowed and left the room.

"Now come over here and relax," he said, extending one of the crabs toward the sofa. He took the armchair beside it. Soft ochre leather of the tall chair showed above Nigredo's broad shoulders, and with the deeply carved palmette at the top, the armchair seemed almost a throne.

"You must have some very good news, since you could not wait for our meeting on Friday."

"Yes, there is good news," said Lagarius.

The boy returned with two cocktails on a silver tray. Lagarius took the clear crystal glass with its rim lightly crusted in salt, a wedge of grapefruit among the ice cubes. Nigredo took his drink, and the boy placed two lace doilies on the low table between them and left.

"That's Tobalá mescal with grapefruit, Carmine," said Nigredo. "*Qué piensas?*"

"It's perfect." He took a deeper sip of the very cold, tart drink.

"So let's hear this news that can't wait, Carmine. Tell me you own the SWIFT system now," Nigredo said with a chuckle at the enormity.

"Ha ha, not quite. As you know from last quarter, my breach of the interbank financial telecom was one of several wake-up calls telling the system that it must be more secure, and I learned that the U.S. company TactiFor got a contract to do exactly that."

Lagarius settled back in the soft leather, cradling his drink.

"OK, so I got in, and now I know that they're going to offer a blockchain solution."

"Ah!" said Nigredo, rubbing his hands together. "*Esa es la noticia, sí?* You can crack that?"

Lagarius wanted to say 'Not if it's done right,' but didn't.

"I see several possibilities for cracking it. The news is that I'm in, and because I'm in, I can see how they're putting it together."

"So, the *possibilities*," Nigredo said, pronouncing each 'i' as a sharp 'e.' "Tell me all about the *possibilities*."

Lagarius took a slow sip of his drink, enjoying the prospect of burnishing his knowledge for Nigredo.

"Right. They're going with blockchain. Their use of it will require smart contracts. But let me back up a bit to explain blockchain for smart contracts. Say an Ecuadorian bank" – here both of them smiled – "wants to transfer money to Dubai. There has to be something which identifies Bank E and Bank D as being really who they say they are, and which assures that the interbank message is trustworthy. Let's call that identification and assurance a 'token.' For two parties, although the mutual identification is not so hard, the message can still be faked. But even if every message is assured, it's still inefficient because really the whole banking system needs to know about it. So, let's put all these messages into one big central system that stamps its OK on every message coming in or going out – great, right? Wrong. Not only does the central system become the focus of attack, but it now runs the show, laying down the rules for everybody – cutting off banks that don't cough up tax info on clients, for example, as the U.S. does. Well, then, let's go the other way: Decentralize and give everybody a copy of every message. Pretty obvious that keeping up with all those copies is crazy, right? Well, it's not so crazy if each token automatically propagates throughout the chain, which is held by everyone who has a token. An error, in which a message needs correction, might offer a chance to insert a faked message, but blockchain stops this by requiring a majority of token holders to agree to fork from that error, never erasing, just forking."

"*Bueno*, can you make the chain think that you're the majority?" asked Nigredo, who had been following with interest.

"For a very short chain, yes, you can create 51% of the tokens, and then issue a rewritten message of your choosing, creating a fork that the rest must accept. But I don't see the system ever accommodating some kind of auxiliary short chain that can fool everyone in this way. That leaves only two ways to go. One is to guess or to steal one of the existing secret private keys that is unique to each person who initiates a transaction on the chain. The other way to go is to fake a token, I think by quickly forging the credentials of a brand-new bank and being first to place its forged token on the chain."

Lagarius drained his drink with self-satisfaction and rattled the ice as he placed his glass on its doily. Nigredo sipped, then cocked his head to one side.

"Carmine, that's wonderful progress," he said. "But really, couldn't the news have waited until Friday?"

Lagarius exhaled and looked down at one of the patterns in the azure rug. He felt his heart beginning to race.

"Yes, but I have to attend the funeral of a friend on that day." Saying this, he looked up swiftly but intently at Nigredo's face.

"Ahg, *amor de dios!*" he said dismissively, putting down his drink. "Young man, we could have had our meeting next week. But I'm sorry for your loss. Was this a close friend?"

"Pretty close, yes."

"Well, I am sorry," he said after a pause, putting his hands on his knees then standing up. "But look, it's time for us get to the wonderful meal that Layla has prepared for us."

Nigredo lightly held Lagarius' bicep and pulled him close in friendship as they walked to the big room's corner table.

"This meal is a variation of one you liked before," he said. "I am sure you will love it."

Lagarius now knew, as well as he could ever know, that Nigredo had nothing to do with the murder of Lucas. At least he felt satisfied that this was so. He relaxed, but cautioned himself not to let slip his discovery of the terrorist files and his indirect contact with the authorities.

An elderly woman was placing on the small table a great glass cube overflowing with white anemones with black centers. The Puerto Rican boy was placing a basket of flatbread and two small bowls of *ash-e jo* barley and lentil soup on the linen tablecloth beside the silver. The hot fragrance rose up with a hint of lemon. A light shone down on the bright setting in the dark room.

"*Mersi, mersi,* Layla!" Nigredo said to the woman and kissed her hand. "*Hamechiz âliye!*"

"*Ghâbel-i nadâsht,*" she said, flattered and smiling. "*Khosh begzare!*"

She dipped her head slightly and left.

Nigredo waved Lagarius toward one of the two seats, then took the linen napkin from the beaded bottle of cold wine, which had no cork.

"Here, you'll love this," Nigredo said, filling the glass for Lagarius then himself. "It's a sauvignon blanc - L'Enclos des Remparts. Another in the refrigerator if we need it."

The soup was soon gone, and half the bread. The small bowls were quickly taken away, replaced with several dishes of sabzi khordan - fresh basil, dill, mint, parsley, radishes, scallions - and kashke bademjan - roasted eggplant with caramelized onions sautéed with garlic, mint, saffron, lemon juice, and turmeric, sprinkled with strong kashk cheese and chopped walnuts. Another basket of hot flatbread was brought forth, this time thin Armenian lavash.

Although Nigredo in previous meals had described the food's preparation, this time he seemed to reminisce, detailing just how Layla carefully followed his mother's recipes from Iran.

"I remember that all the way back to six years old - you know that, Carmine?"

He looked into the black plain beyond the window, with the occasional snap of lightning in clouds to the left and the faint nebulous glow of a city, doubtless Miami, to the right.

"Not so easy, a boy coming to this place," he said to himself, looking out.

The sizzling, saffron-fragrant main course came, Layla bringing the plate for Lagarius, the Puerto Rican boy the one for Nigredo. At the center of each plate was the gold of crispy tahdig rice, alongside the red of barberries over fluffy steaming basmati; along the colorfully painted rim were eight baby lamb chops cooked with saffron, still crackling in their hot pan juices.

Nigredo joyously thanked Layla, and he and Lagarius went happily to work. Another bottle of L'Enclos des Remparts was opened.

"I had to become Hispanic to make it here, you know," said Nigredo as he ate. "I think in every case when a boy must choose between his parents and his peers, he sides with his peers, yes? So, I joined a gang. Actually, we started our own gang, I and four close friends. There is nothing like that, facing danger together, being feared, radiating - what to call it? - *the pheromone of danger.* Ha ha, you like that?"

"Yes, that's good," said Lagarius, laughing, taking up another lamb chop.

"Yes, the pheromone of danger: *Las chicas* are crazy for that. You see today the rock stars, the movie stars, all inked up, pierced, what the hell else – that's all cosmetic for the real thing: The real thing is a man who has triumphed, the killer of another man. *Las chicas* can smell such a man, the one who can kill for them. Ah, well."

Nigredo took a long drink from his glass, brooding.

"Then there was the heist. The five of us had this all planned really well. It was a jewelry store. I was the point man, holding the gun on the clerks while my troops smashed and grabbed the fendi – ha, as we called it. I looked over my shoulder to make sure they all made off, and then the clerk – must have been the owner – whipped out a piece and dropped me. The bullet went in one side of my hip, swished around my pelvis, and back out the front on the other side. Burned like hell."

Nigredo emptied his glass.

"Well. With that, my parents had not only lost their only child with me. They also lost any hope of grandchildren with that bullet. It cut my sciatic nerve. No more *chicas*. I guess you knew the story."

"Only rumors."

"Well, there is much one can do without the distraction of sex. That focus..." – here Nigredo swept his great arm about him like a showman – "none of this would be here without that focus. Also, real friends remain: I took the fall, never ratted them out, and learned that friendship is the superior love, above even sex. But my parents... – they died before hearing their criminal son ask them for forgiveness."

"I'm sorry."

"*Eshkâli nadâre* – ah, sorry – it doesn't matter."

Nigredo extended one hand outside their bubble of light and intimacy and gave it a brief twitch. Immediately the big Puerto Rican with the scarred head strode into the room from the French door and approached the table.

"*Si, jefe?*"

"*Trae algun' silla' cómoda'. Quiero chatea' fuera de casa.*"

The man bobbed his head and went out. A moment later he was visible on the veranda before them, setting up comfortable armchairs with a small table between them.

"I think you may like this," said Nigredo.

When he saw that the table outdoors was properly furnished, he stood up, and opened the veranda door to the cool air and to the singing of insects far below. They sat, and Nigredo merely chuckled softly as he showed the pink box of cigars whose lid indicated Rafael Nodal's Quattro Nicaragua Maestro. Lagarius took one, and at the gestured invitation of Nigredo, took up one of the two butane torches, clipped the tapered end, and began toasting a lasting coal. He slowly tasted the cigar and let the fragrant wreath pass over his tongue. Nigredo raised his brows, querying.

"Magnificent," said Lagarius, allowing the nutty and slightly chocolate and fruit flavors to blossom on his palate.

"And here," said Nigredo with another chuckle, "Guillon-Painturaud VSOP."

He filled both snifters to a third, and they raised their glasses.

"To happiness," said Lagarius.

"To contentment," said Nigredo.

Light flickered in the distant horizon, as if the ponderous black sky and earth were crushing a friction spark between them. After a long wait, the muffled thunder came.

"'Happiness,'" Nigredo said at last. "What *do* people intend for themselves?"

"Why, they intend to be happy - even if they don't know how to go about it."

"'Even if they don't know how to go about it.' - You would think that it's all a matter of 'how,' that we're all agreed on the goal but don't know 'the right way.' I don't think so. Ask a thousand people, 'What is happiness?' and you will get a thousand different answers. Clearly, to say 'happiness' is to say nothing meaningful at all."

Here he paused and took a drink. Lagarius sensed a prologue, and said nothing, waiting. Nigredo continued.

"While I was recovering from my injury, I read the Koran. It gave me peace. But then I asked myself: 'Am I reading from a changed heart, or am I reading to get my mojo back?' In other words, was I defiling The Book by turning it into a kind of magic charm? In honesty I had to stop reading until I could supply the proper answer. I did find the answer. I saw that it wasn't just me. For everyone, the desire to do good is always tainted by self-interest. - Except!' - here he pointed a long finger upward - "Except and unless you deliberately do yourself harm by doing good."

"Agh, heavens, Mr. Nigredo, what good is that? Can't the Almighty look into your heart and see your purity of motive? Can't there be any personal 'collateral benefit' at all? - If we can put it that way...."

"My dear Carmine, don't you know how clever human beings are at deceiving themselves? You don't hear Christians citing Deuteronomy 13 do you? No. It contains clear instructions to stone to death unbelievers. Was there a memo from god to strike out that chapter? I don't think so. All believers 'cherry-pick' Scripture according to some standard *outside* of Scripture, whether it's the 'church fathers,' 'the presbyters,' some televangelist or self-help guru - or some notion turned into an ideology, like love or tolerance. In this way they believe exactly what they want to believe.

"No, my friend. What do you think distinguishes man from all the other animals? His reason? His language? His opposable thumb? Don't make me laugh. Man is distinguished by his capacity for self-delusion. Man is the self-deceiving biped, the self-justifying biped, especially on the subject of 'happiness.' Mao's murder of 80 million Chinese was justified as necessary for the Cultural Revolution; Stalin's murder of 20 million Russians was justified as necessary for the New Soviet Man; Hitler, a comparative *diletante* at six million, murdered to justify the Thousand Year Reich. The worst crimes are baptized in the milk of human kindness, always for the 'happiness' of all. No. The only way to be certain of your purity of motive is to destroy not others but yourself in the moral act. For the truly believing Christian, that means self-destruction for the sake of others. For the Muslim, that means self-destruction for the sake of Allah, may his name be praised."

"Well," Lagarius exhaled, both scoffing and puzzled, shaking his head. "I guess all that has a certain internal consistency."

Nigredo laughed.

"Good heavens, Mr. Nigredo. All this 'destroying yourself'! Did people come into life just to cut their own throats? Damn. Aren't people supposed to be happy in *some* way or other? Isn't *that* their purpose in life?"

"My dear Carmine, you still have the confusions of a young man. Look around you. If women were happiness, pornographers would be happy, and they are not: They are made insatiable by their very appetite - animals, not human at all. If money were happiness, the rich could never be anything but happy, but many are miserable. No, no, no: The purpose of life *cannot* be happiness. Most lives are not happy, most fall short of what they aimed for in life, and every life ends in the unhappy event of death. Life, wealth, everything we can taste, smell, touch, see, hear - our very flesh - all of that is not an instrument of happiness but a veil of corruption, concealing... what? The abyss? Nothingness? It's either a complete blackness, or an invisible something outside life that gives it purpose, something after death, which must be affected in some way by believing it in this life."

"It looks like you might have a chance at being happy if someone else gives happiness to you. I mean, since you say that happiness means 'self-destruction for the sake of others,' someone might sacrifice himself for you."

"No, I said that's what Christians believe. That doesn't work - unless it's entirely random. Otherwise it's a contradiction."

"I don't understand," Lagarius said simply.

"Let's say a rich stranger gives you a sports car - a nice red Porsche Boxster S, eh? Does he give it in order to appease his guilt for having too much money? Or does he give it because he's old and wants the vicarious pleasure of seeing a young man driving it?"

"Ha ha! What do I care? I'm happy because I got the Porsche!"

"Yes, the random gift of happiness is for you to properly enjoy. Yes, too, it makes a wholesome sacrifice of the riches of the giver. But the giver can't take any happiness from it, because he gave it out of some selfish desire. He gets some advantage out of it - in this case, appeasing his guilt or getting the vicarious pleasure. Islam is more pure: It admits of giving without any possibility of gain - a gift of pure sacrifice to the will of Allah, the most merciful."

Lagarius became serious, and he paused, looking evenly at his host.

"'Virtue is enough'. That's what Marcus Aurelius said. But no, what you're saying is even less than that."

"The great stoic? Less than him? Ha ha!"

"Yes, much less. He had his great pride in his own self-control, his own integrity, the very thing that makes us human. This is pure gold - something to strive for. But your guy, what's he got? Less than nothing. Not only must he actively harm himself, but also he must make himself the victim of people who don't share his fine notions of sacrifice. He's an advertisement to really evil people, saying 'Here I am, come eat me up!' He is putting righteousness in the service of power."

Here Nigredo fell silent, and he looked into his glass bitterly.

"Yes," he said with a deep sigh, looking up from his glass. "I have seen that line of thought. You have retraced my own thinking perfectly." He drained his glass and paused.

"Gosh, we've gone off the deep end, Mr. Nigredo. I think I'm to blame for mentioning my friend's death. It's ruining our evening."

"No, not at all. It is fitting. And after all, he was not just a 'pretty close' friend, as you said earlier. On the contrary, your face told me that he was a very dear friend."

Lagarius felt his heart begin to race again. He took a drink, not meeting the eyes of the other. Both enjoyed their cigars for a long moment, their thoughts in two very separate rooms.

"How did you breach TactiFor?" Nigredo said at last, exhaling a wreath of smoke.

Lagarius breathed a sigh of relief and revived at the prospect of casual talk.

"I didn't try to breach TactiFor directly - the site's too hardened. But employee laptops aren't. First I waterholed the Federal Employees Credit Union by sending its familiar email from a similarly-named address to TactiFor email addresses. That's pretty easy, and it's surprising how often it works. But no click-throughs this time. So, I went the hard way. I matched Equifax data for federal employee debtors and came up with a list of TactiFor employees in financial trouble."

"So complicated. - And so many people to target."

"I was looking for TactiFor boy scouts who might come under suspicion for selling access or data. I narrowed the list down by comparing the OPM list."

Nigredo merely smiled and cocked his head, waiting for the explanation. Lagarius chuckled.

"The breach of the federal Office of Personnel Management – OPM – occurred in the spring of 2014."

"How did you get this data, and also the Equifax data?"

"Let's just say that the two sets of data are accessible for mining at a price. When Equifax data on 140 million Americans was stolen in September, 2017, folks were mystified that it never went up for sale. Such a sale would have set off fireworks. No, the owner wisely just decided to market access to it over the dark web, never exactly calling it Equifax data.

"Anyway, I then used DNS poisoning on a known TactiFor foreign affiliate where the foreign country's top-level domain name servers don't use DNSSEC to secure data authenticity. Now, it was only probable, not guaranteed, that one of my TactiFor candidates would visit the affiliate. TactiFor, like OnyxWater..."

"– OnyxWater?" interrupted Nigredo. "The U.S. mercenaries?"

"Yes. TactiFor, OnyxWater – both are kind of retirement homes for Jack Ryan wannabes who can't give up the tree house secret handshakes. OnyxWater takes the washed-up hooahs with tattoos."

"Ha. So, how did you get your software onto the foreign site?"

"The dark web is full of access clues for just about every target-rich site – with better clues and richer sites going for a price. And foreign sites are generally less hardened. Also, foreign sites don't watch the boards as closely."

"'The boards'?"

"The message boards of major software and router companies, where they post their discovered vulnerabilities. Responsible IT departments are supposed to watch them for updates and fixes.

"So as I was saying, after getting access, I placed a little traffic watcher on the TactiFor foreign affiliate until I found my indebted little victim."

"I don't understand how you identified your 'little victim' as he entered the foreign site. I mean, surely he didn't have 'TactiFor' written on his access, did he?"

"The Equifax data had employer names, and employer institutions have IP addresses, which were the key identifier of the access."

"So, kind of a three-way match: Indebted federal employee or associate, secret-rich U.S. institution, foreign site visited by such types."

"Exactly. So, when the target TactiFor employee revisited the foreign site, I spoofed its IP address to point to my server, which looked like the foreign site, and took him there. Once he clicked a link there, I downloaded malware to his laptop, then stopped spoofing him before I could be detected. My indebted little friend dutifully took his laptop back inside the TactiFor firewall for me, with my wonderful little payload for the entire TactiFor tree house. Then I was home free. Well, almost. I first had to find an executable that the employee had access to, and which was widely shared. I replaced that executable with a hacked version that got me to root. At the root shell I wandered the entire site as I pleased, but never sent anything back over the wire – it would have been detected. Instead I cached it for collection on my little friend's laptop, and once he went to work from home, pushed up the data from there."

Lagarius paused and with self-satisfaction rolled a sip of cognac in the hollow of his tongue. He inhaled from the cigar and sent two plumes of smoke from his nostrils. Nigredo pondered it all, his brow furrowed toward the night sky. Then he straightened in his armchair and looked intently at Lagarius.

"But you were not interested in the data," he said.

Lagarius felt a prickle of sweat at the back of his neck as he looked into Nigredo's large dark eyes. He managed a puzzled smile.

"What's that? What do you mean?"

"I mean that you were not interested in the data. You first visited Equifax. You were interested in the man – a man you could sell to a foreign government."

"Oh, I see. Mr. Nigredo, you're good. But no. No, I was interested in a man who would take the blame if my breach were ever detected."

"Not a man whom you could sell? – A man who might destroy the government, who might send American agents to their deaths?"

"No. But even if that were the case, I would be the filter. I would stand between the man and any foreign government that might use such data."

"And you are a principled man who would never bring down a government or send its agents to a very unpleasant death?"

"Never."

Nigredo's eyes narrowed slightly and seemed to take a spark of flame.

"Not even a government that starves the Iranian people with embargoes and drone strikes its own citizens?"

"No."

Nigredo looked at Lagarius for a long moment, then with a slight smile tilted his head toward the veranda railing. He rose and walked there, taking his cognac and cigar. Lagarius followed, bringing his as well.

"So. If you master the SWIFT security upgrade to blockchain, *inshallah*, we own it. Yes?"

"Well, we would own it once, then be gone."

Nigredo slowly took another sip of drink and placed his glass on top of a stone post with a clink. He parted his lips, savoring. He leaned against the iron rail with his freed hand, cigar still in the other. He took a slow puff, the coal illuminating his face redly. After a long look at the city lights in the distance, he spoke.

"Mr. Lagarius, are you a patriot?"

Lagarius gave a mild snort.

"I suppose not. This government has lost its way and doesn't stand for anything beyond its own power. Am I or is anyone else supposed to salute that? Anyway, the Cold War's over. Americans don't give and take intel for ideals; they give it up for money. At a certain threshold of debt, folks stop saluting the flag and start looking for the nearest cash register. - And the history of these folks shows how remarkably low that threshold is."

Nigredo paused, facing him. Then his left hand shot out and gripped Lagarius' right shoulder like a vise.

"Did you come into the hospitality of my family to accuse me of murdering your friend?"

Lagarius could not conceal his fear. He blinked his eyes, his mouth went dry, and he felt drops of perspiration fall from his armpits.

"Sir. I want to say... I came here to reassure you of my loyalty. Had I been guilty of something - what, I don't know what - I, I wouldn't have come here. I would have run. But yes, I do admit this: I had to know if you doubted me, and wished to threaten me through my friend."

Lagarius heard the creak of the decking well behind him and knew that the big Puerto Rican had advanced a step in the darkness. Nigredo did not relax his grip, but looked at Lagarius evenly, and he spoke the measured, carefully-shaped words.

"And had I murdered this friend, what would you have done?"

Lagarius felt his heart hammering in his chest.

"I don't know," he said, blinking only once as he addressed the man. "But you would have had no reason to kill him. I would have left you for that mistake."

Nigredo chuckled, released his grip, and gave Lagarius' shoulder an affectionate jostle.

"You are very brave, my dear Carmine, and you honor your friend."

Lagarius stared down into his glass, not daring to show his eyes. A jagged vein of lightning snapped silently on the horizon, illuminating almost nothing of the black clouds that immediately swallowed it.

Nigredo looked out below the railing and laughed, opening his great mouth, and he seemed to fill the darkness with the booming thunder of that repeated laughter. The oiled ringlets of his hair shook alongside his head. Relaxed, genial, he took up his glass again and raised it toward Lagarius, who raised his.

"Let us salute the bounty of this insane, wonderful nation. May she bless us forever!"

As if summoned by Nigredo's laughter, thunder rumbled, barely perceptible. A light rain began to fall with a soft myriad patter among the nearby leaves.

Twenty minutes later Lagarius was standing with Nigredo on the gravel driveway, beneath a black golf umbrella held by the big Puerto Rican. The plain sedan with tinted windows waited, its headlights showing occasional darts of falling rain. With both hands Nigredo gave Lagarius a parting handshake, then pulled him close to embrace him, swatting his back twice. He stood away for an instant, holding Lagarius' shoulders and looking into his eyes.

"My heart goes with you, Carmine," he said, then swiftly turned away, outpacing the Puerto Rican and his umbrella, striding up the incline through the trellised colonnade without looking back.

Lagarius fished out the goggles from the lambskin jacket that had been returned to him, still watching the melancholy shadow moving beneath the vines. Then it suddenly occurred to him: The man's melancholy was not from his physical affliction, nor from the certainty that his childless name would die with him - a reality for which compensations could be found. Possibly it was from his criminal friends' inability to return the spiritual friendship he now demanded. But more probably, it was from his loss of faith.

4

Leaving the basilica of the National Shrine of the Immaculate Con-
ception about an hour after his arrival on Tuesday morning, Eden Wiser
unfolded the scrap of paper containing his "worry" notes. The sad, earnest
eyes in the lined gray granite face with its athletic jaw seemed to read the
very prosaic jottings as if they were a death notice. He put the paper into his
pants pocket and admired his ONYX RCR electric motorcycle as he took
the helmet from its handlebars and strapped it on. Though not a bike for
either speed or power, it was one of the few luxuries he permitted himself.
He mounted, snapped to life the velvet purr of its engine, and after a quick
swing through the adjacent Trinity Washington University, headed south
on North Capitol Street NW. Immediately he saw the tiny dome of the
Capitol in the distance, almost three miles away.

As he rode he mulled over the details of the notes, mostly the day's
agenda, unconsciously navigating traffic. After the long ride, at the street's
dead end at the barrier at D Street NW, he turned right, onto Louisiana
Avenue NW, where the Washington Monument appeared over the trees of
the National Mall. Once he was headed west on Madison Drive, he adjusted
his mental focus. He slowed down the motorcycle and put aside the details
of the coming day, turning instead to what he personally referenced as his
"big picture" thoughts, and often turning his head left to look at the green
of the Mall and the Monument that waxed larger on his approach.

These thoughts had two fundamental premises. The first was that the
next attack would not be like the last one: Unlike their victims, the enemy
would not be stupidly preparing to fight the last war all over again with the
same tactics. The second was that the attack would have an essentially religious motivation: Only some imperative promise from another world could
make someone wish the destruction of this one. Over and over he tried to
imagine what might take shape from these two principles.

From habit Wiser did not look left just before the Lincoln Memorial but
looked straight ahead as he approached the Vietnam Memorial, which was
not visible beyond the trees in any case. Riding past it, he focused on the
white columns that hid the sixteenth President, gigantic and brooding in
marmoreal sedentary gloom.

He had averted his eyes because he did not care to think about a memorial that he considered not a worthy tribute but no more than a ditch.
What did those sixty thousand die for – and the hundreds of thousands of
others in that war? Then he asked himself, What did those three thousand

on September 11, 2001 die for? He felt his face burning with shame and humiliation underneath the mask of his helmet. In both cases, he thought, for the stupidity of those at the top. At one time after the September attack he could experience burning with anger. Then it had come to him: This anger was deflection of responsibility, a projection onto others of his own shame, of his nation's humiliation by a handful of unarmed men whose grandfathers were nothing but backward, penniless Bedouins. - Bedouins who had given the greatest nation on earth a horsewhipping on the world stage. No, anger and its concomitant bluster and swagger would lead to more stupidity and incompetence, more fatal errors. No: Every day he would remember the humiliation and have his personal shame sharpen the focus of his resolve: It must never happen again.

Every weekday morning at the National Shrine and every evening at home he prayed on his knees, concluding with two entreaties:

Everlasting Father, almighty God, whose Word spoke the universe into being, Shaper of heaven and earth, Judge of all at the end of time, humble me to make me an instrument of Thy knowledge that will turn aside the blow surely aimed even now by the enemies of this nation, a misguided nation that once held Thee in awe.

Holy Mary, soften my anger, and remind me of its roots in my ignorance and shame.

The morning prayer he gave in the basilica either in the Our Lady of Pompei Chapel, at the vestibule just inside the south entrance to the upper level, or in the Immaculate Heart of Mary Chapel in the crypt just before morning Mass there. He especially loved the Pompei Chapel, with its walls of warm golden marble with veins of dark gold, its ceiling of Mary's blue, spangled with eight-pointed gold stars, its images of the five Luminous Mysteries, its south niche mosaic of the crowned Mother and Child under an arc of twelve stars. A Crucifix blessed by Benedict XVI hung on the east wall.

He had chosen his little garage apartment a few blocks away to the northeast in Michigan Park especially to be near this magnificent Marian church. From one window he could see its dome and spire, and on the weekends he could walk to service. He had taken the apartment a month after the September 11, 2001 attack, after selling everything and giving it to the Church.

His wife had worked in one of the north-facing offices on the 96th floor of Marsh & McLennan in the One World Trade Center North Tower. This floor was the very point of impact of the first aircraft at 8:46 am. On that morning, their daughter was waiting in the lobby to go shopping with the mother after her 9:00 am presentation. He often asked himself, Was his wife aware? Was she looking at the unbelievable, insanely growing image of the giant aircraft, roaring to its target laden with fuel for a flight across the continent? Was his daughter reading a woman's magazine, thinking of what she might buy in a few hours' time?

Their bodies were never found. They must not have suffered.

Once over the Potomac on the Arlington Memorial Bridge, just a minute's ride on Washington Boulevard took him to the North Parking lot of the Pentagon. He locked his motorcycle and went through security, exchanging terse morning greetings with the PFPS men he knew well but who remained professionally focused on their work. There would be no penetration of this building through these men.

After several security card swipes, he walked along the hallway of the B ring, toward the center of the massive five-sided complex, the largest office building in the world, and unlocked the door to his small room. There he exchanged his motorcycle jacket for the black sweater on the hook just inside. After a quick check of email he picked up his laptop and went out, verifying that the door locked behind him.

Still on the B ring, he approached the office where his 9:30 am meeting was scheduled, arriving fifteen minutes early. Outside the door the name plaque read: "Capt. John C. Simmons-Humph III." The door was ajar. Wiser paused to comprehend the noise that he heard.

He heard from inside the small, windowless, airless room the sound of a man inhaling, holding his breath, then letting it out. Leaning forward, he could just see John C. Simmons-Humph III – more commonly addressed as "Captain Humph" – standing in profile behind his desk. He was swelling out his chest and throwing forward his shoulders with each deep inhalation, all the while craning his neck to view something on or about the floor.

Wiser retraced a few steps, then stepped forward forthrightly and rapped on the door.

5

"Hey! Ah, come on in, Wiser. You're early," said Humph with a start, kicking the bottom drawer of his desk closed.

Captain Humph was a brown, chunky little chap, with a long body, short legs, not enough neck to hang him, and such long arms that had his ankles itched he might have scratched them without stooping. Through his perpetual narrow squint his eyes moved from corner to corner like a pair of BBs in a tilted glass box. He seemed to nibble on the very point of his tongue, whose pink tip occasionally darted from his taut lips.

"Thanks for working late last night," Humph said as Wiser sat down in the chair before his desk. "The same HUMINT at Taylor Caroline Media that ID'ed the journalist you're following – he got us the data that this freak had been passing around there."

"Who was the person who was passing this data?" Wiser asked.

Humph's beady eyes rolled to a stop in Wiser's direction, and he held himself motionless for a moment.

"He's no longer a problem," Humph stated evenly. He raised his upper lip from the nibbled tongue and tapped his teeth lightly together.

Wiser looked at him without expression, thinking. Was this more of his bluster? Would he actually order the death of someone for what so far amounted to a trifle?

"Was he ever a problem?" Wiser asked. "Wasn't he passing TCM actionable...?"

"– Not actionable data," Humph interrupted. "Just a bunch of wild-eyed stuff."

"So we can close this down..."

"– No, I didn't say that. I want you and your MAINWAY group to stay on the journalist – see if there's some effort there to make a mountain out of a molehill. If my data group comes up with someone else trying to do that, I'll be passing on more trace subjects to you."

"Other than this one journalist, has anyone else at TCM shown even a faint interest in the data so far?"

"Don't think so."

"Maybe I should have a look at the data to better under..."

"– No, let's not lose battle rhythm. Keep the ten-meter focus here. You're doing great. Your work got us the 10-20 on the principals and their meeting yesterday. Got anything more?"

"Once we had their location on Saturday," said Wiser, "I set up Stingray in the neighborhood. We're looking at that information now." He paused. "Is the senator following this for some purpose?"

"Don't worry about that!" said Humph, shoving a stack of papers on his desk with irritation. "Don't misunderestimate the task you've got – stay focused, that's all. Now show me who's had eyes on this."

Wiser pulled out all of the printed authorizations from the tasker folder he had brought, and he spent the rest of the meeting detailing the circle of involvement, which was very small but evidently of great interest to Humph.

As always, Wiser puzzled at this man, at his ridiculous acronym spouting and jargonizing, at his laughable malapropisms, at his insecure obsession with cutting off all of his subordinates from seeing the full context of their work. Especially puzzling was his close association with Senator Al Beddoes, head of the Senate Select Committee on Intelligence. It seemed odd to Wiser that the senator would trust this man. After one especially tiresome meeting with Humph, Wiser had thought of pulling his SF-89 to check his background, but he feared getting caught. He asked another associate on the B ring who was a good friend to take a cursory look for him.

The friend told him that according to the form, Humph had served in the Army during the Vietnam War era without necessarily seeing action, although there was no reference to any DD-214 or DD-256 discharge documents. He had briefly been a cable news "terrorism analyst" by virtue of being an "Outside Paramilitary Special Operations Officer" – a designation unknown to them both. He also listed himself as a speaker at "The Intelligence Summit" held in Washington, DC in 2006, although his name was not on the program. Under the year 2010 on the form, he listed service as the S-2 for CAAT – the Counter-Insurgency Advisory and Assistance Team – at ISAF HQ, Kabul, Afghanistan, an undocumented service. SAP redactions appeared under his listings in the National Clandestine Service.

After this litany his friend had turned to him with a smile.

"If all of this seems a bit sketchy," he said, "just think of this: He was involved in the email discovery of the sex scandal of a four-star general that we know. He wouldn't testify. For lack of evidence this was the brass cleared to become head of the CIA a few years ago."

Well, that was that. Wiser would keep his head down and not complain. After all, this was where he wanted to be: He was the member of a special team that was one step away from the highest power in the Senate on matters of national defense intelligence. He reflected that he was working for a man who, when alone with his superiors, doubtless would take exclusive credit for the work of his subordinates. It didn't matter. If he found something, it would immediately get a hearing, even without his name. He would serve. He would keep silent and keep the gray granite slab of his face expressionless.

The meeting concluded, and Wiser stood up, bracing himself for the stream of acronym-laced jargon that he suspected that Humph had rehearsed before the meeting.

"Thanks, Wiser," Humph said. "Think of what you're doing as a Garden Plot exercise. When you have time send me your FOUO eval on how your MAYWAY might impact ELINT for CDO CONPLAN 2502, CONPLAN 3501-08 DSCA, and DOD 5240.1-R. No command chops on any of this."

"Yes, sir," Wiser said, turning quickly to the door to avoid revealing any hint of a smile.

A step away from the door, his phone sent a sharp, punctuated beep, the Morse code for "RED ONE." He retrieved the phone and read the text. He turned grimly to face Humph, who was standing, waiting. He spoke.

"Another person was at the meeting with the journalist."

.

6

Walking from the Dolphin garage to the North terminal of Miami International Airport, Lagarius refocused his thoughts. During his ride from Nigredo's house to the airport, staring at the blackness inside his goggles, he had indulged that after-the-moment rewind of all the events of the evening. He replayed Nigredo's gestures, the look of his face, the way he had said things. He was satisfied that he had gained the bit of knowledge that he had wanted: Nigredo did not kill Lucas. Beyond that, he was at sea. He grew anxious when he thought that he was farther than ever from bringing his discovery to the attention of the authorities.

Lagarius forced the worry from his mind and looked around him with a sigh. In the terminal there were lovers arm-in-arm, grandmothers in sweatpants, underdressed teenagers in T-shirts, and the inevitable traveling military, mostly in camo. He saw a little girl run to her father, calling "daddy." He smiled to think that in spite of the travelers heedless of their appearance, in spite of the waiting in line and the barking security staff, there was still in the airport the romance of travel, the thrill of being on the threshold of the magic window to exotic places and adventure. He went to the coffee kiosk and bought a mocha and a package of dark chocolate. He found a comfortable chair in a corner near the gate that would take him back to Norfolk. After finishing half the coffee, he placed a square of chocolate on his tongue, settled back in his chair, and closed his eyes to think.

After twenty minutes he took the RF bag containing his phone and its battery from his inside suit pocket and assembled them. He launched Signal to call Ana. After a ring the word pair appeared on the screen as she answered. She spoke her assigned word, "Poisoned"; Lagarius replied "Ethane."

"Hi," he said.

"*Hi-yyen*," she replied, her voice a husky endearment. "*Ça va?*"

"Yes. Are you all right? Tell me where you are now."

"A girlfriend's place," she said. Then, no longer holding back, she raised her voice. "You see? I try to tell you, *ya habibi*, and you won't listen. You tell me what the fuck has happened."

"Lucas is dead."

"Ah!" she said and burst into tears. There was scrabbling phone noise, silence while retrieving a tissue, then a long sniffle. "Goddamn you, Mr. *compartiment* maestro, you got him killed."

"Yes," he said. "It's true."

"What we gonna do?" she said. "Where are you – the house?"

"No, but I will be near there soon. Which girlfriend?"

"Ricce."

"Dear god… the gender fluid Mx Ricce."

"Don't talk about that. She disrupt the gender binary – she's famous. Anyway, where you think I gonna go?"

"Yes, you're safer in a crowd, at least. Too bad you can't be with your uncle. How is he?"

"Like always. He thinks the world going to shit. He's old."

Ana's uncle, Sami Coluthon, was her principal benefactor, the "rich American uncle" – though rich only by comparison. When she was very young, her poor Druze family met him on a summer visit to his home in Yonkers, New York. On July 4 he took them to the park in Washington Heights. There he excitedly reminisced about the "wonderful people" who had stood around him on the day of his arrival in New York City: Independence Day, 1976. For the Bicentennial celebration they had looked down from the heights to watch the tall ships sail up the Hudson. He had taken many pictures and put them in a shoebox. He showed them with such animation that Ana long thought that her earliest recollection, at age two, was witnessing of the passage of the tall sailing ships – a "memory" of an event twenty-two years before her birth.

Uncle Sami arranged for Ana's schooling in Beirut after his angry discovery that she, a skinny and often sick child of seven, was the principal water carrier for her poor family. In their Beirut apartment she would fill up water containers when the water came back on just before dawn. He paid for her tuition and board at the K-12 Choueifat International School in that suburb just south of the city until she graduated. Although she was not academically inclined and really did not know what she wanted to do in life, he managed to secure an F1 student visa for her near his home, at Sarah Lawrence College – a decision he came to bitterly regret. For him, its students were "not wonderful people." They were the ones responsible for her crazily dyed hair, bizarre clothes, and tattoos – of henna, except for the inguinal dragon that he fortunately did not know of. Ana had acquired the dragon when drunk, when her lover Frittata Ricce had taken her to a tattoo parlor and insisted on it. Ana had dropped out of school and was working illegally as a bartender and as a "docent" at Ricce's art gallery. It was Ana who had arranged the party for Stevens Institute students at the gallery, where she had met Lagarius and his colleagues. One of them was smitten enough to quickly marry her. After a marriage of nine months, Ricce found Ana her current job as a "diversity and inclusion officer" at a law firm.

"What we gonna do?" Ana repeated.

"I'm stuck," Lagarius said. "I'm really stuck. I have no idea who Lucas was reaching out to. He said 'a handful' of journalists now have the data for the terrorist attack. I don't know whether to wait for their response or to approach random journalists and risk going to prison. And I *will* go to prison if the data turns out to be false: The data is my get-out-of-jail patriot card. Also, if their editors insist on corroboration, how can they reach me when they have only Lucas as their contact? His laptop might have given some clues, but it was missing from his apartment. I have got to figure out another approach to getting the information into the hands of somebody, anybody high up in the food chain before election day."

"How come? What election day?"

"Have you been asleep? In one week there is going to be a national election here. I think the terrorists have planned something for that date."

There was a long silence. Then Ana gave an excited gasp.

"You got to get the information to the important ones in the *gouvernement*, yes?"

"Yes."

"OK, you get this to your *copains* where you went to school. You said they work for CIA now."

Lagarius hummed dubiously.

"I think they have a good idea of my new line of work," he said. "We're not talking anymore."

"Ha ha, no problem. Listen to me. Ricce is having a big party for *la Toussaint*, Halloween. I mean *serious* party – all her art friends gonna be there. Billionaires' Row: You see the whole damned Central Park from this place. I get your friends there, and you meet them *par hasard*."

"That's the day after tomorrow. You think you can get them there in one day?"

"You kidding? People kill to get this invitation. Also... I gonna give it."

"I see what you mean," Lagarius chuckled. He could hear her slapping her knee with excitement.

"You see, *Hawaja?*" she laughed. "You see? I am moving your bacon from the fire."

Lagarius laughed out loud.

"Ssss!" she hissed loudly for the sound of frying bacon. "You see, you just burnt grease without Ana. I send you the address. And don't worry, your little dragon is safe from Ricce."

Then, out of nowhere came the question.

"You love me, Carmine?"

Lagarius wiped away his previous tears of laughter, then breathed deeply.

"Pretty much," he said.

They exchanged an air kiss and hung up.

Lagarius was about to disassemble his phone when he noticed that a call had gone to voicemail during his conversation with Ana. He looked at the number, hesitating. It was area code 202 – Washington, DC. He pressed the message.

"Mr. Lagarius," said a rather suave-sounding male voice. "Senator Al Beddoes, head of the Senate Select Committee on Intelligence, has information of yours that he would like for you to explain. He would like to meet you for lunch tomorrow, October 30, at 2:00 pm in Washington. Do reply for the details."

Lagarius stared at the screen for a long moment, thinking. He cursed to himself, knowing that he must have been picked up when he used his phone to photograph Lucas' contacts. How much did they really know about him? Lagarius had no illusions about the power of these people, once they had located him. Whatever they knew now, they would certainly find out everything, and they could eventually find him anywhere, given some time. They owned him.

He redialed the number.

Senator Al Beddoes

7

Lagarius felt dazed, disoriented after the thirty second conversation with the suave voice at the Washington, DC number. He was to appear at the International Hotel at 1:45 pm tomorrow and take a seat directly under the middle chandelier in the Benjamin Bar and Lounge, where someone would fetch him. He rescheduled to fly to Washington instead of Norfolk. There was no need to retrieve his laptop from home, since the information of his discovery was already in Senator Beddoes' possession, and there was no time anyway. His motorcycle could remain at the Norfolk parking garage. He would be spending the night in Miami. At the moment he just wanted to get outside, out of the terminal building.

At the cab stand he got into the first taxi and indicated the Four Seasons at The Surf Club on North Beach, where he had stayed on previous visits to Nigredo. The rain had stopped. He opened the taxi window, listened to the somehow soothing sound of the tires on the wet pavement, and breathed the washed air. In ten minutes he was there, and after checking in, walked through the lobby without going to his room. He crossed two walking paths parallel to the beach then took off his shoes and socks.

Beyond the luminous line of low breakers was complete blackness, with no light and no horizon line, the dark clouds blotting out the stars.

Lagarius stood looking into the void, inhaling the land breeze moving toward the blackness, lulled by the incessant soft crash of waves, reliving that same majestic awe that he had felt on his first view of the sea. Then, as now, the sea had not first shown him its sparkling color, but instead its tangible glorious weight sweeping to the unseen horizon, its hint of terror from the mysteries of its blind instinctive life moving now in the endless wheel of predator and prey beneath its waves. He had stood there for an hour as the orphaned brine streamed down his cheeks.

That visit had come in the night as he had walked alone on South Padre Island at age thirteen. It was during his first year at the Marine Military Academy in Harlingen, Texas, where his family had sent him for the start of the traditional military career set for its sons. He would be followed by his two brothers, the nearest five years younger - all Virginia scions of the John Pelham of Alabama, whose full-length portrait hung in the father's library.

Lagarius had hated the academy and all of its senseless military routine –
until he made two discoveries, which had saved him: Football and the
Meditations of Marcus Aurelius, both recommended to him by his beloved
history teacher, Mr. Rosten. Then came the revelation in his final year: The
youngest of the two siblings – both thick-necked and so different from him
– informed him that he was adopted as a baby, not a Pelham at all. He ran
away, not finishing school; he took his laptop and wandered America for
several years; he changed his name to that of his mother's family. Then he
was once again saved by an insightful teacher. After winning a coding con-
test offered by Stevens Institute of Technology in Hoboken, New Jersey, he
accepted a scholarship to attend there, arranged by a professor of computer
science, Artie Gelb.

That feeling of lost identity from his discovery of being an orphan came
to him now. However, now it seemed that it was the world around him
losing its identity, shedding its trusted permanence and solidity. The offer to
meet Senator Beddoes: Was that for a frank hearing – or to lure him to
prison – or to death? But could anyone *not* want information of a terrorist
attack to be known? If not, then why murder Lucas? Had even a word been
spoken to him with plain meaning, or had it all been artifice and insincerity,
cloaked in hidden motives? The airport kiosk clerk, the taxi driver, the
receptionist in the hotel lobby – had they looked at him a little longer than
a real clerk, taxi driver, or receptionist would have done? Were they – and
the host of unseen others – silently watching him, taking notes, reporting?
Crazily he thought: Were they silicon automata, sent against him with such
cunning construction that they could feign the solidity of thoughtful speech,
of a real self-directed personality?

He felt very hot. He urgently wanted to swim, to feel his arms pulling
against a familiar something, to feel the real tiredness in his body after some
effort. There was no one to be seen in either direction on the beach. He
walked the twenty yards back from the water to the beach grass and mangroves and began taking off his clothes. He jerked his head up, thinking he
had heard a voice, then the playful laughter of young women. Between two
mangroves he saw a heap of leaves and he quickly burrowed into it, so
Lagarius thought of himself, like a man who buries a burning log in a black
ash heap to save the seed of fire. He waited a moment in the leaves, listening. There was no one. Was he losing his mind? He rolled up all of his
clothes, put the roll under the leaves with his shoes that contained his
watch, then walked toward the water in his undershorts.

His first step into the dark water seemed to Lagarius as if he were placing
his foot into a sea of black ink. It was cold. He waded quickly to the line of
breakers and plunged in, then stroking away quickly to warm himself. He
swam hard, parallel to the shore for several minutes. He pulled up, treading

water. He looked toward the warm lucent hives of hotels and the city glow behind them, a glowing galaxy afloat in the dark clouds.

Then he turned away to the sea, still treading water. The sound of the waves suddenly fell away. He could hear himself breathing. The blackness before him was a complete as his closed eyes. He thought that the sense of his moving arms and legs might as well have been the illusion of a disembodied consciousness adrift in a starless void – the endpoint of all time, he remembered quizzically, when every object in a fleeing universe will outstrip the light of its neighbors. He felt the unseen immensity of the sea gently lift him on a beach-bound swell.

Then he was struck. He felt the searing burn of a jellyfish along his left side. As he winced, another swell capped and struck him in the face. He coughed out sea water. He crawled powerfully toward the shore. A long strand of seaweed tangled his arms, and he tore it aside angrily. He swam in earnest now, urged by adrenaline. His arms began to burn with effort, and his left side stung. He reached the top of the line of breakers, which seemed to have grown larger. As he went over the top stroking, the wave slammed him down then clawed him back in a powerful undertow. He breached, gasping. He tried again, and again he was towed back, this time well behind the breakers. He was afraid. He stroked powerfully toward the shore and went over the top again. He felt the undertow, and stroked furiously with all the strength left in him. He broke through, slamming his head onto the sand in the shallows, anxiously righting his feet beneath him until the waves shoved him forward to crawl on all fours.

He crawled and fell on his right cheek, gratefully clutching the wet sand. He heard the sound of giggling. He raised his head, wincing at his stings.

Lagarius saw two men capering around on the dry sand, both wearing pink florescent asymmetric thongs of hard plastic. The one being chased stopped, noticing the movement on the shore.

"Oh, *look*," he said in a high mincing voice. "It's a beached whale!"

"That's not a whale, princess, you idiot," said the other with an adenoidal voice.

They approached Lagarius with affected caution, their four hands clutched together.

"It's got jellyfish stings," said the adenoidal voice.

"Oh!" said the mincing voice. "Well, you're supposed to piss on it to make the sting go away. My mother always said that."

Then, unaccountably, like some bizarre dream image, two boys about age seven approached to within ten feet behind the two voices, completely naked, casually holding hands, following the two men in front of them. They looked at Lagarius without a word, without any expression of alarm or sympathy.

The surreal image seemed to Lagarius as if luminous humankind had sent him an example of itself, and asked him to choose between its unreality and the nothingness of the starless sea. It invited him to choose between that blackness: Perfect, with no horizon at sea and sky, no glimmer at the edge of vision; and this light: Luminous, peopled, and yet peopled with grotesque shapes not really conscious but moving in a mawkish pantomime more bewildering for its illusion of consciousness.

"Well," said the mincing voice as he reached into his thong, "I'm going to put out the fire with my little palm stalk."

"Get away from me," said Lagarius angrily, pushing up painfully on his arms - forward limbs only. "Get away from me. Now."

The two scampered off with a squeal of pretended fear, followed by the two silent, naked boys.

8

Sixty-six million years ago in the belt of rocks just inside the orbit of Jupiter, two large asteroids, disturbed by the gravity of that passing planet, smashed together. The collision flung one chunk of the iridium-laced boulders down from the plane of orbit. Ten miles wide, it drifted many years until an accidental confluence of gravity from the sun and the passing Jupiter and Mars whipshot the chunk into a sweeping ellipse. It had years to travel, but without editorials or votes to lament or contradict, its destination was set: The blue bead of water that was the Earth.

It was nighttime in what would become the Western Hemisphere when the boulder, obedient to its nature, entered the Earth's atmosphere at forty-five thousand miles per hour at an angle of fifty-nine degrees, passing from below the equator to a point that would become the coast of the Yucatán Peninsula. Its entry made the sky so incandescent that the dinosaurs that had roused from sleep to look up at its light were instantly blinded. It struck with an impact thousands of times greater than all the atomic blasts combined that would one day be detonated by the planet's clever heirs, who had not yet come into being.

The explosion sent a fireball hundreds of miles north, incinerating the giant beasts that roamed the lower great plain that had recently been up-lifted from the shallow sea, the Cretaceous Interior Seaway, stretching from the impact region to the North Pole. It melted the gypsum seabed beneath it, filling the atmosphere with a sulfuric vapor that would acidify the world's oceans; it lifted a tsunami hundreds of feet high to radiate across the water planet; its impact reverberated throughout the Earth's crust to awaken volcanoes to blacken the sky, blotting the life-giving sun from all the plants and all the creatures who lived by them.

All was not destroyed. Into a hollow, in the continent still skating north-ward a millimeter a year like those boulders pushed mysteriously across a muddy valley by the wind, the seed of a fern fell. In those millions of years that would bring it sixty-six kilometers to its present-day reference of 33.526932°N, -85.028555°W, it evolved. From it a grove of sycamores would flourish, obedient to their nature, to become an ancient witness to the nearby deviation of rivers; a witness to wildfires, to the predations of animals, to droughts and storms.

Nor were the smaller beasts all destroyed. One of the nocturnal-feeding, burrowing mammals especially prospered, its small limbic brain made alert and wary with fear. The stage was set for its evolution. The stage was set for the one at war with his own nature, the wisher for what cannot be, the great hater of all that foils his daydreams, the great liar: Mankind.

9

Senator Al Beddoes looked up from the leather-bound appointment book spread before him on the massive oak and mahogany desk, to the ornate clock on its far corner. Its hands indicated 9:11 am, with a large flourished script below indicating Wednesday. Before the clock lay a stack of bill summaries and a stack of bill drafts. He had been thinking of the battle-ground counties where his last-minute Presidential campaign stops had been scheduled; of who might already be in the Senate chamber, just on the other side of the Senate reception room that was adjacent to his office – of who might be holding out for more concessions for the votes he needed; of who might be a good running mate to replace the current know-nothing "ticket balancer," should that be necessary for a second term; thinking of who might yield to his famous "treatment" of invading their personal space with his massive six-foot-four frame while insisting on "cooperation."

His thoughts had been interrupted by the historic reminder given by the clock.

He wiped his large right hand over his long face, over his prominent nose and fine thin lips, to finally grasp his chin, resting his elbow on the desk with the other arm akimbo on his left hip. Large ears with prominent lobes framed the saturnine, Augustan face.

Yes, he thought, there had been a forgetfulness of that fateful attack by Americans, these most forgetful of all peoples. The minute hand twitched past, to 9:12.

After that attack he had carefully maneuvered for years to at last place himself on what he considered the final stepping stone to the Presidency: Not the Vice-Presidency, but the Chair of the Select Committee on Intelligence. Had the twenty-three years since the attack made those protracted calculations obsolete? Those years in the wilderness must not be wasted. He *would* be the next President of this, the most powerful nation on earth.

It seemed that Providence had sent Captain Humph to him. The man was the perfect instrument: He could claim no countervailing rights of office, since he owed that office entirely to Beddoes; he was inoculated from superiors at the CIA, since he had damning information on its director; he was perfectly deniable, since any of his failures could be blamed on the CIA; his successes were perfectly subject to expropriation, since he was part of no bureaucracy with a vested interest in advertising them; and finally, he was expendable, with no ties or visibility to anybody. Senator Beddoes knew Humph's background, just as he knew the background of every man in the

Senate and every man within his sphere of influence. Even before inter-
viewing him, Beddoes knew him for a blusterer and a fool, but yet one with
enough tools to operate in perfect secrecy, contained within a perfect bul-
wark of untouchability. Were there any examination into their relationship,
Beddoes knew he possessed the ultimate, unanswerable stop to any query:
Sorry, that's classified; national security.

He looked at the pictures of John Adams and Thomas Jefferson on the
opposite wall, their frames mounted far apart. – Quite a few lectures he had
given about those two, when he was a young man teaching history in a rural
Texas high school. – Quite a few noble things he had said about democracy,
too. Experience had tempered all that, as had the extensive reading that kept
him up late, reaching for his Fresca soft drink and fried pork rinds between
each turn of the page, now of history, now of philosophy. *What's it all for?* –
That had been for a time the fixed point of his readings on political power.
More recently it had become *What is it, anyway?* He considered how the
current President had begun his eight-year tenure with a defense of marriage
act and with repeated mention of the word "abortionist" in the same context as "murderer." And then – after merely two years! – he had won his
second term on the diametrically opposite positions. He considered this
revolution not with a feeling of lament – his sole concern now being which
side cast the most votes – but with a feeling of bewilderment. And the
Marxists hooting that they led a "revolutionary society"! Those peckerwoods!
Welcome to democracy, where every principle is overthrown by society with
every generation. And *what is power* when the supposed leaders who hold it
must maintain it by shedding their history, their past, their most basic
principles every year like a snake shedding its skin? Damn, who's running
the show here?

Beddoes wondered about the character of this person who had apparently discovered something of Humph's plans. Beddoes had restrained
Humph: There was no need at the moment to remove him from the picture.
Relax, what's the hurry? Sit down to lunch, won't you? This person could
now be found at any moment they liked. The important thing was to first
find out exactly how deep his knowledge went, and more importantly, with
whom he had shared it. If Beddoes' long experience told him anything, it
was that this afternoon's guest too would become a very useful instrument.

10

After his sting on the beach, Lagarius had dried painfully with his undershirt, put it on, then put on just his slacks. Hotel policy did not allow the concierge to give him medicine, but the man did find a bottle of vinegar and brought it to his room. Lagarius showered under hot water for twenty minutes, dowsed himself with the vinegar, then dried and lay down naked on top of the cold sheets. He stared at the ceiling, thinking, his eyes seeing no more than what he had seen of the black Atlantic an hour earlier.

Again, he thought, the next day's lunch meeting in Washington would put him in grave danger – but danger of prison, not of life, as his meeting with Nigredo had done. He had carefully provided some insurance against this danger by selecting an indebted TactiFor employee. He could say that the employee had approached him to sell classified TactiFor data, and after examining it Lagarius discovered the terror plot. Therefore, Lagarius must maintain that the employee did not know the full significance of the data, else he would have taken it to the authorities himself. Well then, how did Lagarius come to know this employee? Of course, through the foreign af-filiate, which was in Ukraine. Lagarius must document that he was paid as a security consultant for the Ukrainian government. Possibly it was an error of overconfidence that he had not forged these documents previously, but the error could be rectified. If he had time Lagarius could even learn how that government marked its internal documents as classified, to stamp them as such and thus slow the discovery of the truth, which he had absolutely no doubt would eventually be revealed. But by that time the terror plot would be made manifest. Nigredo could provide this documentation, since he had done the same thing for his fraudulent "security consulting" to Mexican companies.

'Danger of prison, not of life': Good god, thought Lagarius, are you forgetting the elephant in the room? *Lucas is dead.* Someone clearly does not want the discovered plot to be known, and is willing to kill to keep it unknown. It cannot be the government: Governments do not allow their own people to be blown up. Obviously government agents had located him using a cell site simulator, an IMSI catcher, which they must have been using to monitor not Lucas, who was too careful in any case, but the journalist. Therefore the journalist was an instrument of the killers – knowingly or unknowingly. Damn, if he could just reach him to determine which it was. Then, a feeling of cold passed over him. Lagarius thought the question as he might have spoken it aloud: *Can you say 'Operation*

Northwoods'? Governments *do* 'blow up their own people.' There was the historical proof. If that were the case here, Lagarius' only defense would be to make it clear that many, many people knew what he knew. He must be very careful to make no allusion to the death of Lucas nor to its implication that he need fear his interlocutors. As with Nigredo, he must once again walk along the edge of a knife to deliver his message while avoiding a fatal blunder.

Lagarius got up and had a look at himself in the mirror. There was a raised welt on his left cheek and neck, a long red blotch along his left side, and several lines of raised bumps on his left calf. He didn't see any stingers. He rinsed his underclothes then dried them with the hair dryer. He set his Jaeger-LeCoultre watch alarm and the room alarm, and once he had slipped between the dense lustrous dobby sateen cotton sheets, he fell immediately asleep.

At 4:00 am Lagarius was up with the alarms, and he ordered a breakfast to be sent to his room an hour later. He showered. His side itched, but there was nothing on his face except for some redness on his neck. After dressing he got the concierge to let him into the business office, where he searched the Internet for the addresses and other details that he would need in six hours' time. He printed out some forms and filled in some of the information, intending to complete them during the flight. He sent to Ana an encrypted email describing in detail his planned movements for the day, and providing instructions for what to do if he failed to call that evening. He also sent to Nigredo an encrypted email, detailing his need for Ukrainian "security consulting" documents. He returned to his room just as the food cart rolled up punctually on the hour. After hungrily eating the smoked salmon eggs Benedict on a dill waffle, with fresh-squeezed grapefruit juice, he was soon on his way back to the airport.

On the airplane Lagarius slept until his watch woke him for the last hour. He sat up and thought. On arrival at about 11:00 am at Ronald Reagan National Airport he took a taxi to the Walmart on H Street NW. There, with cash, he bought a burner phone, a Dremel hand tool with a carbide cutter, a writing marker, boxing tape, a suit of clothes, a gray hoodie, a small overnight bag, and a box to hold the clothes. While going down in the elevator to the first floor he put on the hoodie and drew it up tight under his nose. He placed into the cardboard box the other purchases, along with the forms he had printed at the hotel and filled out on the airplane. The burner phone he put into the inside pocket of his lambskin jacket under the hoodie. On the street he hailed a taxi and indicated the Smithsonian Museum. During the ride he addressed the box, which he did not seal, then busied himself loading Telegram, Signal, the Onion Tor browser, and VPN onto the burner phone.

From the Smithsonian Lagarius walked up Twelfth Street to approach
the International Hotel from the terrace, where he entered the Ishmael's
Coffee Shop there. The lunch crowd was filling the coffee shop; busy with
their orders, the staff had not noticed him slip past the queue and enter the
restroom. He changed into the Walmart suit, putting his fine jacket and
slacks into the box. He stood on the toilet and lifted a ceiling panel. He
removed the overnight bag from the cardboard box, then reaching back as
far as he could, placed the box and the Dremel case in the ceiling.

With the overnight bag under his hoodie, Lagarius walked from the coffee shop to the luggage storage service just a block away. He paid in advance
for a locker, in cash. He placed all his personal belongings, including his
disassembled personal phone and his hoodie, into the overnight bag, and
placed the bag into the secure storage, keeping only the burner phone in his
plain jacket, and his driver's license and ten one-hundred-dollar bills in his
shoe.

As he stepped out the door of the locker service onto Constitution
Avenue, he felt relieved to be done with the fussier details. He breathed a
deep lungful of the crisp October afternoon air and looked up at the
Washington Monument, piercing a sky of cloudless, perfect azure. As he
began walking east, with the National Mall on his right, he turned on the
throwaway phone. It showed 12:50 pm and a temperature of forty-nine
degrees. He called a ride share that took cash, recited his information, and
hung up to use the provided number to call his driver. There must be no
misunderstandings or failure regarding the ride that he must have, he
guessed, at 3:00 pm. He was still talking to his driver, a certain Endale,
when he took a seat on a bench in the National Gallery of Art Sculpture
Garden beside the Smithsonian. Yes, Endale said, he would be there at
Ishmael's Coffee Shop; sure, for fifty dollars he would wait forty-five
minutes; sure, *wenidimi*, depend on it.

The phone showed 1:17 pm. Lagarius looked both directions along the
path, then rose and placed the phone under a rock and some dry mulch
behind the bench. He walked west along Constitution Avenue, north along
Twelfth Street on the far side away from the hotel, finally going east to enter
the building through the middle of its three massive Romanesque arches at
1100 Pennsylvania Avenue.

He walked up to the Benjamin Bar and Lounge and turned from the
stairs to stop and look up at the skylight above the nine-storey atrium with
exposed, rather garish, tan girders in the vast, luminous space. He walked
past the appointed seat under the middle chandelier, crossing to the magni-
ficently stocked bar. Behind the bottles was a wall of old-fashioned metal
postboxes – a reminder of the building's origin as the Old Post Office a century and a quarter ago. He took note of the available scotches, then asked

for a menu from the bartender. He walked away; he sat down in the middle of the light blue sofa under the chandelier to read it.

At exactly 1:45 pm a small, prim-looking Chinese man walked up to Lagarius. He was wearing a white jacket and a bow tie the same dark blue color as the armchairs about them.

"Mr. Lagarius?" he inquired, with no trace of an accent. "You have an appointment with someone here?"

"Yes. With Senator Beddoes, at 2:00 pm."

"I can take your order when you're ready," he said, offering a menu.

"I've made a choice already," Lagarius said, returning the one in his own hand. He ordered crab cake, medium cooked Wagyu ribeye with white truffles, asparagus, and left the wine to the host's choice. The prim man turned to go.

"And one more thing," said Lagarius. "Before dinner I'll have a Royal Salute, neat. What kind of ice is used at the bar?"

"The ice?" queried the Chinese, cocking his head to the side with a slight smile. "Why, it's provided by Clinebell."

"Excellent," said Lagarius. "Please bring that on the side, apart from the scotch."

"Yes, sir," he nodded and left.

As he did, Lagarius sensed a man standing to his right behind the sofa. He looked up to see a lined gray face with a square jaw and earnest, sad eyes.

"Please follow me, Mr. Lagarius," the man said.

The pair went down the lobby stairs and eventually to an elevator with a sign beside it reading: "Museum and Clock Tower." The man regarded Lagarius wordlessly and dispassionately as the elevator ascended. He stepped out and spread his palm.

"Please stand here to be searched. Hand me your jacket and then turn out your pockets."

As he followed the instructions, Lagarius took in the spectacular view. They were on the interior observation deck above the tower clock, as the five narrow windowed columns in each of the four walls attested. To the southwest the Lincoln Memorial was visible; to the southeast, the Capitol dome. At the southwest corner of the walkway circling the perimeter was a very small elevator, more like a cage. The man unlocked its wrought-iron door, sliding it aside with a rattle, then opened his palm again for Lagarius to enter. He pressed a button at the far wall, which gave a jostle and a soft electric hum. Lagarius smelled the light scent of motor oil, paint, and sun-baked wood. The two men stood just outside each other's personal space as the cage ascended. Although Lagarius expressed nothing, the ascent puzzled him: From the street there would not seem to be anywhere to go. A few seconds later the cage stopped; the man slid back the wrought-iron door, then opened the ordinary oak door facing them onto an almost empty room.

Lagarius stepped out into a brilliantly white room flooded with light from great windows in each of the four walls. In front of them just by the door was a square dinner table covered with white linen, beyond which stretched an empty white carpet. The walls were white, with lines of gilt filigree rising up to lose themselves in a tangle of gilt vines. Above the tangle the cream-colored ceiling rose to a central point. Clearly the tiny elevator had ascended in the southwest pinnacle, one of the four that anchored each corner, to arrive at this floor directly under the tower roof. As the glimpse of blue slate just outside the windows told, the window coverings had been hydraulically lifted from the very roof of the three-hundred foot tower to provide the view. Standing close to the south window, Lagarius gazed with astonishment at the bend in the Potomac to the west; at the long verdant rectangle and reflecting pool running from the white columns of the Lincoln Memorial almost to the Washington Monument; at the bright dome of the Capitol; at the panorama of the nation's capital glittering beneath his feet under the clear October blue.

"You should take the west chair," said the man with the gray granite face, indicating with his palm once more. He opened the door to the elevator and was gone.

In the middle of the table was a foot-high piece of quartz, a form made of twenty equilateral triangles, with a smaller hologram of the same shape revolving inside. Lagarius tried to lift this fascinating object, but it was fixed to the table. He returned to the west window, which cast its rectangle of afternoon light on the white carpet nearest the chair meant for him.

Suddenly the door to the elevator burst open. In two strides the massive six-foot-four Senator Al Beddoes was standing very close to Lagarius, almost pinning him to the glass of the window. Looming over him was that well-known public face, now in its familiar pose with the head thrust forward aggressively, with the eyes narrowed, searching not to fix the eyes of Lagarius to impress or to gauge his soul, but searching his face as if to determine where to deliver a blow.

"Mr. Lagaar'us?" asked Beddoes in a Texas drawl.

Lagarius was at eye level with the senator's mouth. He looked up at him as his right hand was enveloped in the man's dry firm grip. He was dressed in a white suit with a long red, white, and blue tie and an American flag pin on one lapel.

"Senator Beddoes, yes, sir."

"Please siddown," he said, turning away.

To the Chinese waiter standing back at the door with a tray of drinks he gave a quick gesture of his hand toward the table. It was the same man who had waited on Lagarius earlier. From his tray he first set a tall glass of ice and a bottle of Fresca before the senator. Before Lagarius he placed two cocktail glasses, one of them half full of whisky, and an ice bucket with a pair of tongs. He turned to the senator.

"Thankee, Wang Wei," said Beddoes. The man nodded and left the room.

Lagarius had already extracted a chunk of the very cold clear ice with the tongs and rattled it into the empty glass. He poured half the whisky over it and brought it eagerly to his lips. The twenty-one-year-old scotch blossomed on his tongue, and kept unfolding its fragrances after he had swallowed. Lagarius quietly exhaled with satisfaction.

"Seems that you're some kinda digital housebreaker, Mr. Lagaa'rus," said Beddoes as he took a drink of the fizzing soft drink. "Is that about right?"

"No, sir. I was working on a computer assignment abroad. An American contractor offered me the files that I believe are now in your possession, hoping to sell them."

"What kinda computer assignment abroad?"

"Computer security. For Ukraine, one of our allies."

"So you pretty much know the ins and outs of how to break into computers?"

"I would hope so."

"And this fella, he knew he had some valuable files, did he?"

"He thought so. He's not an IT person. He certainly didn't know that they contained information regarding a terror attack on the United States."

"Many people know about these files?" asked Beddoes after a pause.

"Not yet. But in twenty-four hours I have set their automatic release to hundreds of people."

"Ah ha," said Beddoes quietly. "I want you to hold off, keep this between us. Can you do that?"

Lagarius nodded in assent. Beddoes took a long drink of Fresca.

The senator then reached inside his jacket and, seeming to swell over the five-foot-square table without rising, dropped a color print into the bright square of sunlight that had reached the table corner near Lagarius' left forearm.

It was a print of Bellini's Christ. Christ's right hand was raised in blessing, his left holding a red staff that extended out of the picture. In his bare torso the almost surgically innocuous scar of the spear wound of the Crucifixion was visible on his right side. Behind him, in the quiet sunrise landscape, were the symbols of the Resurrection in quiet gravitas: Two rabbits, a bird in a dead tree, the three Marys, the steeple of the one Church. But the torso did not bear the original work's head of the young Christ in the thin russet first beard of youth, in russet curls: It was decapitated; a black oval showed at the top of the severed neck. A dinner plate was at his waist, on which lay a Guy Fawkes mask, its V-shaped caricature looking up at the missing head of Christ.

"That there was prominent amongst your files," said Beddoes. "I want you to tell me what that crazy-assed pitcher has to do with a terr'ist attack."

"Yes, sir," said Lagarius, looking down at the image that was familiar to him, not touching it. He paused a moment. "In the digital version of this file, that black oval contains an encoded message. It's very unique. It begins with a public key of 128 hex characters: A mix of numbers 0 through 9, letters A through F. A key like that is used to generate an address on the most common blockchain platform for business, Ethereum. Like an Ethereum address..."

"– Excuse me," interrupted Beddoes. "What's an 'Ethereum address'?"

"It's just an account number. All of the many people involved in a complex transaction have the same account or address. Like the address on the curb outside your house, that's not secret. But just as you let only known persons inside your home, only those who each use a private key to generate a match of that address can get in. – Many persons, many keys, but one secure entry."

"What's the whole point of all that?"

"The point is that while I think that this public key is for blockchain use, I don't think it's used on Ethereum – the platform is too public. After that key are forty more characters that never change across all the messages. I think that's the address. Those two elements must put the large encrypted message below them onto a private platform. Now, that message changes all the time, because it contains one of many transactions, each a separate update by the many workers in the network."

"Why the hell mess with all this blockchain doin's anyhow? Why not just send the encrypted message and be done with it?"

"Ha ha, good question. But that would be a mess if many people were passing around a bunch of encrypted files. And that's exactly my concern: That this is a huge network of terrorists who can instantly coordinate every detail of a complex operation. All they need is this image, which can be anywhere on the Internet. They just download the image, then, with each person's private key, use some custom blockchain software written just for their network to reconstitute the chain. No one outside can crack it, yet everyone inside the vast network is perfectly informed of all the transactions of its many users."

"If nobody can crack it, then what do you want me to do about it?"

"One, the government has the tools to find out where this very unique image is being picked up. Even if it's in somebody's email draft folder, never passed around, and even if the pickup location changes, still it has to be posted by someone. Second, only the government has the decrypting horse-power to possibly read more of the messages."

"But if you're right, that would be just one little message, not the whole picture – like looking through a keyhole to see a speck of an elephant."

"Maybe," conceded Lagarius. "But with a few pixels you can guess a universe."

"You said '*more* of the messages.'"

"Yes, sir. Not that I have a whole one – I've decrypted part of just one of them. In the message the encryption scheme itself seems to change every forty characters."

"And what is that part, Mr. Lagaar'us?"

"It reads: 'magnesium igniters X'."

At that moment there was a knock inside the elevator door.

"Come on in," said Beddoes.

Wang Wei entered, pulling a food cart with two large covered silver plat-ters on it. He placed silverware, then uncovered one platter and set out a plate overwhelmed with a forty-ounce tomahawk ribeye for the senator. A glass of ice and a new bottle replaced his drained Fresca. For Lagarius came the Japanese Wagyu ribeye topped with white truffle butter, and a crystal glass of red wine. Bread and vegetables were set.

"Thankee, Wang Wei," said Beddoes to the server, who nodded and left. The happy clink of silverware sounded as the two men began eating.

At a well-prepared meal, mankind's last universal sacrament, tensions relax and conviviality reigns, no matter on what terms the diners may be with each other. This influence was especially heightened now in Beddoes, who yielded to another profound human feeling: The need to reveal oneself, the irresistible urge to make one's thoughts manifest in the world, whether as a confession for the relief of guilt, or much more commonly as a public justification, an expression of the intersubjective mutuality that founds our language and reason. Beddoes was glad to play his public role as the coarse rube from Texas: It was useful to his realization of political power. But it was a role that left him alone with thoughts that he had distilled from a lifetime of reading and thinking: Fearful thoughts that he dare not share with any-one – except perhaps with this nobody, one of the intelligent "elves" as he called them, in this gifted moment of heart-unburdening communion.

"How's the steak?" asked Beddoes.

Lagarius savored the perfectly marbled ribeye, each strand of which seemed sheathed in butter that melted in his mouth.

"There is nothing like it on earth," said Lagarius, causing Beddoes to chuckle. There was a pause.

"I can guess that you've had some trouble gettin' people innersted in what they might think of as a cock and bull story. Why you doin' it? I mean, you'd be in deep shit if somebody was to think that you was the one stole those files, wouldn't you?"

Lagarius returned his intent look, hoping that he concealed his sudden anxiety. He answered carefully, safely.

"Senator, I sincerely believe that many Americans are in mortal danger with this planned attack. I believe that our very democracy is at stake."

"Thuh!" Beddoes snorted. "Democracy! What's that? Ever read the stuff on the wall of that fella down there?" He gestured toward the Lincoln Memorial. "He said he fought a war for 'gummint of the people, by the people, for the people.' Bullshit. The Union soldiers in that scrap actually fought *against* self-determination."

"But they fought against those who were 'self-determined' to keep slavery, to keep another race from participating in democracy."

"And did that race participate then? Do they now? And looka thar, at the trap you're already in: The fiction that democracy's the happy party for anybody you invite. Democracy, huh! White, black, brown, yaller, polka-dot – no discrimination: It's an equal-opportunity fiction. We trick the old with inflation, since they remember the prices when they was young; we entice the young with gummint bounty that they'll one day be enslaved to provide. And what about them in the middle? The middlin' ones is what's pullin' the wagon – and if they think to stop pullin', why the yappers will put a whip to 'em, the smartest whip bein' to call 'em racists. The general rule for all: The intemperate will be appeased, and the temperate will be blamed."

"But they're free to elect anybody they like to change all that."

"Yeah, and how's that been workin' for ya? Who do they elect? We got Presidents who say 'is a liar' depends on what '*is* is'; Presidents who can't find ten countries on a map; Presidents who think his opponent's father was the goddamned second gunman on the grassy knoll. We got Congress people who don't know what the Internet is, who think that the island of Guam will tip over if 8,000 Marines show up there, who think the USA has landed on Mars."

"OK, it's a terrible system until you consider the alternatives, as someone said."

"That author of Operation Keelhaul was better as a stand-up than a statesman. Democracy put him up there. Democracy put up the federal clowns that send money to the Free Syrian Army, the Syrian affiliate of the very people, al Qaeda, who attacked us on 9-11; clowns who have half the American population dependent on federal assistance. Democracy ain't nothin' but a circus with the monkeys as ringmaster."

"So, we'd be better off with tyranny?" Lagarius chuckled.

"Who's the threat there? Someone who knows what power is, like me, or some twinkle brain who thinks that the gummint is the fucking tooth fairy?

And remember that's a gummint not led by the talented, who went into bid-ness and technology, but led by the dregs. You keep giving godlike powers of gummint to mediocrities and, by god, you *will* see what tyranny looks like."

"Senator, is that the best we can do to keep us from anarchy?"

"You are confused, son. Anarchy *always* exists."

"I don't understand."

"The group that writes the laws always stands outside the law, is without law. What, you think the lawgivers wrote law to put a yoke on *themselves*? Is Congress yoked to hold spending, to avoid a twenty-six trillion dollar debt? Is the Supreme Court yoked to avoid a *Citizens United* or *Roe v Wade*? Is the President yoked to avoid torture when he's got the Zelikow memo; is he yoked by Posse Comitatus when he can whip out the 1807 Insurrection Act? No, the question is not *whether* to have anarchy, but *who* is to have it."

"Really, sir? To act in any way they please, without any standard or absolute?"

Beddoes leaned back in his chair, chewing, waving the huge bone of his half-eaten tomahawk ribeye vaguely over his plate.

"'When society no longer recognizes an absolute, society will then be-come its own absolute.' Yeah, I've read that. But really, who is this 'society'? It sure as hell ain't the people. It's those with power, and the yappers and elves workin' for 'em."

Lagarius managed a questioning chuckle in his bewilderment at what he was hearing.

"Yappers – the second-hand dealers in ideas who couldn't get a real degree at college, but who are useful in whipping up the worshipers of democracy; elves – folks like yourself who have some technical knowledge to keep the gears turning.

"The one thing that everyone aims at is power – everyone, from the sorry shit who beats his wife to the king of the hill in gummint. It tops happiness; it tops 'flourishin'.' What, you think makin' a pile of money, or bein' famous, or draggin' a stack of books onto some desert eye-land and hatchin' some idea is *flourishin*'? Why, that's no more 'n a fart flourishin' in a whirl-wind. Son, flourishin' is *power*, plain and simple – and power ain't nothin' without power over other people.

"Like Teddy Roosevelt said, 'I believe in power, and I have used every ounce of power there was.' Every society requires a class that does not fun-damentally question its own power. Look around and ask yourself, Who are the members of this class currently? Knowing that will tell you the direction your society is headed. Does your society want to abolish that class by hollerin' for 'equality'? If so, it's hollerin' for chaos – not for anarchy, but chaos, the law of the jungle.

"Oh yeah, for now I'll kiss the butt of the solar myth of democracy on Main Street. I'll go online with a zucchini up my ass if it'll keep me in office. But eventually there will come a day when *I* have the power over Americans – not to imprison or break bones. Naw, the days of Lubyanka are gone. – Don't need that. What I mean is to have a special kinda power whereby the citizen willin'ly enslaves and destroys *hisself*. Blamed remarkable how easy it is.

"The first key is the moral sanction. Is he sanctioned to do this or that act, no matter how despicable? The one in power will decide. Did you think that the convolutions of the tax return or the common-sense-defyin' arcana of the laws were a bureaucratic mistake? Huh! Why, that's more 'an half their value. They're there to habituate the citizen to obedience, to the re-flexive acceptance that we own his time and, in the end, his very person, his very mind. We would oppose efficiency and common sense even if they *were* possible. The forms, the licenses, the registrations, the chickenshit have one goal: To gradually inure the citizen to the acceptance of the principle that it is the state – not the superstitions of the church or the silly heritage of his ancestors rottin' in forgotten graves – that gives the verdict on what's right and wrong. We're not there yet, I grant you. Ain't it strange? Modern gum-mints have the power to reduce your person" – here the senator raised his great right hand and gave a loud snap of his fingers – "just like that, to its ninety-odd constituent elements, but typically they don't. Now how come? Over two thousand people go missin' in this country ever' year. Why not add a few troublemakers to the lot? But naw, they don't. There's still some hesitation, some annoyin' sense of the sacred attachin' to this poor eatin', pissin', fornicatin' flesh we're made of. So gummints bumble with the faked suicide, the unto'ard accident, leavin' that oozin' sack of forensic trouble that is you. But we're gettin' there.

"The second key is to say that all things are political. For if all things are political, then all questions will be settled by force. It's all I can do to keep from laughin' out loud when I hear the yappers say, 'It contributes to the national dialog on the question.' – Ha ha, no, wait, 'scuse me! They say, 'It *sparks* a national dialog' – not 'initiates,' not 'inspires' – way too abstract! Oh wait, no, ha ha, here's what they'll say: 'He *or she* will spark a national dialog'! Yes, let's dick it up perfect – sexism-free, abstraction-free. Every little nudge toward my total power counts! Ha ha ha! But a 'national dialog,' by all means. So long as those self-important yappers are amplifyin' our signal, we'll yak up their First Amendment protections. But let them go off frequency and we'll pull that, *pronto*. Let 'em keep up the pantomime of a 'national dialog,' so long as it's a top-down monologue with my power as the final arbiter."

Lagarius felt dazed. This was the man with whom he was entrusting information to turn aside a murderous attack? He looked at his empty plate, shook his head, then looked up to the senator.

"But if power is the name of the game, if ideals, morals, restraint – all of that – mean nothing, then power can randomly end up in the hands not only of 'twinkle brains' or enlightened despots, but of really evil people. – And I'd say that the ones with no ideals, morals, or restraint have a huge head start in the game. You're putting power in the service of chance!"

"Maybe so," Beddoes said distractedly as he thumbed the phone he had taken from his jacket. Then, pocketing the phone and looking up to Lagarius: "We'll have to take this up in hell, Mr. Lagaar'us, where we'll have more time." He wiped his mouth and tossed the napkin beside his plate.

"We will give your information serious evaluation," he said, rising. "But until you hear from me I expect you to keep this between us. Ain't no need for second guessers raisin' needless alarm when an authoritative gummint answer will be forthcomin'."

"Please remember, sir," said Lagarius, who had risen to take the offered hand, "the Guy Fawkes mask in the image. Guy Fawkes Day falls on next Tuesday, election day. That may be significant as the date of the attack."

"Noted," said Beddoes, taking his seat as the service door opened.

Humph and Wiser entered, leaving Wang Wei standing against the elevator's far wall, his hands folded below his waist. Wiser closed the door. Humph picked up the color print from the corner of the table, and with the photo between his two extended fingers, rather imperiously handed it to Wiser without taking his eyes from the senator, who looked at Wiser and nodded toward the door.

"Show our guest out," he said.

Wiser opened the door for Lagarius to enter the elevator. When he did, the senator looked toward the Chinaman standing inside.

"Bring me that crème brûlée and a cup of coffee, would you, Wang Wei?"

"Yes, sir. I'll knock when I return."

Lagarius and Wiser left the room. When the door closed, Humph looked stunned, his mouth open.

"He's leaving!" Humph spluttered. "You want me to snuff him?"

"Shut your upper hole and siddown."

Humph pulled out the chair nearest the senator and sat down in silence.

"First: How far is your assistant into this?"

"Oh, Eden – he's just my tech guy – tracker and researcher."

"Don't bring him around anymore; I don't like the way he looks. And now: 'Snuff.' Don't use that word around me ever again. *I* decide, *I* and no one else."

"Yes, sir. Sorry, sir."

Beddoes forked a remaining bite of meat, swept it through a spot of juice on his plate, and put it into his mouth.

"Why would you want to get rid of your patsy?" he asked, chewing.

"Sir?"

"Mr. Humph, are you a complete dumbass?" he asked, his voice rising. "This Lagaar'us fella walks in here, offers hisself up to cover your tracks, and *you* – you want to get *rid* of him?"

A small wattage light began to illuminate in Humph's eyes.

"What you do is take that data of Mr. Lagaar'us and rework it to make it look like he created all the incriminating files, and look like you discovered him. Got it?"

"Ah! Yes sir, yes *sir*."

"This Lagaar'us will wait a while for results from us. When he sees none, and risks making a last-minute approach to journalists, we will rework that as his desperate ploy to save his skin."

Beddoes paused and ran his tongue over his teeth with satisfaction.

"Now tell me, what is *blockchain?*"

"Uh? Sir?"

"*Ah ha,*" Beddoes said softly. "Just what I thought. Since you apparently cain't find your ass with both hands on this stuff, the work of this Lagaar'us also can provide a check on the folks at TactiFor. Obviously you cain't get gummint elves to help you without, ah, puttin' a little too much light on your plans. All you have to do is tail him so that he doesn't get anybody serious innersted in him. Can you do that?"

"Does a man wear clothes?" Humph smiled and winked.

The senator looked at him fixedly, without expression. He curled his upper lip to give a loud suck on his teeth.

"Ahem, I mean, sir, there's GPS threading in his jacket now. We can't lose him."

"See that you don't," the senator said. "And I'm warning you not to let this person come to harm."

He looked back to his plate, musing as if already alone. He nodded toward the door without looking up, and Humph went out, dipping his head once toward the senator's indifferent profile.

The senator sat deep in thought, his face long and serious like a sentient bloodhound, as he looked toward the Washington Monument in the distance without seeing it, his lips parting and closing for his crème brûlée without his even imagining it.

11

Captain Humph drove back to the Pentagon after the afternoon lunch at the International Hotel. His mind was on the war room that he had established for following events related to the project for Senator Beddoes, but he first went to his desk to check email. Nothing there. Before standing to go out, he pulled out the bottom drawer where a book lay open: *Become Who You Are, Big Man!* He stood and cocked his head to read the large print and to study its accompanying graphic:

> Don't forget the technique of the Forty-third President! As you stand, turn the knuckles of your thumbs in, toward your legs! Feel your shoulders suddenly grow wider! What an impression you'll make, walking into a room like that!

Humph tried the suggestion. Yes, it sure works! He strutted away from his desk with his bigger shoulders, then came back, looking down to make sure he copied the graphic just right. Satisfied, he kicked the drawer closed and went out.

He strode to the war room on the B ring, trying out the new technique, but the one functionary in the room had not looked up when he entered. The "war room" was simply a larger office with two big-screen monitors: One showed a map silently flashing a red dot indicating the GPS location from Lagarius' suit jacket; the other was a Google map for the same location. A bored-looking man with thick glasses sat before the two screens, idly zooming in and out on the flashing GPS with no apparent purpose.

"Got the 10-20 on our subject?" Humph grimly barked out as he approached. He threw his jacket over the back of the empty chair beside the man and began rolling up his sleeves. His eyes narrowed intently, two beads rolling from one screen to the other. The tip of his tongue nervously tapped the bottom of his front teeth.

"Meh," said the man. "Headed north. Highway 29."

Humph sat down. After several minutes the north-bound flashing red dot stopped moving.

"He's stopped," said Humph, leaning toward the screen. "Where is he?"

The man double-clicked the flashing dot, and the other screen centered and zoomed to that location on the Google map. The photograph in the upper left showed the blue awning of a Greyhound Bus station on Fenton Street in Silver Spring, Maryland.

"What the hell?" said Humph. "Is he getting on a bus?"

The other man gave an uncertain grunt.

Humph watched the screens for twenty minutes with impatience. He looked at his watch repeatedly. It was a little after 5:00 pm. Humph stood up.

"I'm going to grab a bite," Humph said. "Text me if he starts moving."

The man gave a grunt of affirmation.

Humph walked to the food court and bought two large slices of already-cooked pizza. He sat down in a plastic chair to eat the oily, salty meal.

As Humph was taking his last bite, his phone beeped. The text read: "Moving." The time was 5:53. Humph threw down the crust and jogged back to the war room. He burst in, out of breath.

"Where's he headed?" asked Humph as he pulled up his chair.

"Route 27 - now turning north on Interstate 95," the man said, turning to Humph and sniffing. "Pepperoni?"

Humph scowled. He pulled the keyboard and mouse closer to him, then opened another tab on the browser and searched the Greyhound Bus schedule. He found the listing for the bus departing Silver Spring, Maryland at 5:50 pm.

"Jesus, he could be headed anywhere," said Humph. "That thing makes stops at Baltimore, Philadelphia, New York, Boston...."

Humph stood up in alarm.

"Holy shit! Last stop is Bangor, Maine. That sucker is trying to leave the country!"

He sat down and snatched up the desk telephone. He would call up the New Jersey Highway Patrol, fly ahead of the Interstate 95 route to join up with the patrol officer, chase down the bus... - And what? he thought. Then what? So what if this Lagarius was traveling somewhere. Humph likely did not have any authority to pull someone off a bus, and certainly he did not have any instruction from Senator Beddoes to do so. To the contrary, his instruction was to simply follow him. He put down the phone.

"As you said," noted the man beside Humph, "he could get off at any stop in between."

"Yeah," said Humph glumly.

He had to think. He was not going to screw this up like last time. His ears burned with the embarrassed recollection.

It happened several years ago, when Humph began his service to Senator Beddoes. After his five-hour interrogation of one Menipu Awak, Humph's Joint Terrorism Task Force "cracked" a "sleeper cell" that was building a multimillion-dollar school to spread the seeds of Islamic holy war to Pakistani immigrant children up and down the Lodi, California farm belt. At no time was Humph taken in by the fiendish Mr. Menipu Awak's guise as the neighborhood ice cream man who drove the beige ice cream truck with Homer Simpson painted on the back. The man had wilted under his professional questioning, confessing on camera to having seen *thousands* of men wearing black Ninja Turtle masks performing pole vaulting exercises, in a basement no less, safe from spy satellites.

After Menipu Awak's further confession to having met known jihadists years after their confirmed deaths, Humph's rescue of the former republic was quickly suppressed. Senator Beddoes leaned on his connections in the media to delete the online stories that Humph had excitedly leaked.

Well, that was not going to happen again. Captain John C. Simmons-Humph III decided to take the bull by the horns. His instincts told him that Lagarius was indeed headed for the border. *That* would put this Mr. Lagarius in the bag once and for all, no matter what excuses he might make to the senator that he was "just traveling." His capture would add to the damning evidence against him – proof that he meant to get away before his perfidious crimes became known. He would follow this Mr. Lagarius in his car – that was the gritty, hands-on approach to this caper. Yes, there would be the long drive, the countless cups of coffee washing down fast food as he squinted relentlessly ahead to his prey. Then there would be the moment of exultation: He would be standing there at the Bangor, Maine station as Lagarius stepped off the bus to meet his accomplices. What would Humph say? What triumphant wisecrack would he utter as Lagarius' face fell in dismay? "Headed for the border, Mr. Lagarius?" Or better: "Dressed for Canada, Mr. Lagarius? I've got a cold cell waiting for you!" Or, the pith of wit: "Why, hello, snowbird!"

Humph stood up with resolve, grabbed his jacket from the chair, and briefly faced his assistant.

"Camo, I'm P-O-V balls to the wall Oscar Mike for the next twelve hours. Stay frosty, 24-7 – I'll be in touch."

"Roger that," said the man.

As he went out the door, Humph thought, "Maybe I should go with 'I don't think you'll be having a Labatt tonight, Mr. Lagarius!' Or maybe 'Short on beaver tails, Mr. Lagarius?'."

Well, there would be time to think about all that during the drive.

12

Wolff, Wolfe, and Lamb was a law firm dedicated to democracy. It was for that dedication that Ana Coluthon landed her position as its "diversity and inclusion officer" – a position won on the recommendation of Frittata Ricce several months ago. Her recommendation amounted almost to an appointment. "Mx Ricce," to use the salutation she demanded, was an academic well known throughout America, who had placed many women in that position in many other law firms and government administrations. These postings were part of several carefully considered campaigns to promulgate change regarding gender and race throughout the land. On another front she was energetic in the selection of those who made schoolbook choices for children in elementary and secondary schools. On yet another front she was active in what she termed "the dilution of the elites": Packing academe with meretricious majors taught by those obedient to the party line that got them their lifetime sinecures. She considered Wolff, Wolfe, and Lamb to be her flagship outpost, and had long been chafing that her appointment previous to Ana had become less than zealous. When Ana divorced from her nine-month marriage to a colleague of Lagarius, Ricce leapt at the opportunity to give the job to her former lover from Sarah Lawrence College.

A general "wokeness" already prevailed at the firm, its principal realizations being a "queer diversity training" requirement and a required signed pledge against "cultural appropriation" by new-hires – for example, abjuring long braids and cornrows by white females. Also established through Ricce's agency was a revised legal lexicon, which for example mandated the expression "justice-involved individual" instead of the pejorative "criminal" or "felon."

However, the appointment of Ana, under the careful tutelage of Ricce, kindled a new enthusiasm for change regarding gender and race at the firm. Now entering into the annual employee evaluations were things such as attendance at "Race to Dinner" events – sessions where exemplars of various races and genders arrived at sponsors' homes to be banqueted in exchange for delivering guilt-inspiring personal harangues of aggressions – variously macro-, micro-, or systemic – suffered at the hands of the bigoted ruling matrix. Another checkbox on the annual evaluation was participation in Ricce's Great Books reading program, which featured titles such as *Oral Sadism and the Vegetarian Personality*, *Lesbian Sadomasochism Safety Manual*, *The Joy of Sex: Pocket Edition*, and *How to Poo on a Date*.

New initiatives extended to the C-suite as well. A board member was fired for his bearing the racially incendiary family name of Lynch. A progressive slate of *pro bono* litigation was drafted. Discrimination lawsuits were set for Michigan men who had been denied licenses for marriage to their silicone significant others, and for the persecuted many whose marriage at a Burning Man festival to themselves – that is, each to his significant other in the shaving mirror – had been invalidated. There was legal defense planned for the transgender man anguished in his birthing class by the phrase "expectant mother," for discriminations against the six-foot-two man who had transgendered to a girl of six, for the same-sex couple barred from reassigning the gender of their four-year-old. And for the firm's branch across the Pond, discrimination suits were planned in defense of the human dog of Salford, of the human goat of London, of the betrothed London lesbians Sharon and Cindy, the latter cruelly discriminated against simply for being a dolphin, and of the woman of Leeds denied betrothal to her chandelier and the woman of Stockport denied betrothal to her rug, her charming Matt.

These initiatives were hardly a joke for Ricce. Yes, she could share a laugh over some of the more preposterous examples whenever they came up during interviews, even mirthfully suggesting that the British cases were vanguard examples of The English Way whose persecutions cried unto heaven for legal remedy. But their greater purpose in her aggressive deconstruction of the sacred she kept to herself. And the line between earnest advocacy and purely desacralizing exaggeration? She kept its demarcation to herself as well.

Ana learned of a still more ambitious program planned by Ricce in her two days apart from Lagarius – one that she was flattered to know depended on her skills and leadership. The coaching had been intense, and a trial of the results would be demonstrated at the grand party in the most expensive penthouse in Manhattan tomorrow evening, Halloween.

Artie Gelb

13

Eden Wiser had accompanied Lagarius to the entrance to the International Hotel's observation deck at street level, facing Twelfth Street. They had not spoken during the descent. Wiser had studied the face before him in the elevator, the face looking past him, lost in thought. This did not seem to Wiser to be the face of a criminal. True, it had missed the morning's shave, but the face seemed open, unguarded, spontaneous, with intelligent eyes and the hint of a smile above the stubbled, dimpled chin. Wiser had simply opened the door for him, and the man had walked out, saying "thank you."

Lagarius walked swiftly north on Twelfth Street and turned right to re-enter the hotel. He walked straight through to exit at the south terrace where Ishmael's Coffee Shop was located. At one of the wire outdoor tables sat a young man with Caucasian features but the skin and hair of a black. His hands were on the table with no drink before him. The thumb of both hands seemed to come directly off the palm, as if its first joint were fused or missing.

"Endale?" asked Lagarius.

"Yes," he said, starting to rise and offer his right hand.

"Wait," said Lagarius, shaking his hand. "I'll be right back. Did you look up the destination?"

"Yes, I have been there."

Lagarius entered the coffee shop and proceeded to the restroom. He stood on the toilet and pushed up the panel overhead. He reached far back and retrieved the Dremel case and the cardboard box. He took off the plain Walmart suit and dressed with his clothes from the box, putting the plain suit inside and sealing it with the tape. He felt relieved to be out of the off-the-rack suit and back into the soft Tagliatore jacket and properly-fitting slacks. He placed the printed forms on top of the sealed box while he glanced into the mirror and combed his hair with his fingers. The Dremel had not proved necessary. He had bought it for the possibility that a hardened bracelet might have been attached to his ankle, which he would have removed. Of course its removal would have alerted those monitoring it, and would have demanded his hurried action to place it into the box with the plain clothes and send it on its way.

When Lagarius emerged onto the patio, Endale did not seem to notice the change of clothing. He was standing, and seemed intent on one thing.

"I know it is not forty-five minutes, but I still need my fifty dollars," he said.

"Will you take a hundred?" asked Lagarius, smiling. "Look at these forms. You see there at the bottom? You will be asked for less than a hundred at the bus station. Pay them from this three hundred, and the rest is yours."

"All right!" beamed Endale. He gave a vigorous handshake.

"You do any work around the house?" asked Lagarius. He opened the Dremel case.

"Oh yeah, sure."

"Well, here, take this. It's a bonus."

"Yeah, man, sure!"

After another vigorous handshake and big smile, Endale was gone.

Lagarius walked quickly south on Twelfth Street then turned right toward the locker service company. Twenty minutes later he was standing in front of the Smithsonian, feeling properly himself now that he had retrieved his phone and could feel the weight of his Swiss timepiece on his wrist. He walked next door to the National Gallery of Art Sculpture Garden. There he found the burner phone behind the bench, undisturbed from its placement there several hours earlier. He began using it to call for a ride share as he walked idly out onto the National Mall, where the light of late afternoon cast long golden light along the hectic green grass. All the drivers would take cash, and none would ask for his identification. It would have been convenient to use them to travel to New York, but for two complications: He would have to show identification to get a New York City hotel room, and the files he needed to show tomorrow were only on his laptop at home, not in the Cloud. He must return home. He would have to switch out in Richmond and get a second driver to take him on to Norfolk – a total three-hour trip. But no matter.

Lagarius looked west at the shadow of the Washington Monument, the blackening finger of an enormous sundial that was sweeping slowly to some horrific, unknown minute of detonation. As he looked east to the Capitol, now flooded in the slanting sunlight, a sadness overtook him. Somewhere inside that golden marble was Senator Beddoes, possibly the nation's next President, whom he felt he had not persuaded of the seriousness of events as impending and ineluctable as the tick of time toward an alarm. He replayed the senator's remarks in his mind, searching for his true motives, turning over each phrase for meaning, anxiously wandering a hall of mirrors. He sighed deeply. Ah, well: At the Norfolk airport he would once again be astride the MV Agusta for the sweet ride home.

14

Thursday a rosy-fingered dawn found Lagarius swimming in the sea.

He had arrived just before 10:00 pm the night before, and as always, had carefully checked the beach house perimeter and interior alarms before opening the garage and gliding in. Once in his study he had launched his tablet and studied Ana's Telegram message that detailed the access information for the Halloween party, loading its QR code onto the burner phone. He had loaded the files to be given to his colleagues at the party onto a thumb drive, and had put the drive and tablet inside his lambskin jacket. He added cash from a safe to his money clip and set out his Alpinestars SMX-1R short riding boots, which he would not need to change for the party. He had prepared a corned beef sandwich and a glass of milk, which he had taken to the table on the upper deck. He had smiled to see the belt and shoulders of Orion due east, low on the horizon. He had smelled the land breeze, heard the soft crash of waves, sitting there for almost an hour. After he had prepared for bed, he had slept without moving until the alarm sounded at 5:00 am.

After his morning swim, a shower, and a toasted bagel heaped with a good dollop of Ana's moghrabieh – still good after the two days – Lagarius placed his two phones inside his jacket and locked a good pair of shoes and a change of clothes under his motorcycle seat. He straddled its one-hundred seventy-four horses, snapping them to life with the button under his gloved thumb. Casque down, he was soon past the Cape Henry Lighthouse and on Highway 13, on the long bridge over Chesapeake Bay. It would be a pretty ride along the Virginia and Maryland coast, at least at the start.

It had been a few minutes after 6:00 am when Lagarius had set out – fifteen hours before his bus package was set to arrive at its final destination at Bangor, Maine.

Lagarius could have trimmed the total time to New York to five hours, but in fact he had time to kill. In Wilmington he took lunch at Banks' Seafood Kitchen, having Clams Casino and grilled Faroe Island salmon, dawdling for two hours as he sat on its patio overlooking the Christina River; then he took a four hour nap at the public library. By the time he arrived in New York and turned into the penthouse garage on Fifty-Seventh Street near Carnegie Hall, it was well after 7:00 pm and dark.

Lagarius secured his motorcycle near the entrance within view of the guard and ran a security cable through his casque, leaving it there. He texted Ana on the burner phone as he entered the expansive lobby of cream-colored stone and gold trim, then pocketed the phone as the elevator doors opened. Stepping inside, he marveled as he pressed the button for the eighty-fifth floor, and felt his ears pop repeatedly during the ascent.

Ana was standing there to greet him as the elevator doors slid open with a wave of deafening music – Annie Lennox singing *Sweet Dreams Are Made of This* – its bass line reverberating in his chest and vibrating the fabric of his slacks.

"*Hawaja!*" she screamed, laughing and extending her palms to his cheeks, fingers splayed. She gave him a long kiss with wet lips. "No hug for you – still working on my body paint."

She was wearing white bath slippers and a white silk dressing gown. The parts of her not covered by the gown – her feet, the backs of her hands, her face – were aquamarine blue with body paint, apparently not completely dried. Her hair was blue, and jelled in waves above her head like loose hair submerged in water.

"Come, come," she said, raising her voice above the din. "You *copains* here already."

Lagarius stepped forward into a vast room that seemed to be at the bottom of a coral reef. Holographic images of brightly colored coral hung magically in the air before him. Wavering blue light played across the space, pierced by shafts of golden beams like sunlight penetrating the waves.

"What's this?" asked Lagarius. He had turned to his right, looking into a grotto dripping with sparks of light running down fiber optic strands to the floor. Inside were many amorphously shaped dark blue armchairs resembling wads of modeling clay. In a few of the armchairs people sat wearing hologram glasses, their heads turned upward, occasionally flinching away from some invisible object, laughing and marveling.

"That's the Lotus room," said Ana, close to his ear. "You can go, but mostly for people who get too crazy or too stoned. Kind of a time-out room from the big production – here I show you. Oh, look! Yoo-hoo!" she yelled, waving her arms to someone far ahead. "Naa, they can't hear me. You *copains* on the other side of security."

Far ahead stood a security scanning gate in a pool of light. The vertical beam of white light bathed the head and shoulders of each guest as he stepped from the gate's metal archway. On the far side stood a huge man, shirtless, bald, and with a patch over his left eye. He held up each of four men, feeling carefully with both hands through the woolen costumes that covered their head and back.

"Here, take this," said Ana loudly, giving him a fluffy bundle that she had retrieved after pointing behind the coat check girl.

"What's this?"

"That your Halloween costume," said Ana. "You and you *copains* are a herd of sheep."

Lagarius laughed. The cap of the costume had a long bill that hung down with the face of a sheep; from its back fell a fluffy woolen rug. He put it on and laughed again. He had to tilt his head back to see where he was going.

"This is outrageous."

"You lucky. Ricce first thought to make you *un troupeau de porcs*, uh, piggies. – Oh look, there she is now!" said Ana. "Ricce!"

She advanced to the short, squat woman who had just approached her, coming out from the security scanner. Maybe it was because of the dim lighting, but it seemed to Lagarius that she had dark rings under her eyes, eyes which drooped at the outside corners. Her pendulous nose seemed to hang over blubbery lips, which she continually pursed. Her short gray hair was spiked in all directions. She exchanged a kiss delivered in the air over each ear from Ana.

"Ana, *ketzeleh*," said Ricce, "what are you doing? You need to get ready for your event!"

"Yes, yes, I go," said Ana, and turned to give Lagarius another kiss on the lips. "Carmine, you know Mx Ricce. She take care of you, and take you to friends."

Ana scampered off, going through the scanner with a wave to the giant with the eye patch.

"So, Carmine," said Ricce, standing close to him to be heard, "it's been a good while since – what was it? – your meeting Ana at the gallery a year ago?"

"Yes," said Lagarius. Although he did not have to tilt up his head to address Ricce, he felt ridiculous in the costume, and pulled it off.

"Ha ha, there you are. Still with those handsome dimples. I trust you've come here to relax, have a good time?" She patted Lagarius on one side with her left hand, smiling. "Have you had anything?"

"Anything? No, I just got here."

"Well, come with me, then," she said loudly to his right ear, slipping her left hand inside Lagarius' waistband, tugging him along with a smile. "We can do a few lines together in my office."

"Ah, no, really," Lagarius said, laughing, grabbing the hand at his waist. "You are too kind."

Ricce held herself against the front of his body to be heard.

"You know," she purred, not taking her left hand away but clasping her right hand over his, "I won Miss Burlesque New Orleans not so long ago."

Lagarius could see it now: The mounds of dimpled cellulite from her flanks to her knees, the sagging teats with each areola ringed with hair. He quailed.

"Ah, I have to confide something," said Lagarius. "Some meds I just started taking have been messing with my libido."

She withdrew her hands and leaned away from him, a random gold beam from the ceiling illuminating a puzzled, hurt face.

"Ah!" she said, her voice falling. "Well, let me seat you. On with your costume, little lamb!"

Lagarius put on the sheep's cap and walked through the scanner. He tilted up his head to see the bald, bare-chested giant awaiting him. The eye not covered by the patch was narrow, inscrutable. The giant reached out to feel the woolen cap and its trailing rug.

"*Lays min aldaruri, Qadim,*" said Ricce loudly, waving him off.

"*Naeam, sayidati,*" he said with a nod.

In the wall before them, an arch covered with a heavy black curtain stood a few yards behind the scanner to the left. The split in the middle of the curtain widened slightly at the bottom onto a dark interior. Far to the right in the side wall were broad fourteen-foot-tall brown paneled doors. Ricce gestured to them.

"There, the restroom and the open bar are through those doors," she said. "Also the terrace and its view of Central Park. Do you know how high up we are, Carmine? We are at the head of a shaft fourteen hundred feet high – a quarter of a mile. The view from there will take your breath away. But you can take that in at your leisure. Let me show you to your friends."

They pushed into the heavy curtain in the arch to the left. As it closed behind them, the din of music fell away, and they seemed to be in a cave, filled with the sound of dripping water and far-away crashing waves. In the blackness, to the left on four raised pedestals, the silver statues of four nude young boys glistened under blue light; on the right, the same, but with the silver glistening on four young girls.

Suddenly Lagarius startled, pulling back from the left.

"Mx Ricce, I want to come down," said one of the boys.

Lagarius could now see that all of the statues were in fact living children covered in silver body paint, the groin covered with a tiny silver leaf.

"A few more minutes, Andy. When the fashion show ends, you can all come down," she said. "You can all get your cookies and play in the Lotus room. Someone will come get you there and take you to the kitchen much later." She walked on.

Ricce divided the heavy curtain at the end of the dark cave, exposing to the astonished Lagarius a vision of hell. A great half-circle stage flooded in light dominated the back half of the enormous room, where a fashion show was in progress. Outside its light, the holographic coral and undersea light wavered darkly to the surrounding walls. Along the walls were two terraces of booths: Low tables painted to look like coral reefs, with dark blue shapeless seats on one side, facing the stage. And there, between the terraces and the stage, undulated a writhing mass of arms, legs, and animal masks – of goats, of zebras, of unknown beasts fanged, scaly, tongued, and popeyed. Shafts of golden aquatic light sifting through the squirming sea of bodies variously illuminated rampant glistening genitalia, oiled mammilla, and prosthetic protuberances bowed, coiled, knotted, and twisted. The glistening mass writhing in the dim light around the half-circle stage suddenly struck Lagarius as a vision of spermatozoa flailing toward an egg.

The music boomed less loudly, giving way to a disembodied voice like that of Truman Capote that marshaled the fashion show.

"And now our final offering in the fashion segment: Xanadu Joe's new line!" proclaimed the simpering, high nasal voice. "Joe would like me to convey his deep regrets at not making it this evening. He's having a bad flare-up of his well-known gut-brain axis disorder. But here's his revolutionary first offering of the night. It is just so *snatched*, so *fire*, darlings: His non-gendered baby bump!"

A parade of men, epicene to brawny, pranced out separately, each exposing an enormous prosthetic distended belly, their nudity veiled by strips of cloth of various fabrics and colors.

Ricce motioned for Lagarius to follow her to the higher terrace at the middle of the back wall. Four persons with the same sheep costume as Lagarius were seated at the low coral table. Lagarius stepped forward and cocked back the sheep's head covering half his face.

"Oh, shit!" groaned the young man farthest left. "It's Carmine!"

Lagarius tilted his head to one side and smiled with mock affability.

"Carmine," began Ricce, spreading her hand to the one farthest right to indicate a stubbled, dimpled chin like his own, "there's Ron Peel, and here's…"

"– No need, Mx Ricce," said the young man with a short red beard next to the one farthest left. "The flock knows its own."

"Great. Look, I've got to take care of something," said Ricce. She indicated the empty seat farthest left. "Carmine, you sit down right here, and I'll be back with you boys in a minute."

Ricce left the terrace as Lagarius stood and acknowledged the group, beginning with the red beard.

"Scott," he said in deference to the red beard second from the left, then nodding from left to right, "William, Tick, Ron. How's Tailored Access Ops these days?"

"Who, us? What – TAO? Tao-te-Ching?" said Scott, feigning ignorance as Lagarius sat down. The others replied with a pantomime of shrugs and raised hands. "Did you put Ana up to this?"

"Yes. I have something serious and urgent."

"Is it catching?" asked Tick, the smaller young man between the red bearded Scott and the black stubbled Ron. He fumbled with a monocle, barely visible beneath his costume but for its retaining cord, which went around his neck.

"There's going to be a terrorist attack," said Lagarius.

"Turning in your friends?" asked William, sitting nearest him, pursing his lips with contempt.

"OK, enough of that," said Lagarius sternly. "This is for real. I need your help."

"We know you've gone dark," said Scott. "We're not looking any closer than that because we like you. Beyond that? Really, why should we even give you the steam off our piss, Carmine?"

A man suddenly appeared at their table wearing a red Borat mankini thong. He had a head of black curls, and thick black hair covered his chest, shoulders, arms, and legs.

"Which one of you gorgeous, beefy lambs can prove to me he's not homophobic?"

"Not me," they all said in chorus.

"It's OK, I *come* in 31 flavors," he said, thrusting his hips forward with the verb. "I may look like Borat, but you can call me Baskin-Robbins. I'm polyamorous!"

"'Slut' is a lot shorter," said Tick.

"Agh!" said the Borat costume with a mincing smack of his lips. He tossed his nose up in the air and pranced off haughtily, wiggling buttocks split by the red thong.

"Comes in how many flavors?" asked Tick. "That dick holster needs to see a urologist."

Ricce reappeared to stand beside Lagarius. With her was a serving girl dressed as a mermaid, who placed before the men five enormous mugs frosted with condensation and rimmed with salt. A slice of lime rested on the blended ice inside each mug.

"I've got a complimentary treat for you all," she said, raising her left hand and dropping it on the back of Lagarius' seat. "This is a special frozen margarita, made with El Tesoro Paradiso Extra Anejo tequila and Grand Marnier 1880."

They all sipped, then hummed and smacked with pleasure.

"You boys are in for an incredible evening," she said.

"Wow, Mx Ricce," said Tick, hamming it up, "you gonna give us some yabb in a three-way with a Nigerian and a pit bull tonight, huh, huh?"

"No, darling. But you missed the warm-up. An Amish boy with a lisp was fisted live onstage by a Mexican dwarf wrestling star."

"Damn!" said Tick, snapping his fingers.

"I see that Xanadu Joe's 'mail' jacket of crushed soft drink cans is leaving the stage," said Ricce as she turned about. She raised her hand again and dropped it as before on the back of Lagarius' seat. "That means we'll soon be having the star event: The three two-spirit sisters doing an excerpt from Billy Blurff's celebrated new opera. After that we'll have a unique dinner: A live human being served 'à la Trimalchio.' The evening will conclude with our dear Ana's debut as master of ceremonies for Il Buffone di Poggiolo, who will create a new work, defecating into stainless steel cubes that he will weld shut, all right before your very eyes."

"'Our very eyes,' dear lord!" said Tick, affecting an English accent and fooling with his monocle, "Ahem, sink me, Mx Ricce, but I could have sworn you had said 'a live human being' for dinner. Is this not a flouting of the health ordinances?"

"You'll see!" Ricce laughed, again dropping her raised hand on the back of the seat. She left the terrace.

Filing out on stage to the introduction of the high nasal voice was another widely-spaced line of models. Each was wearing a dress featuring an inverted nude mannequin, its anatomically faithful crotch just below the chin, its legs thrusting skyward like great antennae.

"Here's what I've found," said Lagarius, turning back to the group. "I've come across a steganographic image with a curious payload. It starts with 128 hex like an Ethereum public key. That's followed by forty characters that never change across all the messages. I think that's the address. Then comes an encrypted block, which varies with each version of the image, although the visible image itself never changes."

"You're thinking smart contract here?" asked Ron, the stubbled, dimpled chin at the opposite corner from Lagarius.

"Yes, of course."

"Why not just look up the address on Ethereum?" asked Scott.

"I did. It's not there."

"Look on QTUM or Cardano," said Ron, swinging his head forward to see past the obstructing column before him. "Ethereum's a dog anyway – doesn't scale like QTUM."

"I looked everywhere."

"Ron, they could care less about scale," said Tick. "I mean, it's not like they're wanting code that they can go public with, right, Carmine?"

"Exactly," said Lagarius. "It must be something custom, not Ethereum."

"What *they?*" asked Scott, turning from Tick to Lagarius. "What makes you think these are terrorists in the first place?"

"In the encrypted block I managed to break one forty-character string. It reads 'magnesium igniters X'. Well, I broke a few others, but they were useless bits like 'all received message' and 'sent parts via FedEx'. Apparently the encryption scheme changes every forty hex."

"Nice," said William.

"Anything special about the image?" asked Scott.

"Yes. It's got the Guy Fawkes mask, looking up at a beheaded Christ."

"The Vendetta mask?" asked William. "Yikes."

"And Guy Fawkes Day just happens to fall on our election day next Tuesday," added Lagarius.

"Big yikes," repeated William.

"Aah, still pretty thin," said Scott. "So what do you want us to do about it?"

"I have all the message variations on that image in my pocket. I would like for you to break the messages, and also search the Internet for who posts the many versions of the image and who picks them up."

Suddenly the music stopped and the amplified crackle of a live microphone came from the stage. It was Ricce, standing there alone in the clear light. The writhing and thrusting of oiled loins slowed in the aquamarine darkness, and many heads turned to listen.

"And now!" she boomed. "It is my distinct pleasure to introduce our before-dinner entertainment, an excerpt from Billy Blurff's new opera for Inuit chorus and hacky sack ballet, *Avenging Spirits!*"

Scattered but exuberant applause answered her.

"Mr. Blurff chose tonight's vocalists for his work after hearing their viral mashup of *Bad to the Bone* and *Let Me Teach You How to Eat*. The group's soprano is Sissy! - One of the most fêted Inuit throat singers of our generation."

A massive white woman emerged smiling from backstage, wearing a rainbow flag around her body, held in place by several hooks that attached to a stiff metal ring around her neck. She waved both hands to the now focused and animated crowd, exposing two thatches of axillary hair dyed bright green.

"The mezzo is Prissy! - The most accomplished Gullah language shouter on the planet."

A black woman whose avoirdupois contended with Sissy emerged, wearing the same rainbow flag dress supported by hooks from a neck ring, and with similar lush green underarms. The crowd stamped and whistled with delight.

"Providing the bass line is alto Missy! – A Mongolian throat singer, whose collection of lullabies has just gone platinum."

Another generously proportioned woman emerged in triumph, dressed and dyed just as her colleagues, but of dark brown complexion. The crowd was on its bare feet, its unctuous, pendulous flesh shuddering with each stroke of applause.

"Those of you who have seen the performance in Lincoln Center will be familiar with the earth, water, fire, and air hacky sack dancers, whom you will see in due course. At the conclusion we have a special treat: The composer himself, who is backstage preparing a delightful finale. And now, brothers and sisters, Billy Blurff's *Avenging Spirits!*"

After the tumultuous applause had died down there was an instant of silence. The audience sat down. The three singers faced each other in a circle, hands joined in the middle at waist level. Then Missy began a deep, rasping, throaty drone. Sissy, the Inuit throat singer, first droned in unison with the bass, then began a series of high, sharp, vocalized inhalations not unlike the braying of a donkey. The joined hands began to slowly rise in the circle, and Prissy began a counterpoint of Gullah song, her face variously contorted with joy and pain. As Prissy began, three men – apparently the earth spirits – body-painted in smears of brown and terracotta with depictions of snakes and other reptiles, emerged from the wings, crouching and wearing only tight loincloths, colored as their skin. They danced counter-clockwise around the circle of singing women, rising, crouching, shaking their arms and legs, until the leader produced a kind of bean bag from his hand, dropped it to his foot, and flicked it overhead to the last man, who caught it on his foot. The last man then returned it to the first, sending the bag arching over the women, cutting a tangent across their circle. This toss and return continued intermittently. Another three men in blue loincloths emerged from the opposite wing, body-painted in various smears of blue, depicted with fish. They joined the circle, moving with the identical dance and bag toss as the earth spirits. Three orange and yellow fire spirits joined them, followed by three red spirits of the air, all performing the same movements and bag toss as they circled.

Signaling the middle section of the piece, the women's voices rose loudly in angry contention, and their arms undulated as their joined hands rose and fell. At the same moment the hacky sack dancers began to fire their bags through the circle, beneath the women's arms, and at spirits not their own, as they danced in agitation around the ring.

At last the women's voices fell to a hush. The Inuit soprano began to coo softly to the others; the Gullah mezzo trilled and babbled lovingly; the Mongolian alto droned endearingly. They approached, touched breasts, and each began unhooking the rings holding the dresses of the two opposite with one unclasped hand. An ample white teat shone in the light, then a brown, a black, until finally a single ring held each rainbow dress that now divided the women's naked breasts. In unison each unhooked the final ring and each rainbow sheath slipped softly to their feet. Looking up, they raised their joined hands to the ceiling as they softly sang a ghostly, sibilant trio. The dance of the twelve spirit men slowed, then halted as they paired at each nude elephantine leg, clutching it to their chests. The singing stopped. The crowd watched breathlessly in a long moment of ethereal silence.

"*Yeah!*" one black man cried out.

The crowd leaped to its feet in a raucous tumult of applause. The uproar continued as the performers bowed, then retreated from the stage. Rhythmic clapping broke out. The earth spirit dancers returned to a burst of applause, which repeated for each of the three other spirit groups as it came out and bowed. Finally the three singers returned to a roar of shouts, still unabashedly naked, and they lined up to wave and blow kisses to the crowd.

There was some movement among the dancers at the back, and everyone on stage looked behind them. They made way for a triumphant Ricce, whose extended hand clutched the composer's elbow, raising it aloft. He was dressed as George Armstrong Custer, with a thick golden moustache and a mass of golden curls beneath a big blue cocked hat. He wore a buckskin fringe jacket and white gauntlet gloves, which he held vertically, stirring them in a discreet orbit like the Queen of England. The performers behind him somehow were convulsed with laughter, some of them covering their mouths and pointing at the composer. One man in the audience stood up and booed loudly.

"Indian killer!" he shouted through his cupped hands. "Spirit killer!"

Custer pointed to him, smiling acknowledgement, then pointed to himself, making a sour face and giving exaggerated thumbs down. He got the rest of the audience into the act, then suddenly reached out his hands to stop them. He leaped into the air, turning himself back to front. The audience now saw the backside of Custer, entirely naked except for the bands of elastic holding up the front of his costume. In the middle of his bare back was a nest of arrows, feathers out. The audience howled with delirious laughter.

Lagarius' companions groaned and laughed.

"Mr. Peel," said Lagarius to the man opposite him, "will you stop bobbing and weaving?"

"It's that damned pole. It's right in the middle of the action."

"OK, Ron, let's trade," said Lagarius, standing up.

They switched seats.

"Brothers and sisters," boomed Ricce, standing alone on stage in a dramatic pool of limelight, "as promised, we will go immediately to our feast of fresh human served 'à la Trimalchio.' Let me reassure you that no felonies have been or will be committed: Our entrée has willingly signed away an arm and a leg for our dining enjoyment." She adjusted the wireless microphone at her mouth, then pulled an antique scroll from her belt and shook it to unfurl two feet of scribbled parchment. The crowd laughed and applauded. "Moreover, no animals were harmed in the creation of this banquet dish." Greater applause, with exuberant whistles. "So now, without further ado, *human being 'à la Trimalchio'!*"

With Ricce's dramatic gesture toward the right wall, her spot of limelight faded out. In the darkness the first three bells of the Fifth Movement of the *Symphonie Fantastique* of Berlioz sounded. They sounded again, then softly a third time. As the tuba deeply intoned the *Dies Irae*, the limelight brightened again on two fourteen-foot black paneled doors in the right wall, from which now emerged two powerful, bald, bare-chested men carrying a man on a stretcher between them. A black cloth draped from it, hiding all its sides. In the pool of focused light the tattoos were visible: Both men were inked with a human having the horned head of a goat sitting cross-legged, and both had a pentagram on the front side of each shoulder. The man on the stretcher was naked, with bunches of grapes along his side and an apple in his mouth. The music continued, with dramatic upward sweeps through the violins. After a moment the man reached up and took a bite of the apple, raising his head to smile and wave to the crowd. The procession advanced along the front of the stage as the music continued, then up the steps at the back, its progress illuminated by the limelight. The stretcher bearers advanced to down center stage, fixed in place the supports under the drapes beneath the stretcher, then began to leave the way they had come. The stretcher and the naked man seemed to be on a table beneath the black drapes, the back edge slightly lifted for better viewing of his body.

"And now!" shouted Ricce, who now stood behind the stretcher in the pool of limelight, "Dinner is served!"

With a great flourish she swept an enormous butcher knife from the unseen side of the table, holding its glinting blade aloft. Then she brought it down and severed the man's hand, which she held before the astonished crowd.

"Now *that hurt*," said the man. Ricce gave him a bite of the "hand" and the crowd roared with laughter.

"*Main en croûte*, with mincemeat stuffing!" she proclaimed with a laugh. Then she stopped in consternation.

"Ah? What's this?" she asked, poking around on the man's belly.

"Hey, that tickles!" he said with apprehension.

"Just as I thought. Bring me that cook!" Ricce shouted. "Bring me that goddamned cook! This is the last time he pulls this shit on me."

Bursting from the paneled doors on cue, the same two stretcher bearers hustled out a small, obese man between them and stood him up in front of the stage. The limelight widened to envelop him.

"How dare you serve this person to my guests without gutting him properly?"

"I... I...," stammered the cook. His arms now free, he lowered his head and began clutching his hands, wiping them nervously on his dirty apron.

"Clean out this pig now, jackass, or I'll slap that ugly wart right off your shoulders!"

The two stretcher bearers grabbed the cook's arms and lifted him onto the stage. Fearfully, the cook accepted Ricce's knife, hesitated, then resolutely sliced into the belly of the prostrate man, who let out a blood-curdling scream. The cook wheeled about, lifting his face fully into the limelight as he held up - not the entrails of the unfortunate man - but a string of sausage. The crowd gave a collective gasp.

"Capocollo, anyone?" the cook bellowed with delight. *Happy Days Are Here Again*, sung by the Comedian Harmonists in German, began blaring loudly in place of the *Symphonie Fantastique*, and colored lights began playing over the stage - the shock of sound and light producing a dizzying, disorienting effect. With the gleeful music, a train of food carts swiftly emerged from the paneled doors. The carts' mermaid servers caught strands of sausage as the cook threw them down, passed them through a slicing machine, and lay the slices on plates of prepared dinners held by the silver statue children. They and the mermaids took them to the raised hands among the crowd, which was laughing uproariously now.

"What's this?" yelled the cook, pulling out another dark rope of sausage. "Ha, ha! How 'bout a nice strand of chivalini, my friends!"

"Don't pull so hard - that tickles!" laughed the prostrate entrée.

"Shaddap, I'm jerking your intestines, you pig, not *that*!"

Lagarius' group had watched all of this, as had much of the audience, in fascinated, rapt disbelief.

"Man, that is some woke shit," murmured Tick at last.

"I think I need to go toss my cookies," said Ron. "Don't take a plate for me, for *godssake*."

He got up and left through the entrance tunnel.

"Will you at least take the files and have a look?" asked Lagarius, addressing Scott, holding out the thumb drive.

"There's a problem there," Scott replied. "Where do we say we got those files? I'm gonna do you a favor and not even ask where *you* got them." He settled back in his seat, appraising Lagarius. "That's why you've come to us. You can't present them yourself because you hacked them from god knows where."

"Listen to me," said Lagarius angrily. "I'm the one putting his balls on the anvil here. I could have kept my mouth shut and gone on my merry, well-paid way."

"Sorry, Carmine," said Scott. "Can't do it."

"OK," said Lagarius with contempt. "I'm pretty sure Professor Gelb can point me to another government agency."

William laughed.

"Good luck finding old Artie," said William. "He disappeared from Stevens several months ago, from what I hear."

"OK, I don't know about the rest of you," said Scott, "but I'm done. I really don't need to see some guy box up his own turds."

"And miss seeing Ana?" asked Tick. "And miss the sproat of hetero-normal moral imperialism..."

"– Tick," William said wearily, poking absently at his phone. "Stop."

"We can get Ron on the way out," said Scott, nudging William to move. "I need to visit the head anyway."

The three shifted around the table away from Lagarius, and went to the exit. At the mouth of the entrance tunnel William seemed to snap his fingers and say something to the others, turning back as if he had forgotten something. Lagarius bent his head and saw the glow of a phone screen on the seat opposite. He rose and fetched it, looking at the luminous text.

"LAY THE DRIVE ON TOP OF MY PHONE," it read. Lagarius erased the message and followed the instruction. He turned to the approaching William.

"Thanks," said Lagarius, handing the phone and drive to him. "Where's Gelb?"

"Las Vegas catacombs, I'm told. That's all I know. Google it."

Suddenly there was a piercing woman's scream from beyond the paneled doors, hysterically taken up by others there. William and Lagarius tore off their costumes and raced toward the tunnel. They emerged to see a wild-eyed mob racing toward the elevators, Ana among them.

"Ana!" yelled Lagarius. He grabbed her arm and pulled her from the crowd as William raced ahead.

"It's Ron Peel!" she wailed, tears smearing blue body paint down her cheeks. "He gone off the roof!"

Several people collided with them. One was Frittata Ricce, who suddenly came face-to-face with Lagarius.

"You!" she said. Her eyes were wild, her mouth open in disbelief. She ran past, into the tunnel.

"What we gonna do!" wailed Ana.

"Here, sit against the wall until this mob is out, or you'll be trampled. Wait for Ricce. I have to go to Las Vegas, now."

He held Ana's face between his hands and kissed her eyes and mouth. She wiped a spot of blue paint from his cheek, laughing through her tears. They hugged, then Lagarius held her shoulders to move her against the wall. He plunged into the stream of people headed for the elevators.

Then suddenly he stepped out of the mob and looked back. He saw the top of Ana's jelled blue hair where she had sat down against the wall. As if disembodied, Lagarius stood back from the others, looking at their panicked faces. He strangely felt a wave of pity flood him - pity for them all: The drugged and drunken revelers; those wanting a moment's recognition before slipping into oblivion; those posing in the most preposterous shapes, violently saying the most preposterous things to fulfill some other, in-expressible, need: The confused, the fatuous, and the damned.

15

One early evening, weeks after an autumnal equinox ten thousand years ago, a dozen fur-wrapped figures climbed a grassy hill. Above it, the top of a full moon birthed itself from the earth and swelled, liberating its ponderous luminosity upward with each approaching step of the human group. When they crested the hill they saw a great sycamore etched against it, as the moon hovered just above the distant black horizon. From the branches of the sycamore, thousands of startled grackles went aloft with a chorus of sharp cries and a rush of wings like the noise of a waterfall.

The band of Indians silently watched the thousands of birds swirl in flight in a dense, mutating cloud above the tree. The cloud of wings elongated, then dilated, then compressed into a globe, then swooped up into a long cylinder that twisted and reshaped itself. The band watched in something like awe, but unpossessed of a question of how or why, unpossessed of a fear that this manifestation was something "other," something completely outside and thus possibly alien to themselves. They watched for a time equal to that of their rowing across their widest river. Then, after the first step of the oldest and tallest man among them, they continued walking, having never uttered a word.

As the man led the group through the grass, he thought of that same tree when he had climbed it as a boy. It was early summer. He had climbed above the silver, flaking bark, up into the perfectly smooth fat limbs – thick maternal thighs. A light white dust was on his hands, his arms and legs, his belly. The luscious lucent leaves had spoken to him, clattering in the breeze, smelling of green. Now the tree had spoken to him in this other way, with the rush of wings like the falling of water. And he remembered its speaking yet another way, when he had pressed one bare hand against its cold heavy trunk, the other hand clutching the animal skins close about him. The tree had creaked in the icy wind, sending a vibration through his hand, along his arm, summoning his very bones.

Without the assignment of words, the man thought of the living signs about him now. – The hiss of the grass as his bare feet slid through it; the petrichor scent of the moist air awakening the earth; the moist air itself, autumnal and heavy. This dense life seemed to enter him with each breath and with each cool step – entering him not with his conscious notation, but rather as much a part of him as the weight of his legs and the obedience of his muscles.

Led by him, the dozen beings walked obliquely down the deep hollow to a cave directly opposite the great sycamore. In the middle of the group was a man dragging two long sticks with a load between them – a travois with the fur-wrapped body of a young girl. He had given the girl her name, so had been first to choose to accept this place of honor. The procession stopped at the mouth of the cave, and he turned, letting the body rest on the ground between the sticks. Three young women came forward to stand alongside the body. They faced each other in a circle, holding a flat basket at the center in their extended arms. One by one, four kindred families approached and placed something of value in the basket: A special bit of quartz, a charm carefully carved in animal bone, a lump of amber with a dead bee trapped inside, a necklace of dried berries. The three women then lifted the basket slowly skyward. The cloud of grackles swooped and swirled overhead, then flew swiftly from the left to the right of those facing the cave. At this good omen the three women gave a voluble soft cry: One cooing, one warbling, one trilling. The basket was lowered, folded shut, and tied with strips of fur atop the body.

The procession reformed and entered the cave. At the back of the cave, two young men from the line stepped forward and took the body from the ground between the sticks, and they placed it in a natural depression in the earth. The family of the deceased girl came forward with an armful of wildflowers, some of which they placed on top of the girl. The others approached, took flowers from the awaiting family, and placed them over the corpse until it was completely covered in flowers and the depression brought level with the floor of the cave. The young men then stacked rocks over the flower-strewn corpse to hide it from view.

The tallest man led the group out of the cave. The sycamore greeted them across the grassy hollow, its branches starkly white in the gathering darkness, etched in glistening blue from the bloated moon.

16

The seven-year-old boy sat on the high stump, drumming his heels against its sides. He heard a low trill, a high trill, then saw the little bird among the green leaves: A warbler with light gray wings and a yellow belly, tilting his head in twitching movements, inspecting the boy in turn. A flash of color went by then alighted, swaying a small limb up and down with its weight. It was a bird with a big beak and, so he thought, a bright red necktie in its white dress shirt. Far away came the drumming of a woodpecker. The boy looked out across the opening in the forest. Dragonflies darted and hovered. He tried the trick his father had taught him: He held his right index finger aloft and sat very still. Tiring, he propped up his elbow with his left hand – then, yes! – long minutes later one of the dragonflies rested on his raised finger. Motionless, the boy wondered how its grotesquely bulbous eyes pictured him. He inspected its six tiny legs, the blue stick of its body, its paired gossamer wings. It darted away. The boy followed it with his eyes, coming to rest gazing on a shaft of golden light where the gnat-winged life of a summer's day entered its theater, then passed out into the nothingness of shadow.

That was where Artie Gelb's parents found him hours later – never having moved from the stump where his father had left him, his eyes still looking about him in wonder, his face rapt and happy.

"Idiot! Look what you've done!" cried his mother, looking back to his father, as she limped up to the boy and hugged him, stroking his head, kissing him all over his face. Still hugging him, she wheeled around on her good leg and unleashed a stream of abuse on the father, who stood there angry but helpless with guilt.

"*Schlemiel! Ihr soll wachsen wie ein Tsibele mit dein Kopf in der Erd und dein Fis aroyf!*"

She began to cry.

"It's OK, Mama!" said Artie as he kissed his mother on the cheek and looked at his father, who could only roll his eyes and repeatedly raise up his hands and let them drop in his helplessness.

That was when his father, at age fifty-two, went on medication. He hated it, and kvetched and schimpfed every time he took his pills. They did help – he never again misplaced Artie – but his lifelong irritability and the verbal abuse of his wife did not abate. It was likely this respite from the turmoil at home that kept Artie sitting happily on the stump that day: He knew from his father that god did not have a face. We're made after his image, but *after his face?* How could that be? Just look at all the faces, flat-nosed, big-nosed, black, white, you name it - *hi!* How many faces could he have, you tell me. So it must be that the forest is another face that he showed, as he showed it in so many different people, but hiding that one face that we can never see, one that was behind everything, one always calm, always sunlit with an un-spoken assurance: *All is well; you belong here; be still and know that you are happy.*

In spite of Artie's realization that day, he had turned out just like his father: Always irritable, always angry with his wife, and even, at age fifty-two, always in need of medication to keep from losing it completely, and always hating his need for it. And so it went until one day, after being off his pills for weeks, he came home from teaching afternoon classes at the Stevens Institute. There was his family waiting for him, already started on dinner, and as usual looking at him to try to determine his mood: His wife and his two daughters, named after the home towns of his Moravian grandparents. The wife looked up from feeding his daughter Ronow, who was in her last stage of high chair life. She looked up to Artie and held out her hands, call-ing "Daddy," kicking her legs. Eight-year-old daughter Morawan stood there hesitating, nervously picking the fingernails of one hand with the other.

He looked at them for a long moment in a transport of love - and of shame and guilt. Look what his irritability and eruptions of anger had done to Morawan! - Turned her into an insecure, nervous girl who had already plucked out her eyebrows. Would he be any different in betraying the child-like trust of Ronow - in finally exasperating his dear wife?

This is our happiness? he thought. This? - Something that could be lost on the absence of a chemical in the brain, on an accident of genetics, on a quirk of diet, on a childhood trauma? What a joke! Life and happiness are nothing but the punch line of a universe of caprice! The large number N balancing the electrical forces of atoms against gravity that allowed creatures larger than insects to evolve; the Epsilon value indicating the atomic forces that made the elements of our world; the Omega of the just-right thickness of the soup of universal matter; the Lambda of the universe's expansion; the Koppa that gave it structure; the Delta of its dimensions - all of it was a stupendously random joke, and the faceless god behind it a chameleon, a Mephistopheles, a Trickster.

"Sweethearts," announced Artie to his dining family, "I'm going to Las Vegas."

17

Over two hundred miles of catacombs run beneath the city of Las Vegas – the bowels of Babylon. These catacombs are the concrete sleeves typically twelve feet high by twenty feet wide, whose two hundred miles do not include the endless length of concrete capillaries as small as two feet in diameter; nor do they include the hundreds of channels, or washes, that feed into nearly a hundred basins that flow into Lake Mead. This cimmerian network was constructed in 1986 to avoid the disastrous flash floods that had destroyed property in the 1970s. Rain from Red Rock Canyon, the elevation fourteen miles west of the Las Vegas Strip and visible from that venue, ultimately travels to Lake Mead, twenty-eight miles east of the city – a drop of three thousand, three hundred feet, or three times the height of Stratosphere Tower, the city's tallest structure. A cloudburst can create a wall of water moving through the culverts at over thirty miles per hour; it is nature's flush of the vast plumbing; it is an excretion that sweeps out addicts' needles, rats, cockroaches, spiders – and the occasional unwary member of its thousand-strong city of human dross.

Such were the details that Lagarius had read online while waiting for his flight from LaGuardia, west to Las Vegas – the purchase of which he knew had compromised his whereabouts. He had downloaded the map of Las Vegas onto his burner phone – the map that he examined now as he stood beneath the scruff of a tree just east of the parking lot of the Masquerade Tower, shading the screen from the outdoor glare. He looked up toward the east and saw the train trestle, part of the railway line across the northwest part of the city, running from southwest to northeast. If he entered there, he would need to walk fifteen hundred feet east, passing under Dean Martin Drive, Interstate 15, and Frank Sinatra Drive to arrive beneath Caesar's Palace.

After his early morning arrival, it had taken him hours of tramping around to glean the vital clue that Artie Gelb might be there. Online information had suggested many entrances, and he had tried them. During the taxi ride to a Walmart for a flashlight, the driver had suggested that Lagarius also buy a backpack and fill it with snacks and cold drinks to barter for information from any catacomb dweller he might meet. It had been good advice. Lagarius finally had tried an entrance at the demolished El Cid hotel. It was littered with needles and other drug paraphernalia, but thankfully an emaciated man leaning against the concrete wall had provided the clue that made farther entry unnecessary. Fifty feet inside, he had been sitting in the light from an overhead sidewalk grating, beneath a long mural of multicolored graffiti. He had been wearing a dirty undershirt, sleeveless with straps, showing needle tracks in both arms. For a bag of potato chips and a liter of cold lemonade he had revealed that someone called "The Professor" was under Caesar's Palace. Lagarius had not phoned his driver to drive on, so he was dutifully waiting there to take him downtown, to the service entrance to Caesar's Palace at Frank Sinatra Drive. Behind that hotel and casino was a loading dock, a parking lot, and between them, a security building – but no obvious subterranean entrance. So Lagarius had decided to go to the next obvious entrance, where he now stood. He had paid his driver and given him an extra twenty dollars, then walked east across the parking lot, past three giant air conditioning fans, and through the broken chain-link fence down a chalky ravine.

Lagarius now walked under the railroad trestle and emerged again into the light. He walked two hundred feet farther and stopped before the rectangle of darkness twenty yards beyond, where the occasional car passed over it. The map indicated that the awaiting hole must be beneath Dean Martin Drive. He checked his phone: 4:30 pm. Fortunately his walk had not been unpleasant: Low gray clouds had completely shielded the sun, and it was not quite eighty degrees. He hitched up the backpack a bit higher on his shoulders. He gave a resolute sigh and thought that he was about to enter the gate of hell, to join those who while living had already abandoned hope.

With the first step of his motorcycle boot onto the tunnel's rubble and broken glass, the dark mouth exhaled on him the smell of wet, dusty concrete mingled with the stench of urine. Each step crunched and echoed down the tunnel. He panned his flashlight left and right, a good beam thirty yards ahead of him.

"Hey! Who's that?" called out an angry voice ahead of him in the darkness.

Lagarius panned the flashlight beam far ahead of him, and along the walls, seeing nothing.

"A friend," he said.

"You cain't come through thisaway," said the voice.

Casting the light around, Lagarius detected a movement low on the right-hand wall. He moved forward.

"I'm looking for Professor Artie Gelb. Somebody told me he was down here."

There was a long pause.

"It's very important," said Lagarius. "I've got some food and drink if you need it."

A wad of rags belched out of a two-foot-diameter opening low in the right wall. The close-cropped head of a man poked out, squinting and holding his hand to block the flashlight.

"Shut that damn light out, or point it some'eres else," he said. His shoulders appeared, then a bare torso. "Whatcha got?"

"Here, anything you need."

Lagarius squatted, placed the backpack open before him, and widened the flashlight beam to create a diffused pool of light around it.

The skinny man, probably in his early forties, poked his thin fingers around inside the bag. On his left shoulder was a tattoo of two snakes twined around a winged staff, with the head of a blind bearded man above it. The skinny man's cheeks were hollow, and he pursed the concavity of his mouth like someone with no teeth. He eagerly took a big packet of beef jerky from the bag, then in his haste to open a liter of Lamb's Cherry Soda, he dropped the plastic bottle, sending a red rivulet across the concrete before he could retrieve it. He put a big strip of the jerky into his mouth and worked it around, as Lagarius could clearly see, to position it between some minimal dental equipment farther back.

"He's on up yonder a good ways," said the man, chewing, nodding toward the darkness behind him. "– If an' you mean the one yclept 'The Professor.'"

"Thank you," said Lagarius, rising and taking up the backpack.

"Thankee for the jerky. I ain't had no good jerky in a *long* time."

Lagarius crunched ahead in the darkness, casting his light before him. After a long walk he heard a faint low rumble overhead – evidently the traffic of Interstate 15. It grew louder. The tunnel bent slightly to the right, and Lagarius could see a spot of light from a sidewalk grating far ahead. Almost ten minutes later he arrived at the light. Bright-colored graffiti extended out of sight on both walls, in both directions. The floor was almost clean of rubble and broken glass, and the urine odor lifted, leaving only the smell of dusty wet concrete. He walked on; the rumble faded behind him, and he could hear the echoing tread of his boots, free of rubble and glass underfoot.

Suddenly a high deafening scream caused Lagarius to throw himself on the floor in terror and to drop his flashlight. It was the Queen of the Night aria from Mozart's *Magic Flute*. The blaring music stopped and there was the snap of a light switch. A dog was barking.

In the blackness, high up the left-hand wall there magically appeared a bizarre diorama, frightening for its unreality. The three-dimensional rectangle of light showed a cozy room with a bed and pillows in back and a low sofa in front. Between the bed and sofa was a row of slowly spinning cylinders. On the sofa a man stretched forward, shining his own flashlight down on the prostrate Lagarius, his other arm around a small dog that was barking yet wagging a bushy tail. The man's head was bald except for a thin tuft of gray hair over each ear; the nose was upturned, and between it and the almost nonexistent chin was an enormous rubbery crescent of a mouth, curving upward.

"Carmine," said an incredulous voice, high and whiny, "is that you?"

"Good *god*, Professor Gelb," said Lagarius, his arms and legs trembling with adrenaline. "You scared the life out of me."

"Heh-heh, my motion alarm. Stop barking, Sargo!"

Gelb reached outside the rectangle of light to grab the iron bar that formed a basket handle in the concrete wall, one in a column of handles reaching to the tunnel floor. He swung down with a practiced motion and rushed up to embrace Lagarius. Standing in his socks, he then stood back, holding Lagarius' arms, still incredulous.

"What in the hell are you doing *here?*" Gelb asked. Then suspiciously, "You're not here to 'rescue' me, are you?"

"No, ha, I guess not. I need you to rescue *me*, if anything."

"Come on up, come on up, come on up, tee-hee-hee," said Gelb. He went ahead, clambering up the iron handles.

Lagarius followed and saw Gelb bounce off the sofa, bicycling his legs in the air, over the nearly motionless cylinders, and onto the bed. Gelb anxiously brushed off his socks and put his left foot into a bedroom slipper with green plastic toes and, on its arch, the head of Shrek, the animated character. The dog, a small short-haired terrier, gray with three vertical stripes on each side like a sea bream, hopped onto the bed beside him. Gelb began rocking the slipper, which had a string going from the big toe down underneath the cylinders, which now began to turn a bit faster. As he stepped onto the concrete floor of the room, Lagarius could see that the cylinders were empty one-pound coffee cans painted with numbers. Belts between them gave a rhythmic squeak.

"Your prayer wheels?" Lagarius chuckled.

"Oh ho ho, yes, and much more than that, Carmine my boy. Sit sit sit!"

Gelb pointed to the low sofa, which Lagarius could now see was really an inflatable pool float covered in tough canvas – probably from one of the hotel pools, he supposed. He sat. He inspected the six vertical spindles, each with two coffee cans whose painted numbers he could not quite make out.

"Ha ha! You want to know the numbers that make the world go 'round, don't you?" said Gelb, smiling. "You want to be the gnat that discovers he's in North America, yes? Tee-hee-hee!"

Gelb pointed to each can's number in turn.

"Top row! N, the atomic electrical strength at ten to the thirty-sixth power! Epsilon, point double-oh seven, on Her Majesty's Secret Service to bind the atomic nuclei of the ninety-four elements! Omega, stirring up a creamy bowl of *ylem*! Little wittle Lambda, just a baby now but out to whip gravity's ass when it grows up! Koppa, the juggler of kaboom and nothingness! And Delta, going on three in the evening, damn you, Sphinx!

"Bottom row! Pi in your eye, the Golden Boy 1.618, a constant fig tree 4.669, a figgy point -1.401155, Euler's 2.71828, *and* ..." – here he gulped, eyes bulging – "the years in a maha yuga: 4,320,000 – man in motion *hut* four, *hut* three, *hut* two, *hut* one, *hut hut*! Go long, baby!"

"Nice, really nice," said Lagarius with a pleasant smile, "but, ah, what's the point of it all?"

"'The point of it all?'" Gelb said, then more loudly, "'*The point of it all?*' The point is that if any of this stops spinning we're all screwed! Damn! You think I'm down here stretched out on my ass doing *nothing*? Ha? – Down here finishing my novel? Carmine, I'm keeping the whole pile of manure from flying apart!"

"Ah, I didn't know," said Lagarius, then leapt at the change of subject. "You have a novel going?"

"Yeah yeah yeah," said Gelb eagerly. "Under the bed, right there."

Lagarius picked up three thin spiral notebooks, one with a green cover, one with a horse, another with a puppy. They were greasy and dog-eared. He flipped through them.

"What? It's all in Hebrew."

"Yeah. Had to get the vernacular right on Yahweh."

"Of course, sure. What's it called?"

"*Forethought of Full Sails Dragging the Anchor of Afterthought.*"

Lagarius cleared his throat.

"Hm. Maybe a shorter title, with a little more punch?"

"Shorter, yeah, OK, maybe. But the punch is there... maybe it gets lost in the length. Yeah, yeah, yeah – I need a jab, piff-piff-piff!" said Gelb, punching the air – "Can't have that roundhouse swing, am I right?

"Ha, or maybe I need a new saint," Gelb suddenly added. He pointed to the wall behind him. "Pick one out for me. Yes, right there."

Leaning against the wall nearest the ladder entrance was a stack of heavy cards – blessing cards of various saints and angels taken from Renaissance paintings, with the name at the top and the virtue or protected group at the bottom. On the wall, resting in a little tray nailed into it, Lagarius saw Gelb's currently favored saint, Francis de Sales, with the word "Writers" beneath the image. He picked up the stack and showed Gelb one he had taken at random.

"It's Saint Cajetan! Perfect!" said Gelb. "Patron saint of gamblers and good fortune, see the name? Yes, yes, put him up there! And look, he's reminding me of what a rude host I've been. Let's go!"

Gelb shook off the green slipper and jumped out of bed. Under the bed he flipped a toggle switch and pulled out a pair of shoes. The prayer wheels kept turning.

"Where are we going?" asked Lagarius. "And what's that switch for?"

"We're going gaming! And you don't think I'd leave the universe in the lurch while we're gone, do you?"

"Professor Gelb, you really don't need to...."

"– Nonsense! Come on!"

Gelb was already down the ladder and half-way across the tunnel. He was headed directly opposite, to another ladder of basket-shaped iron rods. Lagarius left the backpack and went down, flashlight in hand. The little dog stood looking from the height, vaguely wagging its bushy tail.

"Professor, shouldn't we be going this way?" he said, flicking his light to the east.

"No! See that hole farther on? – The whirlpool of death. And here, the four man-eating jaws! Anyway, heh-heh, this is a shortcut."

Going up the ladder, Gelb had replied pointing to a hole in the tunnel some thirty yards to the left, then had pointed to a row of four two-foot-wide drains high in the wall a few yards from where he was ascending. Lagarius could not see the hole, but his flashlight picked out the fence around it made of steel pipes. He stuck the flashlight into his shirt collar and followed Gelb.

At the top of the ladder was a smaller tunnel, where Gelb stood waiting. He had kept his own small flashlight and was shining it into the darkness ahead. They walked quickly together, turned slightly left, then walked farther. Finally Lagarius saw ahead of them a dim light shining down a grate into a cul-de-sac with the familiar ladder of iron rods with some trash and rubble below it. Gelb went up the ladder and pushed the grate aside. Lagarius followed. He emerged and replaced the grate. They were standing in the employee parking garage behind Caesar's Palace. Lagarius knew this because he could see the security building where he had circled in the taxi earlier that afternoon.

"If you had gone straight on from my place," said Gelb, "you would have come up at the grate in the smokers' area right beside the security guards. Not so good, heh-heh-heh."

Instead of walking past security and around to the front of the building, Gelb walked straight up the steps of the loading dock and into a maintenance room. Evidently familiar with the place, he took a small ladder from the corner and opened it under a huge aluminum air conditioning duct. He climbed up, unlatched the access door to let it swing down, then entered the opening. He gestured for Lagarius, who ascended and climbed inside. Gelb reached down and hooked his finger in a hole in the access door to pull it up, then produced a small screwdriver from his pocket, jimmying in the seam of the opening to flick the latch closed. It was very cool inside.

"Now, Carmine my boy!" said Gelb, rubbing his hands together with anticipation, "We, under the protection of Saint Cajetan, are divine spirits in the Citadel of Chance!"

"Professor, aren't we going to cave this thing in?"

"Naa! It's made for beer-bellied maintenance men."

"Right, and what about the noise? It seems like we're making a lot of racket up here."

"Pfft! Metal contracting and expanding – and anyway, we're almost over the gamers' hullabaloo."

Gelb went forward on his hands and knees, Lagarius following. After a long crawl, Gelb stopped at an air conditioning vent and motioned excitedly for Lagarius to come forward.

"Gaze upon the shallowest circle of hell, thou Carmine."

Through the slats Lagarius could see a roomful of slot machines and their flickering lights, and he could hear the bells and noise of gaming action.

"You see? Mostly women feeding quarter after quarter into oblivion. Yet if there were a predictable payout, say a tiny reward after a set number of coins, they would hate it. There must be both random frequency and random size of the reward or nobody would play. And I think there must be the random fail, where the machine gets hacked and drained. Everybody needs that story."

"Mitnick's hack of the unseeded random number generator in old Japanese machines."

"Exactly!" said Gelb, patting Lagarius on the head. "You remember we had a week on that at Stevens."

"And you make your money here that way?"

"No. I count cards at blackjack, 3:2 payout, no continuous shuffle machines, two decks in a shoe if I can find it. You can sometimes see it at a twenty-five dollar table, but that's just fine for me. And speaking of blackjack...."

Gelb crawled forward to a vent overlooking the blackjack tables.

"Here is the middle class circle of hell. Many may know the payout, the number of decks in the shoe, and have the stand/draw table memorized. But they can't tolerate a three-hundred-dollar loss. They remember how they worked to get that three hundred dollars. At that point they are no longer players; fear snuffs out the random joy of the game."

"And the upper-class circle of hell?"

"Are you kidding? This is Vegas. What do you see walking the sidewalks? Notice any dukes or princes among that milling cloud of birds? No, no, Carmine. This is *democracy's* Citadel of Chance, and its wonderful hell."

"'Wonderful hell'?" Lagarius chuckled. "What can that mean?"

"What is the opposite of chance, Carmine?"

"Determinism?"

"Exactly! And unfortunately for most people, that is also hell's opposite. The mob has made a false idol of a heaven where everyone gets justice, gets exactly his due - no chance, no caprice. That is determinism. And for every living thing that has awareness, determinism is death - Game Over. Without randomness, nobody would care to play the game."

"But 'wonderful hell'," said Lagarius, still amused by the phrase, "- I think I see what you mean, but it seems that there should be a better name for it."

"Yeah, well, there's a name for everything, you know. Take for example that stuff between elephants' toes - I mean, there's a word for that even."

"What? 'Cruft,' maybe?"

Gelb came up close to Lagarius' face.

"*Slow natives*. You get it, ha?" he squealed excitedly. "You get it? Slow natives, slow natives, ha ha ha! Slow natives!"

Lagarius groaned. Then Gelb suddenly stopped laughing.

"Hey, you hungry? Come on!" said Gelb, crawling forward on comically quick arms and legs. "Yeah, ha ha, you think I'd forgotten my best student Carmine - dear old Carmine with the smoked hams hanging in the mainframe room?"

"Ah, that was a lunch pickup, only there for the afternoon."

"Ah ha ha ha, *oh* yeah! Come on!" Gelb said, arms and legs churning faster.

After a long crawl pounding through the ducts, Gelb finally stopped at an access panel like the one they had entered. He flicked the catch with his screwdriver, and the door swung down. He extended himself by his arms from the opening, then let himself drop to the floor.

"Wait!" he said to Lagarius, who was preparing to follow.

He brought a ladder under the opening, and left while Lagarius descended. Lagarius found him taping the latch bolt of the maintenance room door. After Gelb closed the access and put away the ladder, they walked down a short hallway to emerge across from the most recognized restaurant on the Caesar's Palace Forum.

"Ah, perfect!" said Lagarius. "That's where I once had a great Chilean sea bass."

"Forget it," said Gelb, turning toward the exit. "Chance was with you that day. You don't ever want any restaurant that plays music that loud.

That means they want you to think it's a nightclub, to cover its crappy food and service. Follow me. I'll get you some real Chilean sea bass."

They went out onto the street, and Gelb hailed a taxi. After a quick left onto Spring Mountain Road and a short drive west under Interstate 15, they got out in a strip mall and entered a sushi restaurant.

"*Irasshaimase*, Professor Gelb," said the young Japanese girl inside the door, smiling.

"*Konbanwa*," said Gelb. "Is *itamae* Hideki busy? I don't have a reservation. Ah, look, there he is."

The chef was preparing for a Japanese couple seated at the bar in front of him, but he smiled and nodded to Gelb.

"Follow the girl, Carmine, and order some hot sake. Let me talk to the chef for a sec."

Lagarius sat where the girl indicated and ordered the sake, watching Gelb chat with the chef. At last he came into the little room to take the opposite seat at the small table. It was quiet. A plucked koto and flute music played softly overhead.

"Nice, eh? - We can hear each other," said Gelb. "This is the place to come to when you're dining alone and paying attention to your food - ha, like me. You sit at the bar and order *omakase* - a dozen or so small dishes made to order, based on the *itamae*'s reading of your mood. We don't want that tonight - not that we could get it anyway: You have to have a reservetion, and no chance for a walk-in on a Friday night."

"So what are we doing?"

"*Okonomi* for you, and two *okimari* for me."

"OK, Professor," Lagarius chuckled. "Break it down for me."

"*Okonomi* is à la carte, so you get your sea bass and whatever else; *okimari* is prix fixe, meaning I take their basic menu but get all the little dishes served at one time."

"But you said two *okimari* for you. You must be hungry."

"Heh, heh, heh. You'll see."

The girl who had greeted them at the door returned with the hot sake and took Lagarius' order of grilled Chilean sea bass, Bafun Uni sea urchin because it was in season, an assortment of sashimi, and some other small courses. Gelb poured out hot sake into Lagarius' small cup, then his own. They raised their cups together.

"*Kompai!*" said Gelb.

"*Kompai!*" repeated Lagarius. They tossed back the drink together.

"Let me get to the point, Professor Gelb...."

"- Say 'Doc,' like you did at Stevens. 'Doc, I need your help.'"

Gelb poured out another round of sake.

"OK, yes. But Doc, first, how are you? You're well known here;" – he waved his hand vaguely at the restaurant – "you can live wherever you want, and yet you're underground like a mole. Have you talked to your family lately?"

There was a long pause. Gelb looked at Lagarius evenly, his mirthfully upturned crescent of a mouth now drawn straight.

"You're trying to 'rescue' me, aren't you? Carmine, I told you I've got serious work holding this manure pile together. Don't make me angry."

"OK, Doc, but can I at least get your phone number? I need to hear from you sometimes."

Gelb reluctantly pulled a phone from his pants pocket and held up the screen, displaying his number.

"OK, here. Call me."

Lagarius did so; Gelb held his phone to his ear.

"Pete Townshend speaking," answered Gelb seriously.

"Who?"

"First base."

Lagarius gave an exasperated laugh.

"What's on your mind, Carmine? It must be serious enough to threaten to unhinge the universe."

Lagarius sighed thankfully at Gelb's return to focus, as the girl placed small dishes on the table for them: Miso soup, half a lemon rind filled with seaweed and radish and topped with a thin spiral of cucumber, some crunchy *jakoten*. They began eating.

"Doc, I have discovered some files – no need to say how – but they show evidence that someone is planning a terrorist attack on this country."

"Well, then. Take them to a journalist; take them to the government; take them to one of your friends in the Stevens gang – most are in Tailored Access Ops now, you know."

"Doc, I have done exactly those three things. Scott won't take them because they're stolen; the government is not moving fast enough; and the journalist may have gotten...."

Gelb leaned forward, shaking his head with a querying shrug.

"Gotten sick? Gotten laid?"

"– May have gotten Lucas Meeth killed. You knew him."

"Damn! Of course I did."

"I went to meet him and the journalist on Monday at his Hoboken apartment. When I got there I found Lucas stabbed through the heart and his laptop gone."

"Why not call up the journalist?"

"I can't; I don't know who it was. Lucas had set up the contact..."

"– Ah! Because if old Carmine had made these contacts himself, he might have found himself in handcuffs for hacking."

Lagarius gave a guilty nod.

"'Wonderful hell'," mused Gelb. "Yes, you're right, we need a better term."

"Doc, really, if we could think about..."

"– Goddamnit, do I look like a thinking machine?" snapped Gelb angrily. "You leave me to think about your problem the way I will!"

"I'm sorry. You're right. I apologize."

Lagarius looked at the rubbery, now happy crescent of the mouth of his broken friend, and tears began to well up in his eyes. He thought that the man must always eat alone, and that this was a sacred moment, when his friend could reveal himself to a kindred spirit, to someone who loved and understood him, while sharing a splendid meal. He blinked his tears away before they fell, glad that Gelb was not looking at him but at the ceiling, pondering.

"A perfect heaven," mused Gelb. "– One where no chance or caprice can turn aside perfect justice for each soul: That's the ideal, isn't it?"

"I think we're headed for a 'Does god exist' conversation," said Lagarius with a soft smile.

"'Who' again? God who? A hawk or a handsaw? A veterinarian or a bartender? A giraffe walks into a bar, and says...?"

Lagarius cocked his head, puzzled, silent. He shrugged in answer.

"*Highballs are on me!* Ah ha ha ha!" Gelb squealed with laughter. "Get it? Highballs, *high balls?* Ha ha, get it, get it?"

Suddenly Gelb stopped laughing.

"And that's the problem, Carmine my boy. We're not having a 'Does god exist' conversation because 'god' is even worse a term than 'wonderful hell.' Does it mean god the vet who looks at high balls, or god the bartender who serves up refreshing highballs?

"Imagine two winners at the gates of heaven. The great slot machine is rattling out coins on the streets of gold. One is Isaac Newton; the other is a syphilitic clay eater, a moron who died of smallpox. Both are equally devout, checking the identical tick boxes on the most fashionable catechism of the season. How are they both to enjoy perfect happiness throughout eternity if they both retain their personalities? Now of course if they lose their personalities, then what the hell are we talking about? – Happiness without a distinct personality is meaningless."

"I think Dante said that both remain unequal in station, but equally and perfectly happy in contemplating the presence of god."

"Right, then their station, as shaped by their earthly life, counts for nothing in terms of happiness. 'Not by deeds are you justified,' blah, blah,

blah. Their true happiness is in that contemplation, and it must be perfectly equal. Or would god want a moron perfectly happy contemplating a finger painting by a gorilla and a genius perfectly happy contemplating the Mona Lisa? Would a just god want each person stuck at unequal contemplative powers throughout eternity? - Or worse: A divine bamboozlement where the moron *really believes* his contemplation is equal, while god and all the angels laugh up their white robes behind his back? But then if there is an advance in powers, there must be some ultimate limit when all are equally possessed of that highest power. And worse yet: All must have that equal power while retaining their distinct personalities."

"I believe the Church simply says: 'It is a mystery'."

"Yeah, well, in that case I can say that the universe sits on the backs of four elephants who stand on the back of a giant turtle, and if you question that truth, I will say, 'It is a mystery.' Any number can play that stupid game. Ha, and they do."

The girl arrived at the table with the main entrées. Before Gelb she placed a gray slate geta serving a *kuruma ebi* giant prawn on a bed of arugula, covered with garlic sauce, chopped spring onion, and the roe of flying fish. Before Lagarius she placed a similar large geta with his grilled Chilean sea bass, topped with ginger, green onion, and soy sauce. Between them she arranged many small dishes: Lagarius' bright red Bafun Uni, torched scallop with sweet fresh *yuzu*, sakura oak smoked radish, *akagai*, baby yam, various sushi and sashimi - with tiny chrysanthemum blossoms among them. With a pair of tongs she laid *oshibori*, hot towels, on a plate beside each diner. Then on the table close by she placed a dish with a large pyramid cover of yellow *kintsugi* ceramic with a bright band of cherry blossoms painted around it.

"What a beautiful cover," said Lagarius. Then, reaching for it: "It's a pyramid like the Louvre."

Gelb's arm shot out and gripped Lagarius' wrist before he could lift the cover.

"No," said Gelb. "The Louvre has four triangles, not counting the base. This has three. Anyway, since you're eating, you wouldn't want to see Schrödinger's cat, would you?"

"I can't see the cat?" said Lagarius, laughing. "Is it alive or dead?"

"No. You have resolved the superimposed possibilities as a sea bass, without trusting to chance at all. You are now wanting the impossible: A meal that is both a sea bass and something else at the same time."

"OK," said Lagarius, laughing at Gelb's device. "I promise to obey the laws of quantum mechanics. I will enjoy my magnificent sea bass."

He took up a big flake of the fish between his chopsticks. He savored the live yeast smell of fresh soy sauce. The steaming, fluffy chunk of flesh with the hint of ginger and green onion seemed to melt in his mouth.

"Unlike yourself," continued Gelb while chewing, with another great mound of prawn queued up on his chopsticks, "in this one city the demo-cratic flock has embraced randomness. They are happy to let the Great Chef choose what meal they will enjoy. As I said earlier, in the absence of ran-domness there is no joy in the game at all: There is determinism, perfect justice, and perfect equality. In other words, death, Game Over."

"But most people worship a god who offers perfect justice, equality, and of course, immortality."

"Yes, for the largest of the three groups in this last age of Kali Yuga, that's true. But their misunderstanding of first principles, as in every case, results in perversion. Look at the result! – An age where hysteria sweeps across the multitude like wind wavering the tall grass; an age where the most learned are the ones most lacking in wisdom; an age of self-doubt; an age of confusion from top to bottom, from the most basic principles of science to the most basic concept of self and sex. Slightly better, for a smaller group there's gratitude and identity: Its members just want to express their grati-tude for the great random game that they've been blessed to receive, and want identity, which they misunderstand as immortality."

"Doc, that's hardly a misunderstanding. After all, how could you have identity if it doesn't have an immortal container? If you didn't, at some point your identity would go out of existence."

"Family, Carmine, *family*. No one understands what that means. It's not just 'having kids.' It is that uniquely random event that casts your ripple across the smooth surface of all future time. It is completely outside the symmetry of time; it is non-'time-symmetrical'."

"You're putting chance in the service of family."

Gelb emptied another small bowl that was around his geta and took up a bite of pickled ginger.

"As you say. Nietzsche imagined that a demon might sneak into your subterranean loneliness and whisper in your ear: 'This gift of life of yours – your every sigh, every pain, every triumph, every despair, every transcendent and every cowardly thought – all of it, in every minute detail, will one day be repeated; and after an oblivion of ages, repeated yet again, and yet again for time everlasting.' To that demon he replied, 'You are a god, and never have I heard anything more divine!' *Don't you see what he was doing?* His supreme, towering strength of will to happiness sought to strangle despair by em-bracing determinism. A mistake! Despite it, he deserves to be a member of that third and smallest group: Those who embrace randomness and chance. For only the mechanically reversible, time-symmetrical, events will be repeated in eternal return, in the despairing sense tempted by his demon. But randomness is unique and immortal. Randomness is the only thing which cannot be undone."

The girl took up empty bowls and plates and laid out more hot *oshibori* with her tongs, taking up the cold ones. Gelb took up a fresh one, wiped his hands and mouth, and leaned back.

"I look at a human being and expect an ocean of possibilities, of unmet desires, of untried ideas, of adventures yet to be sailed upon. But instead I find something like an automaton - a narrow smear of shit on the great spectrum of human wonder. I find a furtive glance cast to the herd, to some dead idea, to some 'oh, look at me, my so-expressive me!' poseur, to an effigy of some media-spawned plastic idol. Oh god, yes, give me a *real* automaton where at least the plastic is authentic, instead of one where I have to dance a minuet around his precious ego, one possessed of some delicate fraud of self-esteem, one who would rather avenge his envy instead of yield to a superior. I refuse to join the age of Kali Yuga. I will burrow in darkness, uphold the immortal laws, and see the face of the divine."

Gelb tossed back a round of sake. Then suddenly he sat upright with a jolt. He sniffed the air in alarm.

"Rain!" Gelb said ominously. "I smell rain!"

He raced to the window where, as Lagarius now standing could see, it was pouring down hard. Gelb ran toward the door, waving frantically to the Japanese girl at the register. Lagarius followed him.

"*Gochisosama deshita, gochisosama deshita!*" said Gelb to the girl as he stuffed a wad of cash into her hand and burst outside, waving for a taxi.

In the downpour Lagarius followed him to the curb, where fortunately a taxi was rolling to a stop. He leaped inside behind Gelb, closing the door with a thump on the taxi's snug dry bubble, the rain still thundering on its roof. In just that moment of getting inside, their clothes had been drenched to the skin, and their hair soaked.

"Service parking lot behind Caesar's Palace," said Gelb to the driver; then to Lagarius: "We may be in trouble. - Depends on what's been coming down, farther west."

After fifteen minutes of slow driving in the blinding rain, the taxi turned off Frank Sinatra Drive, into the parking garage marked 'Associate Parking and Deliveries.' Under its cover the roar suddenly dropped off, and the wet taxi tires gave an echoing squeak on the concrete floor as Gelb directed turns to the driver. Gelb paid and leapt out of the taxi, Lagarius behind him. They were standing some distance from the security building, which was outside the garage, where Lagarius could see water pouring into the grate beside it. The grate at their feet, where they had emerged earlier in the evening, was dry in the covered parking. Gelb pulled it off and went down the iron rungs. Lagarius followed, pulling the grate back in place behind him. Lagarius followed the bobbing beam of Gelb's flashlight as he ran ahead of him. He heard music echoing down the tunnel, growing louder as they ran. The sound soon was unmistakable to Lagarius, who recognized it from Ana's collection: Reverend Horton Heat's rockabilly hit, *I Can't Surf*, blaring from Gelb's motion alarm. The barking of the dog became audible. Then they were there.

"Thank goodness the numbers are still turning!" said Gelb to Lagarius, raising his voice over the music.

The two soaked men stood catching their breath. Directly across from them was Gelb's bedroom, a warm dry rectangle of light illuminated by the table lamp beside his bed. The dog stood on the edge, wagging his tail in anticipation. To reach Gelb's den they would have to return down the iron rungs on this side and up those that ascended to Gelb's space, crossing twenty feet of torrent that could be heard in the blackness above *I Can't Surf*. They played their flashlights on the fast-moving water below.

"Look at the rungs across there!" shouted Gelb above the din. "I think only the bottom one is underwater. We need to go now. Remember, if you get swept downstream," – here he leaned out of the tunnel and shined his beam along the near wall – "the four man-eating jaws get you! And farther on, the whirlpool of death!"

Lagarius shined his own light on the row of four two-foot-wide drains high in the near wall, now spewing water almost half-way across the twenty-foot span below. Farther downstream he could see the fence of steel pipes surrounding the ominously unseen hole.

Gelb descended, flashlight in his mouth. He turned to cross, and Lagarius fixed his own beam as a goal to the opposite rungs, as Gelb's light flickered over the sweeping water. Lagarius could see that it was above Gelb's knees, and that he was extending his downstream leg to brace against the force of the flood. Stumping carefully through the water, Gelb reached the other side and scampered half-way up the rungs, squealing with delight. He gave a thumbs up to Lagarius.

Lagarius descended. He extended his arms for balance, holding the flashlight aloft.

Then the air about him seemed to buffet and waver at his ears; a low roar shook the tunnel floor under his feet. He looked up with his beam to see Gelb point upstream and seem to yell as he scampered to the top of the ladder. Lagarius turned his head, directing his light upstream. A wall of water a sickening four feet high was racing toward him. He worked his legs vainly in a frantic quick-walk. The torrent slammed into him, its weight driving him down and off his feet. He emerged gasping and heard Gelb yelling to him.

"Grab the pipe rail! Grab it!"

Lagarius readied his arms to grab the pipe fence while thrashing to stay above the flood. He flicked his beam right, left... – a blink of painted green steel pipe was the last thing he saw as his head slammed into it and thick darkness covered his eyes.

18

"The 3522 bus should be here in fifteen minutes, at 1:05 am," said Wiser as he took the passenger seat and closed the car door against the cold. "It will pull up right in front of us."

While trailing the bus on its journey from Washington, DC to Bangor, Maine, with four stops in between, Captain J.C. Simmons-Humph III had called for Eden Wiser to fly ahead to Bangor and take a taxi to its bus station. He was to wait for him in the Dysart Restaurant, which was inside the same building, on the opposite side, facing the gas pumps. The bus had been expected hours earlier, but there had been a breakdown outside Portland, and Humph, in exasperation, had driven ahead to meet Wiser, alerting the GPS watcher in Washington to call him at once if Lagarius' delayed bus moved. In the restaurant they had ordered coffee - the fifth cup that evening for Humph - and had walked out the single glass door on the bus station side, through the striped, uncovered boarding zone to Humph's car. It was backed into a space where a row of uncovered parking was marked along a low hill facing the building, so that the entire length of the green and white building was visible through the front windshield. For the third time, Humph had sent Wiser back inside to make queries at the gas station's convenience store counter, since the Greyhound information desk was closed.

"And there's only one door on the bus?" asked Humph, eyes narrowed, nervously nibbling the tip of his tongue.

"The bus has only one door, and it will face us when the bus pulls up," said Wiser evenly, trying to conceal his impatience. "What exactly are we trying to do here?"

"'Trying to do'? Hell, we've gone over this," said Humph.

"I mean, are we here to make an arrest, or what? And on what charge?"

"Yes, by god, we're here to make an arrest - on the charge of interstate flight regarding an issue of national security. You're not going blue falcon on me, are you, Eden?"

"Of course not," Wiser scoffed angrily.

"OK, then, don't get ate up on the details. I don't see this going kinetic, but we don't know who he might meet here."

Earlier, in the nearly empty restaurant, Humph had discussed with Wiser the possibility that Lagarius might meet someone who would transport him to the Canadian border, or that he might talk some truck driver in the restaurant into ferrying him. Humph's plan was that after their initial identification of Lagarius, Wiser would run around to the opposite, gas station, side of the building and wait for Lagarius to exit with his ride. Humph would do the same at the bus station side of the building. They would remain in phone contact until one summoned the other for help in making the arrest. Both of them would be in three-way contact by phone with the GPS watcher in Washington, so they would know the whereabouts of Lagarius and their partner at all times. As for the larger context that was the real point of Wiser's questions – a context limited by Humph's "need-to-know-only" sharing of information – apparently Lagarius was complicit in an attack that could not be prevented until he had made a revealing move, such as trying to flee to Canada. Other questions about Humph's operation had plagued Wiser during his flight to Bangor, but he had decided to keep them to himself for the time being.

It had gotten cold. With the engine off and the windows cracked to keep the windshield from fogging, Wiser was glad to have the coffee in the foam cup, and his trench coat about him.

"Let's go condition red," said Humph. He placed his coffee in the console and took out his FBI service Glock 17. He snapped the slide to chamber a round and holstered the pistol under his left arm. Wiser had not carried his weapon on the airplane; Humph had given him one that he kept in his vehicle. Wiser likewise armed and holstered it in his shoulder harness.

Humph adjusted his phone headset at his mouth.

"R-r-rock-a-bye, R-r-rock-a-bye, do you read me?" he muttered into the mouthpiece, staccato and grim. "How's the baby?"

Humph had elaborated a set of operative words for the "caper," as he termed this ruse of Lagarius to escape into Canada and his plan to thwart it. "Rock-a-bye" was now the war room in Washington; the "baby" was Lagarius; in the write-up that he had mentally drafted while following the bus, the "caper" would become Operation Cooked Canada Goose.

"Subject's rolling in," crackled a voice in Humph's headset.

Bus 3522 rolled into the boarding zone, into the pool of neon light there. Its jake brake sounded, giving a loud blast of pressurized air as it firmly stopped. The door on the right front side opened. After a long moment, a hooded man wearing a jacket with a Greyhound Bus patch over the left front pocket stepped out and raised one storage panel low on the right side. Just a stubbled chin showed beneath the shadow of the jacket's hood. The bus door remained open, but no one came out.

"R-r-rock-a-bye, R-r-rock-a-bye, *where's the baby?*" muttered Humph anxiously.

The stereo reply crackled electronically in the phone headsets of Humph and Wiser:

"He's right in front of you."

"R-r-rock-a-bye, no visual," muttered Humph. "What's on your screen?"

"Red dot of subject is fifteen yards northeast in front of you. Blue dot Eagle One side-by-side with green dot Eagle Two. No dots moving."

"Wiser, ID yourself to the driver and search the bus!" ordered Humph.

Wiser got out of the car, FBI badge already in hand, calling to the startled driver, who had stood up a two-wheeler and was about to reach into the storage area for packages. Humph watched him show his badge. The driver nodded, and Wiser entered the bus, his right hand at the opening of his unbuttoned coat. The driver began stacking the two-wheeler.

"Eagle One, subject shifted three feet west."

What? Shifted where? thought Humph.

"Eagle Two," said Humph with alarm, "is subject crawling under the seats?"

"Not possible," said Wiser. "I'm looking inside the toilet. The bus is empty."

"Eagle One, subject is on the move northeast."

What? thought Humph. All he could see was the back of the driver, wheeling a stack of packages around the back of the....

"Got you, you bastard!" yelled Humph into the mouthpiece as he burst out of the car, pistol drawn and raised skyward in his right hand.

The driver had gone out of sight around the bus, but Humph quickly rounded the bus and ran up to the driver's retreating back. With his free hand Humph grabbed his right shoulder, spun him around, and tore back his hood. The two-wheeler and its packages went flying as the terrified black driver opened his mouth and stammered.

"Wh-what choo doin', my man?" he said angrily. "What the hell's a-matter witchoo?"

"I, I, I'm," babbled Humph as he put away his gun. "A dangerous man. National security, on the loose. I'm sorry, I'm sorry. Let me help you with...."

Wiser rushed up and began helping collect the scattered parcels.

"Subject just flew twenty feet and stopped," came the stereophonic crackle between the two headsets. "Damn, did you knock him out of his shoes?"

"Here, look at this," said Wiser, holding up one package with one hand and clawing through the others. "It's the only package originating in Silver Spring."

Humph snatched it away and began tearing it open.

"Hey, hey, you cain't be doin' that," said the driver. "That ain't your'n."

"National security," said Humph as he popped the boxing tape and pulled out Lagarius' GPS-seeded jacket.

"Goddamnit," said Humph, throwing the jacket to the pavement in disgust. "A goddamned soup sandwich. We've been owned."

Wiser began a scarcely concealed slow burn of anger as he glowered at Humph.

"Hey, stand by," crackled the headset. "I think we got something."

"Whatcha got, whatcha got, whatcha got?" said Humph excitedly.

"Wiser's group just came through with this. Carmine Lagarius just bought a red-eye to Vegas. The plane took off ten minutes ago."

"I got that," said Humph, nibbling the tip of his tongue with renewed enthusiasm. "Bravo Zulu, Rock-a-bye. Eden, contact me when your people have his Vegas hotel check-in. As for you personally, you need to catch a plane and Charlie Mike at Virginia Beach. I want you to stake out this fool's beach house."

Arusha LePepeyon

19

The light of the full moon breaking through the clouds awakened Lagarius.

He squinted, blinked, then gazed absently at its bright disk, its pattern familiar to him as a badly carved Halloween pumpkin with drooping eyes and a mouth mournfully off to the left. A light rain fell upon his face. His whole body was being gently, lullingly rocked, to the slapping sound of lightly ladled water.

He jolted upward and winced in pain. He cautiously felt the lump on the right temple of his head as he sat and looked around, bewildered. He was in a wooden dinghy at the end of a small marina – a jetty with about a dozen berths on either side, all taken by boats less than twenty feet in length. A walkway from the jetty went over a rocky shore to the patio of a tile-roofed building. Milky moon glow covered all and wavered on the low waves reaching to several other inlets in front of him. Along the inlets were single docks and behind them, palm trees and substantial tile-roofed houses. Lagarius turned painfully to look behind him. In the highway of moonlight he saw an expanse of water, churning more as it reached away from him.

He took an inventory of himself. His boots were missing, leaving him in his socks, and his pants were shredded. One pocket was gone – the one with the money clip – but the other was intact with his credit cards and driver's license inside. His lambskin jacket was soaked and ruined, but the two phones on one side, and the tablet on the other remained. His watch was still on his wrist, indicating three minutes after midnight, Saturday, November 2. He had a terrible headache around the lump at his right ear.

He took out the burner phone that he had used to accept Artie Gelb's phone number in the restaurant and turned it on, hoping for the best. Surprisingly, it worked, and illuminated with fifteen percent battery remaining. He redialed Gelb.

"Yes, Carmine?" answered Gelb, calm and unperturbed. The prayer wheels turned in the background, squeaking softly.

"Thank goodness! You sound high and dry. Are you OK?"

"Sure. One hell of a water park ride we had, though."

"Where the heck am I?"

"You're down from the Lake Club at Lake Las Vegas."

"How did I get here? Don't tell me I went through the tunnels and came out here."

"OK, I won't. You went through some concrete plumbing and got shat out a septic tank twenty miles east of downtown."

Lagarius groaned.

"I thought you were a goner when that wave hit you. I jumped onto the sofa and threw myself into the angry face of Poseidon. Hung left and barely missed the four jaws of death. Godamighty! You were out cold, with your head on top of the pipes and your arms slung around them. I was full cowboy with my legs around that sofa, zipping along – yeeha! The speed was kinda good, though: When I grabbed you, you came away with me right onto the Shithole Express. I had my flashlight in my mouth, and we went through the pipes like a locomotive in the night. Lucky you were zonked: With that light dying ahead in the blackness, and raging, roaring waters all around – damn, I've never been so scared in all my life. Finally we got belched out into some wetlands, then slammed through basin after basin. Some of those basins have big concrete bumps, tank traps, can you imagine? And what for? Any invading tanks coming up that way? Jeesh. Anyway, we got into the calm waters of Lake Vegas. Nice golf course along the water to the left – you golf? Forget it: Twisting on the lower back will kill you. I paddled like hell to get out of the middle current. We came up onto a little boat at a jetty. You were mumbling and groaning, but still like a sack of concrete for me to get you into that thing. It seemed like you were going to be OK, though. Sorry I couldn't stay. Apologies, but one man in the balance against the entire spinning universe – you know what I mean?"

"I understand. No problem."

"Did you email Lucas in the last few days?"

"What? Doc, you know Lucas is dead."

"Yes, I know that. Which one of us is forgetting stuff? You asked me to think about your problem, should I forget? His laptop was taken. I think you should send email to him. If the person who took his laptop can get into his email, you'll be in touch with them."

Lagarius gave an enormous sneeze.

"Sorry for that," he said with a sniffle. "So, I want a conversation with his killers?"

"Did you see someone kill him and take the laptop?"

"No, but..."

"– Then quit assuming so much. Even if bad people have done all this, they may reply and give you a clue. Clever morons like to boast about how clever they are. But you don't know who really does have it. Sending an email is casting bread on the water, sure, Bar Kappara be praised – but it doesn't cost you anything. – And send it in the clear, I shouldn't need to remind you. I'm sure you encrypted all your previous stuff."

"True. OK," said Lagarius, keeping his doubts to himself. "I'll give it a try."

"Look, Carmine, I've got to get a drop of oil onto Lambda, do you mind?"

"No, it's all right. I'll let you go. Call if you need anything, Doc."

The rain had stopped. Lagarius hung up and sat thinking. He would use one of the emergency throwaway numbers available to him on Nigredo's network. But first he must carefully compose what he had to say in order to keep the message brief, in accordance with protocol. After a few moments he took up the phone, dialed, and left the message:

"Desperate. Wet with rain. No cash, no transportation, no clothes, no shoes. Standing by outside the Lake Club at Lake Las Vegas."

He thought long about Gelb's suggestion to email to Lucas' address. He launched Tor over VPN then accessed a dummy public email account. He typed in the Lucas address then stared at the blinking cursor in the luminous screen. He continued typing.

I have broken the messages in the image of Bellini's Christ. You should contact me before the events planned for November 5.

He re-read the message several times, from the point of view of someone planning the attack, and again from the point of view of someone intent on stopping it. Of course he had not broken any significant number of messages, and he was only guessing that November 5 was a meaningful date. But bluff and surmise were the only gambit left for him to play. He clicked to send it.

Lagarius looked around the boat and raised the lid on a storage box in the stern. He took out several life jackets to make a pillow and mattress, and a sheet of plastic as cover against the chill. There was nothing more to do but lay back and wait. He looked at the moon and idly imagined the astronauts of long ago hopping around on its surface, playing golf, dropping a feather and a hammer to prove Galileo's law of falling bodies. Somehow he felt profoundly at peace: The endless gnawing replay of Beddoes' remarks and its motive-guessing hall of mirrors had ceased. In his moonlit face his heavy eyelids blinked, blinked, then closed. He fell asleep.

Soon he dreamt that one of the astronauts was ringing a bell at a fellow astronaut standing a few yards away in the moon dust. He gave the bell a slow-motion vigorous shake, but the other playfully cupped his hands at the sides of his helmet, shook his head, and shrugged. The other threw the bell at him and it seemed now to travel a hundred yards to slam into his helmet.

Lagarius jolted upright, shoving off the crackling plastic, pawing for the phone now ringing in his jacket. He read the text message.

At 5 am stand at the north entrance to the Lake Club on Grand Mediterra Blvd.

The timestamp showed that it had been sent just thirty minutes after his voicemail appeal. He opened the Las Vegas map on his phone and saw that the designated point was only two or three hundred feet from where he lay, and clearly accessible. It was almost 1:00 am. He set both his watch and phone alarm for 4:30 am. He felt almost happy, and even the throbbing knot over his right ear seemed tolerable. He lay down again, covered himself with the plastic, and was almost instantly asleep.

❦

Lagarius woke up several minutes before his 4:30 am alarms. He put the life jackets and plastic back inside the dinghy's storage box then walked up the jetty, over the narrow walkway, and out along the south side of Grand Mediterra Boulevard. Walking east, the faint pearl blue of first light showed over the palms surrounding the Lake Club parking lot. He arrived at the north entrance and stood on the manicured grass in his socks, looking around, feeling foolish. A dark-colored vehicle with deeply tinted glass was backed into a parking space directly south, under a clump of trees. He checked his watch: 4:48 am. Probably unseen passengers in the vehicle were looking at him, calculating, verifying, waiting. He thought it prudent to stand in the open and remain calm.

At exactly 5:00 am the vehicle under the trees rumbled softly to life and inched slowly forward with no lights, approaching Lagarius. At the exit to Grand Mediterra it stopped and the driver's window hummed, lowering two inches. At the opened slit a brown hand appeared with a key fob. Lagarius approached. Two steps before his reaching it, the hand pressed the fob and two sharp whoops sounded, synchronously with two red flashes of light from behind the clump of trees where the vehicle had been. Lagarius took the key fob, and the window zipped closed. The vehicle eased onto the boulevard, turning right as its headlights came on, then right again behind the trees, a low searchlight headed south in the shadows.

Lagarius walked to the clump of trees. He could make out a low red sports car in the faint light of morning as he turned the corner. Then he laughed with happy astonishment.

"No, no, it can't be," he said aloud to himself. He threw back his head and gave a loud laugh.

There it was, backed in, facing him now: The red Porsche Boxster S that was casually mentioned during his supper with Nigredo.

Lagarius opened the door, taking pleasure in the snug firm action of its handle, in the anticipation of the engineering that awaited him inside. On the driver's seat was a fluffy towel, which he took up to dry his hair. Underneath it was a change of clothes and a pair of shoes. He stripped off his wet clothes, dried, and changed, appreciating the circumspection that had positioned the car beside the trees to allow him to dress without anyone's notice. He got in and stowed the wet things in the rolled up towel behind the seat.

The expensive thump of the door sealed him in a bubble fragrant with leather, illuminated by three gauges with a row of instrument lights beneath. Lagarius laughed again when he saw on the dash the deluxe Escort Max 360 radar detector. He opened the glove box and saw the registration in his name. On the passenger seat was a folded note on top of a leather satchel. He unfolded it and read the handwritten message:

Your happiness – and mine. MN

He opened the satchel flap and a soft linen bag slipped out. Loosening the drawstring, he took out the Persol PO 714 tortoise-shell frame sunglasses and laughed aloud as he unfolded them, then refolded them into his shirt pocket. Inside the satchel he saw a manila envelope marked "Ukrainian security consulting receipts." Beneath it were three crisp packets of one-hundred-dollar bills, each mustard-colored strap dividing the face of Franklin, each a stack of one hundred hundreds.

Lagarius did not laugh as he re-read the note, but smiled with deep satisfaction and gratitude: He had never seen Muhammad Nigredo put his name on anything, much less write out something in his own hand, and here the man had done that, scanning it in Miami and having it printed in Vegas. And he had thought of everything besides, including a phone charger with adapters for any device. Lagarius brought the engine to life and listened to its subdued boom; he adjusted the seat and mirrors, and set the GPS on his phone for Washington, DC, thirty-six hours away – thirty if he forced it.

He wondered what news Ana would have when he would stop to call her six hours later, when he would take gas in Gallup, New Mexico.

20

"*Chouchou*, this gonna be my big moment. You gotta be there."

Lagarius chuckled softly into the phone, looking past the blur of digits on the gasoline pump, basking under the cool, dry, cloudless New Mexico sky.

"I don't know, Ana," he said. He looked at his watch: 11:09 am. "I can't promise before three o'clock. More likely it'll be closer to five. And you realize I have to drive all day and all night to make Sunday."

"Why don't you park your new girlfriend and get on a plane? You could spend tonight with your little dragon, get big breakfast, then see the whole show.

"You don't miss your little dragon?" she purred.

"Ha, yes, I do. I need to drive, though. At least for the next few days I have to cut as low a profile as possible. After that, it probably won't matter. Are you in Washington now? It would really be nice if you could take an anonymous visitor."

"Sure, sure. I'm at the International Hotel. I can put envelope behind front desk with key."

"Thanks. And maybe a change of clothes? I know I'm pushing it."

"I'm really busy – practice every minute, this is so big. But I will try."

"When do you come on? And tell me again what's this all about – it all seems a bit weird to me. A bunch of women are going to meet on the National Mall to tell about their sufferings in the wealthiest, most liberated nation on earth – is that about it?"

"You see? You just a racist, un-woke pig, *habibi*. This is big. Where you been? The Green people now see this is more than climate change. This is Gaia geophysiology."

"You've been talking to Ricce," Lagarius said disdainfully.

"Women are wearing the pants now – smarty pants and thinking cap too. We got too many binaries now: White-nonwhite, man-woman, capitalism-socialism. All this is from patriarchal dominance. We gonna shut all that down. Shut it *down*. You can't even see that, can you?"

"OK, OK, so what's your part in all this? When do you come on?"

"Remember the three singers at the Halloween party. Ricce says that they are *har*-bingers for the semiotics of the new age, and that I am the first speaker of the new semiotics. I come on just before she gives a big talk – at six, maybe six-thirty."

"Well, then," said Lagarius. "I guess there's no way I dare miss it."

"I'm still sad about Ron Peel. I can't think how his body must have..."

"– Yeah, don't," said Lagarius. He exhaled audibly. "And then there's Lucas."

"I'm sad," said Ana with a sniffle.

"OK, I'm sorry we brought that up. Look, I've got to go pay for my gas and get back on the road."

"Give me a kiss," she said.

"Call only on this throwaway phone number if you need to reach me."

They traded air kisses and hung up.

Lagarius walked into the convenience store to pay for his gasoline. Behind the counter was the station's big red and white logo – Full Fill – showing an energetically smiling gas station attendant from the 1950s wearing a red service cap like the blue ones worn by policemen. He picked up a salty snack and a bottle of cold fruit juice, then went to the counter.

"What's this thing I passed on the road – 'Phil Fill'?" Lagarius asked. "It looked brand-new, with robots lined up in front of a pillbox."

"Yeah," said the clerk, a young black man whose head was shaved but for a shaggy crown of dreadlocks hanging to his ears. "'Phil' be the name of the robot that come out to you. He gives you a tablet of all the stuff in the store while he puts in the gas. You click on what you want, and he bring it out to you."

"You can't go in and look around?"

"Naw, naw, none o' that. No bathrooms neither. And no cash like you just laid out here – card only. Top o' that, you don't mess with Phil: That place is full lit up, with cameras ever'where. You try to outsmart Phil, and the cops is out there in a minute."

Lagarius thanked him and went out. In the sweep of concrete driveway a gasoline tanker truck had parked. On its side was the silhouette of a lantern separating the words "Dark" and "Lantern," with the word "Petroleum" beneath it. A man with a green Mohawk-with-mullet haircut and a sleeveless denim jacket and gloves was laying out lengths of hose behind a row of orange safety cones. Lagarius did a double take when he noticed that the 'man' was wearing purple lipstick, and had body mass more at the hips than at the shoulders. She held her arms out like a gunslinger as she walked around the truck to the other side.

In five hours the Boxster zipped through the fleeting green spot of Albuquerque and the following wasteland to Amarillo. He passed more 'Phil Fill' stations, with their row of robots in front of their white boxes with no human openings. After passing the ten half-buried cars south of Interstate 40, the "Cadillac Ranch," something of a landmark west of the city in the utter flatness of the prairie, he stopped again – at 'Full Fill' – for gas and a break. The city seemed deserted. Many businesses were boarded up. Only a few cars were moving along the business roads north of the Interstate.

Another flat expanse took Lagarius to Oklahoma City, past its two sky-scrapers, to Fort Smith, Arkansas, where he fueled again and slept for less than an hour at an Interstate rest stop. He woke up a few minutes after 10:00 pm, and was driving again. All along the way to his next Full Fill stop in Nashville, his headlights illuminated lines of people walking in scattered clumps along the roadway. They seemed to be laden with their belongings, which they carried in trash bags and shopping carts, and with dirty children, who stumped along with the adults or rode in toy wagons pulled by older ones. They never looked up at his passing car, but walked with their heads down. Lagarius slowed a bit when entering Memphis, about half-way to Nashville. On one side of the road was a billboard with the face of a man seemingly an amalgam of races, next to the message: *Are you too racist to vote for Bill Black?* On the other side of the road was a billboard with the grim face of Al Beddoes, next to the message: *President Beddoes will keep us safe.* Like Amarillo, Memphis too seemed deserted and boarded up, except for the occasional person staggering into or out of the hundreds of tents and cardboard homes filling every sidewalk that he could see. Between Memphis and Nashville, again he saw the destitute people and their children along the roadside.

Before entering Nashville Lagarius pulled into another Full Fill just as morning light was showing. He set the pump to operate while he went to pay. The driveway was dirty and the trash bins were overflowing. The convenience store windows seemed to have been shot several times with bullet holes, which were mended by bolts holding a bit of plywood on either side of the glass. At the door a huge cardboard placard greeted him through the glass, reading: WE DON'T DIAL 911, with the picture of a man looking down the barrel of a shotgun at him. The door stuck at the upper corner; Lagarius forced it, and it waggled open. He approached the counter. There was the now familiar Full Fill logo on the wall behind the counter, its red paint peeling from it.

A tall thin elderly man stood at the register smoking, looking nervously out at Lagarius' car. Behind two enormous ears his long, yellowing white hair was tucked, reaching almost to his plaid shirt.

"Don't worry, I'm a-watchin' your car," he said, his Adam's apple bobbing the gray stubble on his neck as he spoke. "Come on up."

"Is there a crime problem here?" asked Lagarius.

"Ain't a dawg got ticks? Yeah, I'd say we got issues in that department." He looked Lagarius up and down. "Where you be from?"

"Virginia."

The man gave a mild snort, apparently unconvinced. A length of cigarette ash fell onto the counter, which he swiped away.

"I passed so many destitute people along the highway," said Lagarius. "What's that all about?"

"Them's gypsies - least, that's what folks call 'em. Though they ain't proper gypsies in my book. They just country people with nowheres to go."

"Why, don't they have homes?"

"Naw, don't nobody hereabouts got a proper home. They's a slew of trailer parks and RV parks, but not what you'd call a Christian home - not nothin' like what I growed up in, nohow. - And we was pore.

"Them gypsies just wander about, askin' for a scrap of food, sleepin' in they clothes. Kindly heartbreakin' seein' the littlest 'uns, what with dirty faces, snot runnin' down. But they git up to any size and you'll find 'em mean as the dickens. That's how come me to be watchin' your car."

The fill handle clicked outside at the fuel tank.

"Sixty-eight seventy," said the clerk.

Lagarius placed a hundred-dollar bill on the counter.

"Hm. Ain't you got no twenties?"

"No. Look, I wanted to pull up somewhere and close my eyes for a half hour. You can keep the change if I can park here, and you keep watching my car."

"Why hell yeah, OK. Pull your car up here close by the winnder wheres I can see."

Lagarius went out, replaced the pump handle, and parked the Boxster close to the clerk's window as he indicated. He gave a wave to the clerk, leaned back his seat, and was instantly asleep.

After about twenty minutes Lagarius sat up with a start as the Boxster jolted, and a child screamed and ran past the right front corner of his vehicle. Behind his vehicle stood the old clerk, waving a stick angrily.

"Git off from heahn, you little bastard!" he yelled at the child. He came alongside the driver's window.

Lagarius straightened his seat and saw the bent wire just outside the passenger windshield. He got out.

"Dad gum, the little fart got one of your wiper blades, or tried to."

They walked around to look at the metal arm, now bent upward.

"I can straighten out the arm, pretty much," said Lagarius. "The rubber's still there, but a bit of it is torn off. Do you have any replacement blades?"

"Naw. Shore don't. You want some money back, seein's how I let that little cuss git the better of me?"

"No, that's OK. Don't worry about it. I need to get up on the road anyway."

"Well, let me git you a coffee and a bear claw, anyhow. Take that as some amends."

Outside Nashville Lagarius saw the matching billboards alongside the road. To the left, again the face of indeterminate race, with the message: *Bill Black: Maybe he's not, but he identifies as one.* To the right, another grim Beddoes, with the message: *Are you with Al? – Or with the terrorists?*

Lagarius continued east along Interstate 40, climbing into the Appalachians, resplendent now with autumn colors in the morning light. He put down the windows to keep himself awake and to enjoy the clean November air in the cockpit. The mountains flattened a bit into the rolling green Shenandoah Valley as Interstate 40 became Interstate 81. Lagarius could not help thinking of the legendary exploits of Stonewall Jackson on this majestic stage, the most famous soldier in the world that summer of 1862, after routing 52,000 Union soldiers with a force less than a third that size. A flood of memories from the constant retellings of the John Pelham family and the Marine Military Academy in Harlingen, Texas came upon him. He wondered which filled his eyes now with solemn tears of awe: The morning enchantment of the great valley on his altered state born of sleeplessness; or the green hills ablaze with red, gold, and orange that swept vastly into a mist where impossibly heroic ghosts awaited on horseback among the trees; or the blood-soaked futility of it all.

At Lexington, Virginia, Lagarius gassed up again at Full Fill. Like the station at his first stop in New Mexico, it too was being serviced by a Dark Lantern Petroleum tanker. He went in to pay and get a cold fruit juice, and stood behind another patron at the counter. Before them a man, evidently the tanker driver by the logo on the back of his jacket, took up his clipboard and took back the pen that the clerk had just used to scribble his signature on the receipt.

"See you next time," the driver said with a nod. He did not notice something fall from his jacket pocket as he turned to go. The patron in front of Lagarius stooped to pick it up.

"Hey, here's the necklace you dropped, friend."

A half-second snarl passed across the driver's bearded face as he turned to take the strand – a round-beaded strand with two square red beads and a pendant.

"Careful, though," joked the patron. "That bushy pendant might be a bit ticklish on your girlfriend, tee hee."

"Ha ha, yeah, maybe you're right," said the driver, rolling the "r."

Back on the road, Lagarius drove three more hours along Interstate 66, taking it into Washington across Theodore Roosevelt Bridge, then down Constitution Avenue, past the Lincoln Memorial, past the Vietnam Memorial, past the reflecting pool, all now thronged with women in festive colors, carrying placards. As he turned into the International Hotel parking lot he checked his watch: 3:11 pm.

21

The cloudless azure of a perfect November day greeted Lagarius as he walked out through the massive central arch of the International Hotel and crossed to Twelfth Street, headed south. His burner phone showed 4:11 pm and sixty degrees. Ana had found time to provide him a new change of clothes, which she had placed on the corner of her hotel room bed for him. After a hot shower followed by cold, he felt completely refreshed, no longer tired. He had texted her as he had entered the city, but had received only a terse reply: "Very busy. Bastards have fenced Lincoln." He decided to leave her alone until he had walked near the steps of the Lincoln Memorial, where the speakers for the grand event would be – an event that welcoming signs in the hotel lobby proclaimed as "Washington Monument Renaming: Pocahontas Bliss."

After crossing Constitution Avenue and passing between the two buildings of the Smithsonian, he emerged onto the National Mall, where a festival atmosphere prevailed. East toward the Capitol dome the mall's great lawn was an open expanse but for several dogs and their owners playing Frisbee and children playing chase. A woman wearing soccer shin guards was struggling to put a tutu on a boy who was energetically kicking her, his face a petulant scowl. West toward the low hill of the Washington Monument the crowd thickened, milling toward the Lincoln Memorial, not visible from this side of the monument and its surrounding trees. In the crowd furry costumes of cats, mice, and other animals danced along; a giant ball with the face of George Washington painted on it arced slowly above them, which descended to meet flailing arms that punched it skyward in a burst of laughter; a wire rainbow formed by multicolored balloons wavered westward; and joyful women in every variety of green costume and rainbow-colored costume milled about with many carrying hand-painted signs. One read "First Year Students, Not FreshMEN!"; another, "Save The Northern Quoll – No More Toad Legs!"; another, "AIDS Research Cuts Never Heal!"; and another, "Vaginas Are Beautiful!"

To avoid the crowd Lagarius walked west on the sidewalk along Constitution Avenue. At Seventeenth Street he returned to the mall, emerging at the World War Two Memorial. He marveled at the sight before him. All along the reflecting pool stretching a half mile to the Lincoln Memorial were women in green and rainbow-colored costumes as before, with multicolored balloons and placards held aloft. Near him, crossing Seventeenth Street, which was blocked from traffic at both ends, a giant papier-mâché image of George Washington and another of Pocahontas, both supported by several women holding long sticks, bobbed above the crowd. Washington was bug-eyed with alarm, holding his bottom as Pocahontas rammed him with a giant penis, which sent up a howl of mirth each time she hit home.

Evidently Lagarius had entered upon a lull in the agenda. Everyone was facing west toward the Memorial, anxious with happy anticipation. He overheard a woman say, "Ricce's on next!", her prayerful hands clapping excitedly, bouncing on her toes. He pushed his way west through the crowd, reading signs along the way: "Inclusive Traffic Lights, NOW!" held by two large women wearing tank tops with the message "I'm with Ze," each with an arrow pointing to her partner; "I Can't Even Think Straight!" held by a woman with rings pierced into her mouth, nose, and ears; "Wolves Are People Too!" held by a woman with black hair below her nose and along her cheeks, wearing a green dress covered with buttons reading "Stop The Coal Greenmageddon!"; a thin, ghostly pale woman held the sign "Meat is murder!"; he saw the sign "Syphilitic Lives Matter!" held between an unsmiling couple of indeterminate gender, wearing dark sunglasses; "Jesus Had Two Dads, Praise God!" held by a person cavorting about in the costume of a satyr; "Interracial Marriage Comics For Kids!" held by a black woman who laughed with a white woman carrying a café au lait-colored baby asleep in a chest carrier; "Librarians For Trans Drag Story Hours!" held by someone with hairy arms and legs wearing a dress; two burly women with sagging breasts in matching rainbow T-shirts laughed together, one with the sign "Size Matters! Fist Her Tonight!" and the other with "Burgle One, You'll Enjoy It!"; a woman cradled a sullen-faced toddler while holding the sign "Fight For Woke Babies!"; someone with a shaved head tattooed with a blue spiral-shaped triangle held the sign "Pedo Bashing Is Racism!"; a burly woman holding a wolfhound on a chain held the sign "Bestiality Is SIN-sational!".

By the time Lagarius reached the far west end of the reflecting pool it was 5:15 pm, and the sun had fallen just below the treetops behind the Lincoln Memorial. In the middle of the one-lane circle surrounding it, a flimsy chain-link fence stood, supported by inverted T-shaped pipes and marked with signs cautioning: "Under Maintenance. Hard Hat Area. Do Not Enter." Descending about fifteen feet from the circle to the reflecting pool were three broad terraces, divided in the middle by three flights of steps. On the top terrace, to the right near the trees that ran the length of the reflecting pool, was a screen about forty feet square, its projected image of a wavering rainbow banner now more evident since the sun had fallen. An identical screen on the left showed the same image.

The majestic focus above the terraces was the Memorial. Portico backlights behind the twelve forty-foot columns along its front now etched them against the dimming sky, whose light blue was dissolving to iridescent mother-of-pearl. Behind the middle four columns a spotlight fell over the nineteen-foot statue of Lincoln, luminous against the dark square opening like an old man sitting in a darkened doorway waiting for his children, his bright brow tilted forward in reverie, his eyes in shadowed gloom.

The change in the afternoon lighting signaled a bustle of activity around the three microphones on the top terrace, as several young technicians ran about, moving wires and waving to each other, and making adjustments at the mixing console and to the cameras nested in front. Lagarius saw Frittata Ricce with a sheaf of papers, standing beside a scaffolding of speakers, talking to a group of women around her and gesturing emphatically. He resisted the temptation to call or text Ana, who surely must have been busy in preparation for her "big moment," as she had called it.

An excited hush traveled through the crowd as a woman came forward and bent over the center microphone, which had been lowered for Ricce's height.

"And now!" she said with a pop of air and a quickly squelched feedback squeal. She paused between barely controlled excited breaths. "Our leader... the woman who needs no introduction here... the scholar... the fireball of passion... the one... the one... *the one*... Doctor Frittata Ricce!"

A tremendous roar shook the mall as Ricce gave a hug to the woman and came to the microphone. The forty-foot screens at either side now showed Ricce in high-definition aliveness. There were the eyes with dark rings beneath, the dark eyes drooping at the outside corners, the continually pursed blubbery lips overhung with the goitrous nose, the short spiked gray hair. In veristic crispness too were the scattered liver spots and the salt-and-pepper hairs of her eyebrows.

"Thank you," she murmured, pursing her lips and raising both hands. "Thank you."

Rhythmic clapping broke out to the shouted "Ric-ce! Ric-ce! Ric-ce!"

"Thank you. Thank you. Please," she said.

Another fifteen seconds of shouts and applause went on. The backdrop of the Memorial now glowed warmly against the bright pumpkin sky behind it, with the dramatic sunset surrendering to cobalt. Lincoln, a brooding spot of light in the distant dark threshold, seemed to ponder as he listened, seated just above Ricce's shoulders. The small figure flanked by her two forty-foot, mercilessly focused heads continued.

"Thank you," she said as the crowd fell quiet. She pursed her lips. Then she lifted her voice to a shout. "Girls, are we here to disrupt the gender binary?"

Again a tremendous roar went up. Ricce stepped back, laughed, and lifted her hands. As the shouts, whistles, and applause died away, she came back to the microphone.

"Tonight we are here to celebrate the renaming of *that*," here Ricce pointed violently at the Washington Monument, "as the *Pocahontas Bliss Clitoris!* We have renamed that cisgender phallus of the root binary: The binary of man/woman! The *Pocahontas Bliss Clitoris* is our revelation, our triumph!"

The crowd shouted, screamed, and hooted in a happy deafening tumult as a rainbow suddenly began to flow up continuously from the bottom of the monument, projected from lights at its base. Ricce tried to speak again, but the cheering went on for a full minute.

"Last year... last year – thank you ladies – last year was our triumph in getting a great American hero on the new five-hundred-dollar bill: Our own Andrea Rita Dworkin!"

There was more cheering.

"But now, this year, thanks to the passage of the Sangre Menstrual Act – a legislative victory won on the intellectual power of the *Manifesto for the Visibility of the Period* – we now have at the Federal level..." – here she spread her left hand and began striking digits with her right index finger, each count interrupted by cheers – "hundred-thousand-dollar fines for the misuse of preferred gender pronouns... fines for the meat-is-murder deniers... legal protections for the cultural misappropriation of locs, Bantu knots, baby hair, Senegalese twists, box braids, and cornrows... a new cabinet-level position to *hunt down* and *shut down* environmental racism... ten thousand national safe spaces for recovery when toxic masculinity overwhelms the nerves..." – here she switched her left and right counting hands – "and a new initiative that will provide a total of one hundred billion dollars in funding, for Trans maternity care... for elective nipple removal... for reparations for offenses suffered from bestiality deniers... for child Trans prosthetics... and for a fully-funded Mermaid Act that at last puts infant sex changes within reach of the poorest families in America!"

A thunderous roar went up, fists pumped into the air, and thousands of multicolored balloons went skyward from the crowd.

"Yes, those are the legislative triumphs. But never forget the real source of our strength: Our revolution in culture – our cultural triumphs. You have heard earlier this afternoon from many in the vanguard of crushing the gender orthodoxies, especially those in the Christian church. You heard Justin Bivalve from the Church of England, a leader in the struggle to promote experimentation with the many cloaks of gender identity in English parochial schools. You heard Sue Succubus and Mikael Negrom from the Church of Sweden, who at last have forced the adoption of 'hen' as the proper pronoun for Jesus. And you heard my own intimate friend Gretta Cloaca from the United Church of Canada, whose powerful intellect has deconstructed the idea of God, demolishing the walls of hatred that once denied Christian fellowship to atheists.

"Yes, the world is at last awakening to us! Our power has swept away old customs, old culture, old habits, and old ideas. It is a power that allows us to be gracious to our enemies..." – here she was interrupted by hoots and boos – "yes, I know we have suffered, my dears, but we must allow for contrition, for the truly repentant to join the new transformation, the new Union. We must, yes, we must allow for the purification of hearts even such as *these!*"

Ricce spat out her last word with a snarl, turning to face a group of people now assembling far to her left. These men and women seemed at first to be nude, but it became evident that they were wearing minimal flesh-toned swimwear – so minimal that the men covered the groin with both hands and the women stood in the familiar pose of one hand shielding the pudendum and one arm across the breasts. For all of them, the head was lowered and ashamed.

"These... these seem to have awakened to the fact that they have nothing to stand upon, not any *thing* to take hold of; that there is nothing between them and our contempt but the air; 'tis only our consent and mere pleasure that holds them up."

She pointed at the group, addressing them directly now.

"You probably are not sensible of this; you don't see our hand in it, but you look at other things, such as the good state of your bodily constitution, your care of your own life, and the means you use for your own preservation. But indeed these things are nothing; if we should withdraw our moral consent, those things would avail no more to keep you from falling, than the thin air to hold up a person that is suspended in it. If we should unleash our contempt, those things would have no more influence to uphold you than a spider's web would have to stop a falling rock."

One man was pushed forward by a burly man, shirtless, with a patch over his left eye – the same giant, Lagarius could now see, who had tended the security gate at Ricce's Halloween party. Another man, whose bare chest was tattooed with a man sitting cross-legged and having the horned head of a goat, came up to the burly man carrying a small can of black paint with a brush in it. Taking up the brush, the first man painted the word 'RACIST' on the forehead of the one he had pushed forward, then pushed him to the closest microphone. As the camera showed his forehead on the two forty-foot screens, the crowd began shouting angrily in unison, "Racist! Racist! Racist!" Ricce held up her hands for quiet.

"You, sir! Mr. Sportscaster, you used the 'N' word during a sports broadcast, didn't you?"

"Y-y-y...."

"Come on, *biao tai!* Declare your position! Don't try mansplaining your way out of this. Do you think that the seventy-five million viewers here and around the world are too delicate to hear the details? The evil must be purged and cleansed through your mouth, your public confession! Speak!"

"Yes, yes, yes, I admit it!" he blurted out suddenly in shame. "I said 'nitty-gritty' live on the air during a soccer match! I did! I referenced a black man; I said that Samuel Eto'o was giving a nitty-gritty performance; it was racist! Forgive me! Please, forgive me!"

"Do you wish the ugly word erased from your forehead?"

"Yes, anything, please!"

"What do you see at your feet?"

Before him was a heavy wire cable about four feet in length.

"Sir, do you want your transgression removed? Those you have offended cannot do this. You must do it out of your own sense of contrition."

"Yes, yes, please!"

"Sir! Pick. It. Up."

At last understanding, the man picked up the cable. He looked questioningly at Ricce. Then he took one end in both hands and whipped the cable violently over his right shoulder. As the cable struck his left kidney, drawing blood, he let out a yelp of surprised agony. The crowd roared in angry satisfaction.

"Very well! Girls, shall we let his stain be removed?"

"No! More! He's a racist!" they shouted variously in anger.

"No, ha ha, really, girls, we must be magnanimous!"

From the crowd came a groan of disappointment, mingled with boos and shouts of "Lash the bastard!" and "More!"

Ricce nodded to the strongman with the eye patch, who led the repentant sportscaster down center. He took a sponge from a bucket held by his bare-chested assistant and wiped off the word "RACIST" from the man's forehead. The man fell to his knees, shaking his hands clasped in prayerful gratitude to the crowd. The assistant led him off to the right, out of sight.

With the example clearly before them, the other barely-clothed members of the group stepped forward one by one, received the marking of their crime on their foreheads, inflicted lashes upon themselves, and gratefully received the sponged ablution of their crime to the acclaim of the crowd. A classical scholar was shamed with the word "RACIST" for citing Basil Gildersleeve, a classicist who had served in the Confederacy. A network administrator at JPMorgan Chase was likewise shamed for using the terms "blacklist" and "master/slave computers." A female children's fantasy author was shamed with the word "SEXIST" for saying that only women can have babies. A fired Walmart employee was shamed as a "SEXIST" for directing a

man to the men's room. A man was shamed on multiple counts –
"RACIST", "SEXIST", "ABELIST" – for calling Suey P. Kim, who had
recently sprained her ankle, a "douchebag," with his inscribed offenses overflowing to his cheeks, and earning himself three lashes to appease the fury of
the crowd. A woman named Mary Müller was shamed as a "XENOPHOBE"
for suggesting that migrant rapists are anti-feminist. For defying the
Wojcicki Laws of Diversity and Inclusion, a CEO was shamed as a "CAP-
ITALIST," as was Geoff Urban, in his case for not doing enough to promote diversity investments. A therapist for the London Tavistock Centre
was painted as an "ANTI-PEDO" for suggesting that the Mermaids organization was politicizing gender diversity in children, with the enraged crowd
demanding and getting five lashes for him. And a woman – a former Ohio
state senator who opposed a bestiality bill, despite its protections for victim-
ized animals – also inflicted five lashes on herself after being painted as
"ANTI-BESTIAL."

Ricce's face replaced the chastised foreheads in the two giant screens
either side of her central microphone – a face beaming with satisfaction.

"There now! With that the world sees what a furnace of wrath, a wide
and bottomless pit, is the withdrawal of our moral consent.

"But now it is time for us to delve a little deeper. We have renamed that
phallus of the root binary: The binary of man/woman! 'The conceptual
penis as a social construct' is proven! Behold our triumphant, revealed
Pocahontas Bliss Clitoris!"

The crowd cheered with exultation at her words, which were emphasized
by a flickering, dancing display of rainbows displayed along Washington's
stone obelisk.

"Yes, the *Pocahontas Bliss Clitoris* proclaims our jurisdiction over the
symbolic environment. But! But it is merely a semiotic for the great advance
of consciousness to come. Listen to me, *listen!* Tonight I have a greater
revelation for you. We must pass through two more states to reach ekatma,
the final state of Union. *Listen well!* From wokeness we must pass through a
dream, then through a deep sleep, before finally achieving it! Yes, girls, this
is difficult to comprehend. But we need not discuss postmodern con-
structivist/deconstructivist critical theory in relation to the Sapir-Whorf
hypothesis here. The difficult words that I will supply are not necessary for
your understanding. Fortunately for our march to Union, a way has been
made for us, a way that shatters the binary semiotics! I am now pleasured to
introduce Ana Coluthon, a being who has broken through with communication that is – I don't use this word often, but it is – *genius*. Ana is our
bodhisattva who remains to teach us that we convey meaning not through
reason and logic and the entire systemic patriarchal claptrap of repression,

but through noumenal empathy. Do you feel it, fellow spirits of the para-matman? This is prajna. Behold and hear!"

At Ricce's right, one terrace lower, Ana Coluthon strode imperiously to the microphone wearing red high heels and a spandex bodysuit of shimmering fire engine red. Her hair was swept up into a bun atop her head like the second brain of Buddha's bodhi. A soft, excited gasp swept through the crowd. Standing with her long legs apart, she closed her eyes. She pointed her fingertips to her navel, then slowly began to turn her hands palms upward as she hummed meditatively into the microphone. Her heavy brows, prominent nose, and square chin filled the two forty-foot screens. As she opened her mouth roundly to intone the Om mantra, the camera zoomed to her plump, glistening lips and the live pinkness of her wet tongue.

"Aaa," repeated Ricce. "The first syllable of wokeness, as light as the air!"

The crowd was now hushed as Ana more loudly intoned the mantra, filling the great space all the way to the shaft in the distance in its wavering rainbow of color. An eerie vibration began to rise within the half-mile volume of air as the crowd hypnotically joined in.

"Uuu: The syllable of dreaming, dreaming of the vivid jets of flame, that gush and eddy forth from this immense pile of earthly distinctions, earth's holocaust, consuming any man with the demeanor, the habitual and almost native dignity of one who had been born to the idea of his own social superiority, and had never felt it questioned till this moment. Dear ones, this burning they will call lawlessness, crime, and riot – *do not listen, feed the flames!* Ha ha! It is worn-out Trumpery! Now we shall have a glorious blaze! We shall get rid of the weight of dead men's thought, which has hitherto pressed so heavily on the living intellect that it has been incompetent to any effectual self-exertion. Well done, my girls! Into the fire with them! Now you are enlightening the world indeed!

"Mmm: The deep sleep at the bottom of the sea, after you have cast marriage certificates upon the waves, and declared yourselves candidates for a higher, holier, and more comprehensive union than that which had subsisted from the birth of time under the form of the connubial tie. Sleep beneath the waves – the deep, dreamless sleep that informs you that for you there is no law, no guilt that might inhibit the application of revolutionary justice – that lawlessness, crime, and riot *do not apply to you!*

"Until finally, with the last vibration, your consciousness rests in the final state of ekatma upon Mother Earth. The wood-paths shall be the aisles of our cathedral; the firmament itself shall be its ceiling. What needs an earthly roof between the deity and her worshipers? In the ekatma upon Mother Earth we have found the way to purify that inward sphere, and the many shapes of evil that haunt the outward, and which now seem almost our only realities; but if we go no deeper than the intellect, and strive with merely *that* feeble instrument to discern and rectify what is wrong, our whole accomplishment will be a phantom, so unsubstantial that it matters little.

"Yes girls, we have said, 'let's disrupt the gender binary.' And our ideal has been '*Man/woman becomes gender fluid.*' We have also said, 'Let's share, heal, connect, and get grounded in a space that is not dominated by whiteness.' And our ideal has been '*White/black becomes the warm tan of a single humanity.*' Have we not also said, 'Smash the capitalist one percent'? And there our ideal has been '*Capitalism/socialism becomes corporate stewardship.*' Have we not also said, 'Avoid the climate extinction in 2050!' And our ideal has been '*Exploitation/sustainability becomes geophysiology.*' We also said, have we not, 'There is no Planet B.' And our ideal has been '*Climate terror/climate justice becomes Gaia reverence.*' Do you begin to understand? We must make a leap in thinking beyond intersectional critical theory and realize that *those are all binary semiotics.* This is not us! We transcend the binary dialectic! *Do you begin to understand?* We are marching to a new unity, a new union, a reabsorption, the ekatma of a New Being!"

An audible gasp swept through the hundreds of thousands of people, from the terraces to the rainbow-colored obelisk almost half a mile away, followed by terrified murmuring. Ricce seemed puzzled. But the awe-struck multitude was not looking at her. They were looking – some of them pointing – at the Lincoln Memorial behind her. She wheeled around.

Lincoln was standing up! The marble had become alive!

The statue of Abraham Lincoln had risen from its seat and now stood as a white colossus against the dark doorway behind him. A blaze of white light poured over his head and shoulders, casting dark pools in the sockets below his brow and in the hollows of his gaunt cheeks.

"'Union or slavery,'" said the statue, shaking its head sadly, speaking in a thin tenor, or rather falsetto voice, almost as high-pitched as a boatswain's whistle. It was a piercing voice, heard clearly at the farthest reach of the half-mile of air now stilled and solemnly motionless before it.

"'Union or slavery,'" the voice repeated. The marble giant took a few steps in the silence, and stood before the columns of the Memorial and, now, in the two forty-foot screens at the terraces below. "Tonight I hear it again, this perennial confusion that has stained every society like an Original Sin. – As if to say that 'Union' were the negation of 'slavery,' that is to say, freedom; or as if to say that 'Union' somehow transcends freedom. And yet Union is not freedom, nor does it transcend it. For that confusion I stand here before you tonight to make a humble apology on my own account and to chastise its perpetuation by tongues filled with this blood sin of our humanity.

"It is true that I did preserve this political Union of two hundred thirty-six years. But I can no longer sit in lithic silence and do nothing to correct those who mythologize me, those who would make of me a god – a perversely inverted god, where the worshipers bend not to the god but instead bend the god to their own devices. The dead do live; the dead do listen. Whatever their everlasting reward or punishment for actions in this brief life, they have another: Their everlasting exultation to hear their names spoken in truth; and their everlasting torment to hear their names give wings to falsehood.

"I was not, am not, a god. Let there be no mistake regarding my failings. I was a racist, consistently 'in favor of having the superior position assigned to the white race.' Never was my goal that of 'bringing about in any way the social and political equality of the black and white races.' And while I may be redeemed by the fact that I came to hate slavery, it must not be forgotten that I wished those freed slaves to remove themselves from the polity of whites to Chiriquí, Panama; to Île-à-Vache, Haiti; to Liberia, Africa; and that my bitter counsel for what might become of those unlettered and propertyless unfortunates was 'root, hog, or die.'

"As one of your living historians has averred: You must 'accept that it was possible in nineteenth century America to share the racial prejudices of the time and yet simultaneously believe that slavery was a crime that ought to be abolished.' In this duality I am one with my opposing President and many of his generals, the noble, kindred dead from whom our 'mystic chords of memory' swell in a chorus of praise for that unique thing in all history: The American. Find that duality in your histories; but do not search them for syllogisms or dialectic; for history is the dark world of caverns steeped in blood and human failing.

"I have exalted Union above all else, and for this I beg forgiveness. Union is not freedom; union is not diversity; union is not the unique individual. Union is oneness, the conforming of the different, the standardization of the unique; it is Leviathan and Moloch. The root of freedom is the close, the personal, and the familiar; it is the love for one's own Georgia, Virginia, Vermont, and Illinois; it is the voices and dear faces of one's own kin, those ancestors of one's own unique identity; it is one's own flesh and blood made immortal in reverent memory, rescued from the devouring earth. This is the shared ideal that makes us all Americans: That the individual, and the familiar roots that make such possible, shall not perish from the earth."

Suddenly the colossal image of Lincoln shimmered in a wavering film of static, translucent to the seated, unmoved stone now visible behind it. The vapor of static seemed caught in an endless loop, breaking up in the air, silently mouthing the words "shall not perish from the earth."

"It's a hologram!" shouted a voice through a rubbed microphone that crackled and popped with interference. The face of the senator from Georgia snapped onto the two forty-foot screens, bouncing and weaving as it was followed by a hand-held camera. The hand of a business-suited security guard among the six who surrounded him occasionally blotted out the screens. Where Lincoln had stood, the group of seven struggled with Ricce's bare-chested, tattooed entourage and the screaming mob of women behind them, striving to reach the black SUV parked at the northeast tangent of the Memorial circle, just outside the chain-link fence.

The tangle of bodies, now animated by wildly thrown punches and flailing arms, milled down the slope from the Memorial, crashed through the chain-link fence, and became a full-scale brawl at the top-most terrace. The throng of hundreds of thousands of enraged women surged toward the terrace.

"Racist! Sexist! Tear him to pieces!" they shouted variously. "Kill the motherfucker!"

Lagarius, who had witnessed everything from the line of trees parallel to Constitution Avenue, raced then fought his way to the nearest of the three microphones. He reached it as women jostled past him.

"You are in great danger!" he shouted into the microphone, his voice wavering with adrenaline. "You will be trampled to death if you do not *sit down, now!* Everyone must please *sit down!*"

The microphone was knocked out of his hands with a squeal of feedback as women covered the steps, pressing forward. A snarling face came close to his.

"Who the fuck are *you*, dick head?" shouted the woman. She punched him in the face.

At that moment Lagarius felt himself crushed within a sea of bodies, all screaming, choking, and gasping. He felt his shoes trampled off his feet as he was lifted up and moved forward. He fought to pull his arms up from his sides and cross them over his chest so that he could breathe. The powerful current of bodies carried him up the terraces as the screams of rage and mortal terror became deafening. The heads of the nearest women packed around him bobbed limply, unconscious.

Then an opening broke through the tangle of bodies.

Twenty feet away Lagarius saw the naked, dismembered torso of the senator from Georgia, lifeless but somehow upright, recognizable only by the remaining half of his pale face and its florid cheek. He saw women with their chins dripping blood, their bloody fists flailing toward the lifeless man. One of them turned to him, her hair disheveled, her eyes bulging with fury, her mouth bloody. As the torrent of moving flesh swept him away, their eyes met. It was Ana.

22

The powerful and the notable will arrive at the church in the countless black limousines, eminences not just from America but from around the world. Attendants in white-gloved livery will move swiftly and deferentially to open the heavy black doors, to direct the black-suited mourners to their places, to immediately provide the walkers and wheelchairs to those known in advance to have need of them. They will enter the majestic building with its white interior and luminous clerestory, its many stained-glass windows, its image of Christ triumphant attended by two seraphim in the blue dome above the altar, and its life-size wood carving of the crucified Christ on the east wall. They will walk forward, where at the end of the aisle at the center of the church they will see the casket, previously blessed, covered with a black pall embroidered with one equal-armed Roman cross, and flanked on each side by three long beeswax candles. In the right front pew they will see the gray-haired matriarch, stern and unemotional, with the eight men and three women she has born of the Georgia senator that they will bury that day.

The woman and her family will have their thoughts divided in the hour to come, divided between the service and their remembrance of the words spoken by the elder brother of the senator at the previous night's vigil. They will see his somber and thoughtful face; they will again hear him speak in eulogy.

You are my kin. After his family died of smallpox, your great-great grandfather walked from my native Greenville, South Carolina to this place southwest of Atlanta with not a penny in his pocket. He was fourteen years old: In that day, already a man, ready to do the work of a man.

From the outset the congregation will see that a memorable service is before them: The musical setting of the *Dies Irae* of Arvo Pärt, without organ, will be sung perfectly. The priest and his servers will move confidently and in unison through the missal, never faltering, never touching the face with the hands. They will begin with softly spoken prayers at the foot of the altar, backs to the congregation, then the priest and servers will approach the altar, and the priest will lift his voice clearly to read the Epistle and the Gospel. During those murmured prayers the family will have again remembered the eulogy from the vigil.

He fished, trapped rabbits, and ate whatever peaches and berries hung over the public road until he found work at a sawmill. In two years he was manager of that sawmill; ten years on from that, he was its owner. He saved; he had but two suits of clothes and one pair of shoes; if he had an extravagance, it was for candles to read borrowed books by at night. By the time he reached middle age he was the byword of every man and woman in this county for fairness, wisdom, and far-sightedness. His son was an honor to him; the son of his son, your father, likewise.

With the incensing of the altar the Offertory of the Mass will begin, making the church redolent of the resinous and darkly fruity frankincense and myrrh smoking in the thurible. Finally, at the Epistle side of the altar, a candle will be lighted at the showing of the consecrated sacrament, and the congregation will take the Eucharist.

Your father was the richest man in Georgia, and richest of all in knowing that his abundance flowed not from coin, but from his virtue. In that sense of abundance you sons and daughters of this man are truly of his seed. Several of you so wisely administer a network of private hospitals that it leads the nation in providing indigent care; one of you is a renowned scholar of this nation's founding document; several of you are builders who are providing the best-valued homes for first-time buyers; others are mathematicians, translators, and scientists; and many of your children are similarly distinguished.

Not one of you owes a penny of your abundance to the favors of a politician or demagogue; none owes his place to shibboleths told to a tenure committee; none owes a thing paid in the clipped coin of lies, irreverence, or dishonor.

Arvo Pärt's *In Principio* will provide the musical setting for the combined homily and Last Gospel of John 1:1-14. The casket will be blessed again and the congregation will proceed to the burial.

At the graveyard the congregation will walk up a low hill by a stone path through uncut grass, and cresting the hill will see a broad hollow with a great sycamore at the near edge, the living celebration of the seed of the seed of dead generations, and starting from it, a murmuration of starlings. They will see the revered father lowered into the earth where, far below and unknown to them, lie the bones of families and tribes, pressed down with the dried petals of numberless spring blossoms and with the black moldy leaves of numberless autumns.

The unrighteous proclaim their baseness out of their own mouths by the envy they bear you; yet what a gall it is to them that you cannot be destroyed. Yes, your father has fallen, the victim of evil. But even with his death, which is the more substantial? – The glorious weight of the remembrance of this good man, or the hollow echo of clichés from souls so fleeting that you might pass a hand through them? They are as flies, creatures of a day, shadows of a dream; and he the granite floor of a heaven that is eternally unshakable.

The voice of Koyles Popoff, the Pulitzer-Prize-winning journalist, awakened Lagarius at 9:11 am Monday. It was an indignant, insistent voice, exaggerated now almost to outrage as the man walked among the televised ruins on the terraces below the Lincoln Memorial, now a trash heap of broken signs, torn clothes, and piles of shoes. The voice was amplified within the cavernous interior of the Walter E. Washington Convention Center where, thirty feet above, steel joists, plumbing, and air conditioning ducts hung in the black unfinished ceiling. Lagarius now sat up on one of the hundreds of makeshift cots arrayed in rows on the vast concrete floor.

The compact mass of stampeding women had swept Lagarius from the top terrace, down Henry Bacon Drive, to at last deposit him on the grass above the Vietnam Veterans Memorial. He had been fortunate in being able to lock his fingers at his chest so that he could breathe within the crush of bodies. All around him there had been less fortunate ones, scattered limp in their green and rainbow-colored costumes, some of them groaning in pain from broken bones and internal injuries. Sirens had wailed, and soon police and emergency medical technicians had arrived to move expertly among the scattered victims. Their quick triage had sent the seriously injured to MedStar hospitals north of town and in Georgetown; those who were conscious and apparently uninjured, like Lagarius, had been sent to the Convention Center for observation; and some had been covered with sheets where they lay motionless.

Lagarius and others in the rows of cots looked up to the seventy-five-inch television mounted on a huge central column.

"I am standing at the very spot of what may be one of the low points in our nation's history," said Popoff, holding a wireless microphone. He looked miserable in the cold, hunched down into his coat as the wind whipped his hair. "It was to this terrace that the senator from Georgia walked to taunt a largely peaceful group of young women, surrounded by his personal militia. This was in spite of being courteously asked to go to his awaiting vehicle and leave them in peace. Without apparent provocation, these hired thugs began punching. In an act of selfless heroism the women, all unarmed, managed to overwhelm the men before they could draw the pistols concealed beneath their suits - *all fully loaded, mind you* - to unleash mayhem into the helpless, unsuspecting crowd. Imagine it! - Unarmed women heroically flinging their very lives against an impending volley of bullets, sacrificing themselves to save the defenseless thousands behind them!

"And down here..." - Popoff walked down to the next lower terrace - "another act of heroism took place. Apparently some disgruntled male, possibly a provocateur from the senator's gang, rushed from the trees and grabbed a microphone, hurling sexist slurs at Professor Ricce. One valiant woman - we don't know her name as yet - knocked the microphone away from him and with remarkable quick thinking instructed the crowd to sit down, saving hundreds of thousands of lives from being trampled to death. This is the kind of people who make up the new movement led by Professor Ricce: Ordinary people who rise to the occasion to become American heroes."

Lagarius blinked, shook his head as if waking himself, and looked around at the dozens of rapt faces staring up at the television screen. Several women stood in the familiar pose with their arms crossed at their waists, then raised one hand to cover the mouth that was open in astonished admiration.

"Yes, in all objectivity we must say that the dismemberment of the senator was unfortunate. But we must keep in mind the context. These unarmed women were set upon by violent armed men and defended themselves valiantly with the only weapons they had: *Their bare hands*. The wonder of this feat deserves our admiration. Of course we can dismiss the conspiracy-mongers who have tried to fan the flames of sexist hatred by suggesting that parts of the man were eaten. The social media companies have been quick to delete the accounts of those who have posted such disgusting allegations.

"But just how was the senator able to mastermind this murderous provocation?"

The screen split to show images of the interior of the Lincoln Memorial alongside Popoff.

"There, there you see our exclusive shots before the crime scene was closed off, just below the revered, immortal words of the Gettysburg Address; the greenroom at one end... and at the other end... yes, there, the holographic cameras set at various angles and the mixing console. And there in the ceiling... you see the projectors that beamed the image, as well as an outdoor array of them along the exterior edge of the roof. Apparently the senator stood against the green backdrop wearing a suit of positioning sensors and a lavalier microphone. The cameras recorded his body movements, which were mixed at the console with pre-drawn animations of Lincoln, then projected from the ceiling to beam down the interior shots, then from the roof to beam down his image standing at the portico. - That is, until one of Professor Ricce's valiant followers sniffed out the charade and smashed into it."

The inset images dropped off, and the screen enlarged to the view of Popoff on the terrace.

"But what dark motive could have possessed this man, until last night a respected member of the Senate? How long were these sinister thoughts festering in his mind before erupting into that rambling, unintelligible diatribe? Until last night the man was considered one of the most thoughtful and patriotic members of the Senate, a man steeped in history and the author of a dozen books on political theory. Then last night something must have snapped, spewing out as a racist, sexist rant – fighting words shouted in a crowded theater – that could only have provoked violence.

"Yes, my fellow Americans, this may seem a low point in our nation's history," said Popoff, his face somber in the close-up that now filled the screen, "with over two hundred dead at last count, cruelly trampled to death because of one sexist instigator who unaccountably tried to project *his own racism* onto America's greatest President, the Great Emancipator, Abraham Lincoln. But then, we Americans are a spunky bunch. These women, these heroes, have shown us how to rise above the hatred. Let us hope that they or *ze* will *spark a national dialog* on the great issues of systemic sexism and racism that still plague our great country, this noble experiment in democracy. This is Koyles Popoff, signing off for now. Remember: Stay alarmed – and stay tuned."

The reporter's familiar five-word signoff had been doubled, murmured by some of the viewers who were sitting in their cots or standing alongside.

A blip sounded on Lagarius' throwaway phone. It was Ana, wanting to talk over Signal. He did not answer; he put down the phone. He still felt the horror of seeing her disheveled hair, her bloody mouth, and her bloody hands tearing at the strangely upright corpse of the Georgia senator. He imagined her now sitting on the bed at the International Hotel, tearful, remorseful. She would be wanting to meet him, either at the beach house or at the hotel. He could not bear to deal with her now in the hotel room, and although he badly wanted a shower, there was no need to retrieve anything: Only the cast-off clothes that Nigredo had given him were there; his personal phone and everything else were locked inside the Boxster in the parking garage.

He took up his phone and launched the Onion Tor browser to check his email. There it was. There was a reply to his "bread on the water" message sent from Las Vegas at Gelb's suggestion. He opened it.

Please reply revealing some information that only the owner of the files in question would know, then fully identify yourself. We hope to meet you in New York.

Another blip sounded on his phone. It was Ana again, this time with a Telegram text: *BABY! CALL ME!*

Lagarius returned to composing the email reply: '*Magnesium igniters* X'. *Carmine Lagarius*. He typed in the numbers of both his phones. He thought of what might be added, especially to clarify the meeting, but left it as was. He tapped to send the terse reply.

Another blip sounded. Ana's Telegram text read: *URGENT!*

He launched Signal to call Ana. After a ring, the random word pair appeared on the screen as she answered. She spoke her assigned word, "Spoilage"; Lagarius replied with his, "Vermian."

"Baby, I have to tell you...," she began, sniffling and ready to cry. Her voice seemed to echo.

"– Ana, wait," said Lagarius. "Dear, first tell me where you are and who is with you."

"I'm in the bathroom at hotel. Some girlfriends outside in the room."

"OK, listen. Lock the door, then turn on the shower and the ceiling fan. Then it's OK to talk."

Lagarius heard the shower's background patter, then the remote whirr of the fan.

"Baby, something's wrong," she began. "I overheard something very bad, very bad."

Lagarius had expected tearful contrition about the night before. He waited.

"Ricce was with some friends. They were talking about you – I heard your name. Then Ricce said something scary. She said, 'Lucky we didn't kill the bastard at the party after all.' You see, baby?" Ana choked, suppressing sobs. "Ron Peel was killed. But they didn't mean to kill him. They meant to kill you."

Lagarius let out a soft, falling groan. Of course! How stupid he was not to think of it. Ricce's dropping of her hand to signal to someone at the party that this was the one to be murdered; his switch of places with Ron; the easy mistake that beneath their hooded costumes they both showed an unshaven dimpled chin; and, yes, Ricce's astonishment on seeing Lagarius alive when the party broke up. But why "lucky"? Why was the failure to kill him now a lucky blunder?

"Baby, I feel so bad. I want to be with you...," Ana said, her voice rising sharply with 'you,' keening, bursting into tears.

"For last night...," she sobbed. "Do you hate me?"

"No, Ana, sweetheart, listen...."

"That wasn't me last night, not really. I felt myself huge.... I was a big power, like I wasn't me, but a big animal with hundreds of legs – the legs of all those girls; not my little voice, but a big roar. Oh, but I took a bite," – she wailed miserably and stamped her feet – "I took a part of that man like the Christian people take a bite of Jesus! I'm so stupid! It *was* me, I am so evil, I going to die and go into the body of a whore!"

Ana wailed inconsolably.

"Ana, Ana, listen. As you said, that was not you. You lost yourself for a moment. You must not blame yourself now."

Lagarius waited as Ana's sobbing died down.

"I feel so bad. I want to be with you," Ana said, sniffling.

"You are safer in a group. I am a target. With me you become a target, too. – Maybe not by Ricce, I don't understand that, but by someone – god, I don't know what to think. What – did Ricce or some of her group think that you overheard them, you know, when they said 'Lucky we didn't kill the bastard'?"

"I don't know. I don't think so. I didn't ask what they meant."

Ana took a deep breath and blew her nose.

"I want to be with you," Ana whimpered.

"OK, all right, just go to the beach house. I'll be there soon, but for now I have to go from here to New York."

"When? I can go with you."

"Ana, just go to the beach house. Go jogging on the beach, it will make you feel better."

"OK."

"And one more thing, very important. Do not check out of the hotel – I may need the room. Just reserve an extra day and then leave."

"OK," Ana said and paused. "You love me, Carmine?"

Lagarius felt the tightness in his chest and felt his eyes dimming with tears.

"Never doubt it," he said.

They exchanged their air kisses and hung up.

Lagarius looked ahead at the rows and rows of cots, seeing none of it. Did he love her? Of course he could not say otherwise in her moment of need. But the pang at his heart: Really, was that love? No, it was not; it was a great sorrowing pity for the confused, silly, beautiful, incoherent bag of longing that was Ana, who deserved love – love, her birthright and what should have been a property as inherent and unquestioned as gravity, the speed of light, and Professor Gelb's Epsilon, Delta, Lambda, Omega, and the rest of it – but wasn't. Love was the most vital human property, and yet a random elective for her as well as for those others on the National Mall: The tattooed, the pierced, the grossly fat, the syphilitic, and even those who would degrade themselves with animals – all of them giving words out of their mouths that they would never have spoken had they been born in a different place or even a few years before or hence – inflected noise, echoed from some catchphrase in a video or pop song or from somewhere, not meant to carry a thought but to signal that unfulfilled need – as universal and inarticulate as Ana's long mantra of Om.

Just then a nurse with a clipboard walked up among the nearby cots.

"Folks, if I could have your attention. Your row is the next to see the doctors. If everyone along here," – she gestured with a long stroke of her arm – "will please follow me to the waiting room. We're doing our best to get you back home as quick as we can."

Lagarius, along with about thirty people in his row, filed in behind the nurse. Like some of the others, he had only socks on his feet. After a few minutes' walk they went into a partitioned room with no ceiling and sat down on metal folding chairs. The long wait began.

A half hour later a blip sounded on Lagarius' phone. It was a reply to his last email.

Mr. Lagarius, I am the journalist who met Lucas Meeth, and who took his laptop for fear that it most certainly would have been impounded by the police. The analysts contracted by my employer, Taylor Caroline Media, finally broke into Mr. Meeth's email, in search of corroboration of the evidence of an imminent terrorist attack suggested by your files. It is indeed fortunate that you have emailed, as this now affords us an opportunity for you to make your case to TCM editors, who remain skeptical of the evidence known so far. Accordingly, I hope that you will reply with a simple affirmative that you can meet in the TCM lobby in New York at 11:00 am tomorrow, November 5. Please do not attempt to phone or elaborate electronically, as I and the entire staff are quite busy with election coverage. I also consider it more appropriate to relate personally the details of Mr. Meeth's demise. Sincerely, Arusha LePepeyon.

Lagarius read the message many times. He knew that he must suppress the temptation to email or phone in defiance of the clear instructions not to. It was frustrating, but there was simply nothing more he could do. There were no options left. Time had run out. He could only hope that he was wrong about the suspected date of the attack, sometime on November 5, Guy Fawkes Day, or that he was foolishly, altogether wrong about some impending attack, even though the absence of an attack would remove his only barter against going to prison for breaking into TactiFor. With sick foreboding he gave a deep sigh and sent the email reply: *Meeting accepted.*

It was after 1:00 pm when Lagarius, after a temperature check and quick palpation, finally signed the release to leave the convention center. A nurse had given him a pair of throwaway slippers, and he stood on the curb in these to hail a taxi in the windy cold. He was starving, but first he had to go to Alden Shoe on F Street. By the time his newly-shod feet were under the table at Plume on Sixteenth Street, it was 2:30 pm. Although it was not on the menu, he asked for rotkohl, a simple red cabbage side dish that he loved but could rarely find cooked properly. Chef Schlegel graciously agreed to prepare it. Lagarius began with poached Maine lobster tail in Thermidor sauce followed by the entrée of veal chop in red wine with baked artichoke and hazelnut, which came out with the rotkohl. He chose a glass of velvety intense Volnay to go with it all. He took the dessert of marzipan mousse with tayberry sorbet, accompanied by Grand Marnier and coffee.

During the meal he thought about his options for the four-hour drive to New York. He could have left now and slept in Manhattan, but he couldn't bear the hours of being dirty in dirty clothes. Furthermore, he would have to show his credit card for the hotel there, and there would be a rush to buy if he got his clothes the morning after. Also, he wanted to install a stash in his vehicle for the satchel of money and documents as soon as possible. So, feeling properly stoked after his meal at Plume, he took a taxi to buy new clothes and a leather jacket at Michael Thomas on Thirteenth Street. After that he bought cheap running gear and several screwdrivers at Walmart and went back to his car in the garage at the International Hotel to install a hiding place under the dashboard.

The hotel room had been cleaned and the bed made. Lagarius went for a jog around the National Mall in front of the Capitol, avoiding the reflecting pool, which was not visible in any case beyond the hill of the obelisk now to be called Pocahontas Bliss Clitoris. Then he took a hot shower, laid out his clothes for the morning, and was soon asleep.

❦

Eden Wiser had ample time to reflect after setting up his stake-out of Lagarius' beach house Friday morning.

He had rented a room nearest the beach house, in the hotel a mile south. On the balcony he had set up a land telescope with 60x magnification, but more usefully, he had dressed as a jogger and gone to the dunes north of the beach house to install a cluster of sensors: Motion detector, sound pickup, video, and infrared camera. Any disturbance from any of the sensors would chirp a notice in the small packet of electronics that he could clip at his waist, or zip into his jogger's fanny pack so that the sound pickup in the dunes could be heard in his earpiece. The motion detection, video, and infrared he could see on his laptop. In addition he had bought a National Audubon Society goldfinch sweatshirt and cap, in case he needed another explanation to anyone curious about the attention he was directing north from his balcony.

But after learning how to ignore the false alerts from the laughter and walk-bys of seagulls, he was idle, all Friday afternoon and all day Saturday and Sunday. He stretched out on his balcony with a blanket ready when his body went into shadow. He looked at the Atlantic through his sunglasses and thought.

Why were there not more resources devoted to this operation if Lagarius presented such an imminent threat? A formal court order could secure more in-depth surveillance, and a FISA court was a rubber-stamp authorization that could get resources immediately. On the other hand, if Humph and Beddoes did not want other parts of the government to know about their activities, could that mean that they feared a mole within their own bureaus? Lagarius was not being detained: That would seem to indicate that they did not consider his freedom of action a serious threat. In that case, what could he do that would not be dangerous in itself yet would simultaneously expose actors who *were* very dangerous?

As always, his thoughts ended in the reminder to himself that he was one step away from the highest power in the Senate on matters of national defense intelligence, that he was trusted, and that he could take that one step to bypass the inept Mr. Humph if he saw a true threat to the nation's security.

On Monday at about 2:00 pm he leapt up from his balcony recliner, threw off the blanket, and stepped indoors to his laptop. His sensor had chirped on the sound of a door being closed at the beach house. His video there, which could see only the north side of the house, showed through a window the silhouette of what seemed to be a woman changing clothes in a back room downstairs. A half hour later, he heard the sound of a sliding glass door closing. He took the laptop to the balcony while he peered through the telescope. In the distance a head bobbed through the tall dune grass leading to the water. Then he saw a beautiful woman in bright red spandex running gear, with a wire from her earbuds to her waist. He smiled wistfully at her powerful thighs, her long legs, the swing of her pony tail as she ran. He thought of his wife and daughter. He refocused his attention on the sensors. They did not indicate anything at the beach house. Wiser supposed that the woman had come to the house alone, although he couldn't be sure. After the woman returned from her jogging about two hours later, there were no signals from the house.

Wiser had just gone to bed when he heard a chirp from his sensors a few minutes after midnight. He leapt out of bed and opened his laptop to see several figures in shadow on the video – five when seen more clearly on the infrared, glowing against the black mass of the house. Oddly, he thought, they were not at the west side of the house facing the road, but were moving from the ocean, passing along the north side of the house to the west door. There was silence as they clumped together there, evidently waiting for entry. The bedroom light downstairs came on. He heard the door open, then the voice of a woman.

"*What?* What you doing here? It's cold. I'm asleep."

There was an indistinct reply, the sound of feet tramping, then the closing of the door.

After ten minutes there was a burst of noise as the glass door at the back slid open. Wiser heard muffled screams and saw in infrared a writhing figure held erect among the other five. He dropped his phone in shock as he heard the sound of voices speaking in Arabic, subdued yet urgent. *Damn, it might all begin to make sense!* he thought, as he picked up his phone and immediately dialed 911. As he swiftly put on his sweatshirt and jogging gear, he calmly gave the address of the beach house to the 911 officer; he said he was having a midnight jog on the beach and heard a woman scream, attacked at her back door; he said that he was afraid and ran, that he would run back. The voice told him not to approach, that the officers, already on the way, might mistake him for the assailants. Wiser said that he must hang up.

Wiser grabbed his service revolver, chambered a round, and wrapped it in a towel since it would not carry in his fanny pack and since he did not want to brandish it. He placed a second magazine in the fanny pack with the electronics and his FBI badge, plugged in his earbuds, and ran out to the elevator. As he ran through the soft sand to the water he heard the sickening sounds: Muffled screams followed by the grunt of a man heaving his weight against something, then silence.

On the beach Wiser listened as carefully as he could to the audio sensor as his feet pounded the wet sand, his breath heaving as he ran. The Arabic was louder now, with some voices subdued as they entered the house, returned with volume, and conversed outside, evidently verifying the cleanup of evidence. A hundred yards from the beach house he saw the five figures moving toward the water. They were moving not in the manic flight of common criminals, but with the measured swiftness of deliberate killers. He did not have a target, but nonetheless tore off the towel and fired a warning shot toward the sea.

"Stop! FBI!" he yelled at the top of his lungs. "Stop where you are, *now!*"

The heavy zip of slugs tore the sand around him. Wiser flung himself flat onto the hard sand and heard the trailing report of the AK-47s. The firing continued as the sound of a speedboat roared to life then faded. The firing stopped.

Wiser got to his feet, picked up the towel, and sprinted to the beach house. He ran through the soft sand between the dunes then stopped with his foot on the first step to the decking. There at the south corner of the house, hanging from the outdoor shower with its neck bent at a right angle, was the body of the woman he had seen jogging along the beach. He did not want to advance into the evidence, and in any case he was sure that there was nothing he could do for her. He heard the approach of the oscillating police sirens.

As he walked back to the beach he heard the sirens clip off to silence at the driveway in back, saw the flicker of their colored lights against the dunes, heard the slamming car doors. He kneeled on the hard wet sand, wrapped his service revolver in the towel, and placed his FBI badge on top. He placed both hands on top of his head and waited for the officers and their shouted commands.

24

A cold slate sky hung low over the Baltimore-Washington Parkway as Lagarius sped north in the Boxster before dawn Tuesday morning. He thought about the rather punctilious email message sent by journalist Arusha LePepeyon, clearly an Eastern Indian woman. He wondered how much attention the Taylor Caroline editors had actually given his files, especially in view of the distraction of the election season. Curious too was her reference to Lucas' "demise," which she must have either witnessed or come upon, since she took his laptop immediately after his death. It seemed evident, at least, that she was not complicit in his murder.

Billboards along the highway proclaimed the virtues of the several Presidential contenders, one of whom would be elected that day. Staring with blow-dried, telegenic earnestness at the drivers speeding past, the faces all promised to restore some vague greatness of the nation's past, or launch it into a visionary future greatness equally vague, or do both at the same time. Lagarius reflected that somehow all of that expensive greatness always seemed to be paid for by people who were not voting: An unborn future generation who would pay off the borrowing, or a dead past generation whose estates would be pillaged. And after all that promising, after the promisers had taken their turns at making good on the promises, it never seemed to work out. Promise after promise after promise, the destitute "gypsies" would still be wandering the heartland, the smaller cities would be abandoned as boarded-up ruins, weeds would grow in the forsaken malls and rusting factories, and the homeless and the destitute and the displaced would continue to pack the larger cities.

To perpetuate that endless fraud marketed on the glories of America's past: Was that the purpose of the danger he was facing, Lagarius asked himself. He wanted to save *that*? He wondered where he would be if he hadn't taken the discovered files seriously. Snow skiing in Gstaad? From there over the Alps to that Michelin three-star in Basel? Or maybe "down under," enjoying a New Zealand summer with Ana? Instead he had gotten good people killed: Lucas and Ron and, who knows, maybe even himself and others before it was finished. - All fallen to some unseen power that might have best been left alone to destroy itself.

As he drove he felt grimly sick, but oddly, at the same time felt a peace, an inner "cleanness" as he termed it to himself, a sense that he had done the needful - that the faint nausea was for matters outside himself. The anxiety that he had felt after his first contact with Beddoes - the feverish need to penetrate the duplicity, the divided motives, the whole house of mirrors – had been washed from him. In spite of all the powers, he had upheld himself.

He gave a deep sigh and turned his thoughts to how he would get his MV Agusta back home. Since Thursday it had been parked in the penthouse garage on Fifty-Seventh Street. He could have flown to New York and ridden it back to the beach house, but he didn't want the six-hour ride in the cold; and anyway, the Boxster had a tow hitch: He would rent a light trailer.

He drove. He mentally rehearsed his 11:00 am presentation. He thought about Ana, sleeping through the morning at the beach house, her mouth half open, softly snoring.

It was a quarter to nine when Lagarius sighted the toll booths at the end of Twelfth Street in Jersey City, where Interstate 78 plunged beneath the Hudson River before resurfacing in Manhattan. Ten-foot letters above the booths announced the Holland Tunnel. Lagarius checked his gas gauge as he sat in the slow six-lane queue. Ahead at the corner of County Road 637, the last crossing street before entering the tunnel, he saw the Full Fill gas station logo on the right. He wasn't sure whether the other stations along Twelfth Street would take cash, so he merged right and after ten minutes entered its driveway at the near corner of 637.

Lagarius went inside to pay cash in advance. He roughed the crisp one-hundred-dollar bill as he held it between his hands, then laid it on the counter. There he saw a clipboard, holding a receipt from Dark Lantern Petroleum. When he came out he saw that a motorcycle had pulled in front of him. It was a Kawasaki Ninja H2 R Arrow. The rider, a Japanese man maybe in his late twenties, had just filled his tank and was racking the pump handle, taking up his helmet.

"Nice ride?" said Lagarius.

The rider lifted his chin and gave a proud nod.

"And you?" he said, looking at the Boxster with a smile.

"Meh," Lagarius said. "It commutes."

The two men laughed. The rider straddled the machine and brought it to life with a roar. Setting the pump handle to fill, Lagarius went to the front of his vehicle to get the windshield squeegee but dropped it. As he bent down in front to retrieve it, his wrist came forward from his leather jacket to reveal his watch: 9:11 am.

At that moment came a deafening explosion and fireball from the driveway behind the Boxster. The motorcycle rider was flung down the driveway and across County Road 637, striking a traffic lamppost; Lagarius skidded across the pavement and struck the curb near him.

Lagarius lifted his head from the pavement, dazed, feeling that out-of-body disorientation fueled by adrenaline. Behind him the Boxster was standing upright on its front bumper, a rear wheel spinning in the air, wedged crazily between the driveway and the steel beam above the island of gas pumps. The blast had lifted up the back of the vehicle, whipping the body vertically to providentially shield the two men from the fire. The side of the station away from them blazed to the sky, and Lagarius felt the heat of the flames on his face.

As Lagarius shakily pushed up to his knees, a car came flying around the corner from Twelfth, turning right onto 637, missing his head by a foot. The right side of the car was on fire. Lagarius saw the crazed, bulging eyes of the driver as the tires squealed past. A cacophony of car horns klaxoned around him; he heard the thump and shattering glass of accidents from vehicles driven by those mad to escape death from the inferno. An enormous crash came from beyond the toll booths, at the entrance to the tunnel, followed by the deep bass sound of heavy metal bouncing on concrete.

He looked at the motorcyclist, who was sitting against the traffic lamppost, a metal panel about two feet wide. The facemask of his helmet was shattered, and a thread of blood trickled down the right side of his face. He groaned in pain, holding his right arm, which was clearly broken below the shoulder. The motorcycle was still running, but not moving since the chain had come off the back drive sprocket. Lagarius reached to the handlebar and switched it off.

"Can you hear me?" Lagarius asked the rider. "Your right arm is broken. What else?"

The rider looked at him, flexed his legs a bit, and probed his torso with his free hand, but moaned and returned his hand to holding the broken arm.

"Nothing. I think I'm good," he said with a wince.

"OK, hold on. I'm going to drag you to the other side of the post. It's safer."

After grabbing the man's jacket and pulling him to the shielded spot, Lagarius looked at his watch. He thought of what he must do, as much as he hated it. He took out his driver's license.

"What's your name?" Lagarius asked.

"Phil Tousei."

"I'm Carmine Lagarius," he said, holding up his license. He fixed his eyes on the man sternly. "Listen to me, Phil. I work for the government. I'm on a task force related to containing the terrorist attack that we have just witnessed. I must be in Manhattan in one hour. This will happen. I am going to take your bike for one day and return it."

"The fuck you say."

"Phil, look at me. *Look at me.* People will die if I'm not in Manhattan."

"Fuck yourself. It can't even run. Chain's off."

Lagarius took out a packet of one-hundred-dollar bills from inside his jacket, and took the key fob to the Boxster from his pocket. He put both on the man's lap.

"There's the money and the car. That's one day's rental."

"Jesus Christ, then. You're going to take it anyway. If you can string that," he said, nodding toward the motorcycle, "I'll believe who you say you are. – And give me your phone number."

Lagarius called the offered phone number, which rang inside the man's coat. Then he gently took the gloves off his hands. He pulled them onto his own. Then with the bike's rear wheel against his chest, he gave an adrenaline-charged pull of the chain, rolling it onto the drive sprocket. He pulled the bike upright, snapped on the engine, and nodded to injured man. He revved the engine once, then shot forward, zipping through the nearest toll lane.

Half-way down the slope where the six toll lanes narrowed to two lanes, Lagarius skidded to a stop. A dozen cars had crashed, and a flatbed trailer had jack-knifed into the left wall. The trailer was bare, with broken strapping hanging from the sides. In the gap between the flatbed and the cars, the flatbed's load of galvanized steel culvert pipes, each about five feet in diameter, lay in a line. Lagarius counted twelve of them, beyond which the tunnel lay open, with no traffic.

Lagarius revved the engine and angrily waved off the man standing in front of the line of enormous pipes. The man shook his head, waving his hands over his head in reply. Lagarius put his chin down near the Arrow's handlebar and twisted the accelerator down hard, smoking the back tire and setting the engine screaming forward at full speed. The man waved, then leapt aside at the last moment.

Lagarius counted twelve Doppler-compressed zips as he accelerated through the culvert pipes then burst into the open tunnel as if shot from a cannon. He opened up the Kawasaki Arrow as the speedometer needle rocked past one hundred.

❦

Eden Wiser struggled to suppress his exasperation as he sat in front of Humph's desk at the Pentagon Tuesday morning. They had met at 8:30 am to review Wiser's first draft of the report for the events of the previous evening at the beach house. For one thing, it was annoying just to look at Humph's tanned face – a tan that he had acquired in Las Vegas while supposedly waiting for intel on Lagarius' whereabouts. The awaited check-in by Lagarius into a hotel in the early morning on Friday never came, yet Humph insisted on staying there, convinced that the subject would reveal himself.

Humph indicated that he was searching for Lagarius in the casinos, but did not disclose that in the course of his dutiful searching he had lost over a thousand dollars in the slot machines. Equally annoying to Wiser at the moment was Humph's divided attention to his computer screen. Evidently he was monitoring a news channel, which chattered softly as they conversed.

"So," said Humph while looking at the computer screen and absently toying with a plastic bag of shell casings, "this brass you policed from the AKs.... You're sure it's recent? Not from somebody who aired out their rifle into the dunes for practice?"

"Well, no," Wiser scoffed, "and I can't imagine anybody dumb enough to stroll the beach with an AK-47, especially one still rigged for full automatic. The question remains: Why did five Arabic speakers descend on the man's house in the middle of the night and murder his girlfriend? You've got my audio record in the other bag there..."

"– Right, and I'll be the one who resources a translator. Look, Eden, I think you're looking at this too simplistically. You're making a suppository assumption that the girl and her camel jockeys are related to what we're doing with Lagarius, and I don't think there's a tie-in at all. Could be that she crossed some Middle Eastern mafia in a drug deal gone bad – who knows? How are the local police writing this up?"

"After an agency call to the police captain in charge, they're putting it down as a suicide. It seems that the girl spoke at the Sunday event on the National Mall, so they're saying she was likely depressed about friends being trampled to death there. Of course I had to reveal the surveillance, but I didn't mention anything about Arabic speakers. The girl's body is in the morgue, awaiting identification by Lagarius. We texted him a few minutes ago, but he hasn't replied."

Humph had stopped listening. He stood up at his desk, staring at the computer screen in alarm. It seemed to Wiser that the tan had suddenly drained from his face.

"Not that!" Humph choked out. "No! Just one explosion, just one!"

Wiser impertinently grabbed the corner of the computer monitor and turned it into view.

"Turn up the volume!" Wiser said.

The panicked newscaster was announcing explosions at gasoline stations all across the United States, which all seem to have happened at 9:11 am. A map of the nation showed red dots for the explosion sites, with new red dots popping up in the dozens from coast to coast as they were reported.

"The *magnesium igniters!*" said Wiser aloud, suddenly realizing. "Lagarius discovered igniters – they must have been placed in the gas storage tanks and detonated at 9:11."

"'*Discovered*'?" Humph shouted. "Goddamnit, he planted, he master-minded it all! He did! He and his Saudis!"

"What are you saying? You just denied such people had anything to do with anything. And what did you mean by 'just one explosion'?" Wiser took a step backward in horror. "God in heaven, Humph, what have you done? Have you let a false flag operation go out of control? Are you trying to frame Lagarius for all of this?"

"Get out of my office!" Humph screamed, red-faced and trembling. "Get out!"

Humph angrily swept his hand across his desk, sending the sheaf of papers in Wiser's report fluttering against the wall with its plastic bags of documentation.

❦

Lagarius immediately braked the Kawasaki when he emerged from Holland Tunnel, entering the cold daylight in Lower Manhattan. People were rushing across the street singly and in packs without regard for traffic. He picked his way up Sixth Avenue toward his destination at the Taylor Caroline Media building at 242 West Forty-First Street. At Thirty-Fourth Street hundreds of people were running in a panic west toward Penn Station. He turned right to Madison Avenue and proceeded uptown from there, turning left on Forty-Second Street. Near Times Square the milling crowd became impassible. He turned back and found a parking garage near the Public Library. He took a picture of the parking receipt and texted it to the Japanese motorcyclist, then walked west along Forty-First Street, ducking into doorways whenever a panicked group headed west threatened to trample over him from behind.

As Lagarius approached Forty-First and Broadway suddenly a burst of screaming from a crowd went up in front of him. A panicked mob streamed toward him, filling the sidewalks and street. He ducked into the doorway under the sign that read "Pho Bar." As the mob rushed past, an old woman tripped and was slammed against the glass storefront of Pho Bar. When Lagarius pulled her into the doorway, she looked at him with the wild eyes of an animal and began flailing at him.

"Let me go, you sonofabitch!" she screamed, then stepped back into the stream of bodies, which snatched her away into the swift current of its trampling, yelling mass like a leaf in a river rapids.

Lagarius entered the pho restaurant, and as the door closed the screaming din fell away. He turned to face an elderly Eastern Indian man holding a menu.

"Good moarhning. Seating for one?"

Lagarius shook his head, nonplussed at the man's calm demeanor. He looked around, dazed too at the incongruity of the Indian man serving in a

Vietnamese restaurant. A red bar with fixed red stools ran along the glass facing the street, and in parallel rows behind it were three more bars with stools, all garishly red. Over each eating place hung a string of red paper octahedrons, ending with a gold tassel. Four big screen televisions, paired on either side of the door, hung from the ceiling near the glass storefront, flickering with news images, but silent and captioned. The restaurant seemed designed to serve many people for a simple lunch. An Indian woman sat at the bar farthest away, enjoying a bowl of pho, and concealing her laughter at Lagarius' encounter with the waiter.

"Sir," said Lagarius, "does it occur to you that this city is under attack? What are you doing?"

"So it would seem. I find it much safer to refrain from activity at the current juncture. And in any event," he continued with a head bobble, his right hand waggling like a fish swimming toward the ceiling, "what is written on the forehead...."

Lagarius slumped onto the offered stool, and the waiter placed on the bar in front of him a dingy, single-sided menu. His watch showed 10:09 am. Only then he noticed that his palms were scraped and that the bottom forearms of his leather jacket were shredded. Mechanically, he reached inside his jacket for his phones. There were no messages on the burner phone. He reflected that since his warnings of an attack had been amply justified, there was no need to conceal himself any longer; he might as well check his personal phone. He assembled it and read the text: *Mr. Lagarius, the Virginia Beach Police Department requires your response to an urgent matter.* There was no text of any cancellation of his 11:00 am meeting with the journalist. He read the list of recent calls, several just repeated from an unknown number. Just then that same number displayed as his phone rang. Thinking it might be related to the text from the police, Lagarius answered.

"Well, well, there you are, Mr. Lagarius. You mad bombers are so hard to get a hold of. But then, you've had a very busy day today, haven't you?"

"Ricce?" answered Lagarius, puzzled. "What are you talking about?"

"Why, you've been blowing up hundreds of gas stations all across the country! How can you be so forgetful? The government has all the files on your dastardly plot."

"You had Ron Peel murdered, didn't you?"

"Ah, hmm. Well, that was a close call for both of us, wasn't it? It really pays to keep your blockchain up-to-date, as you well know. I mean, the last word was that you were a threat that needed to be snuffed, then poof, suddenly you become the scapegoat for the firebombing of America. Glad we could save you – until you check in at the Federal supermax prison in Florence, Colorado, that is."

"The beheaded Christ, with the Guy Fawkes mask - that was the block-chain key, wasn't it?"

Ricce began to sing happily in reply.

"Remember, remember!
The fifth of November,
The gunpowder treason and plot;
I know of no reason
Why the gunpowder treason
Should ever be forgot!
Threescore barrels - times a hundred - laid below,
To prove Uncle Sam's overthrow.
But, by god's providence, him they catch,
With Dark Lantern Petroleum, and magnesium match!"

"That had to be quite a group you put together," said Lagarius. "Who helped you?"

"A group that *you* put together, Mr. Lagarius, who helped *you*. The Muslims who were tired of the drone strikes on their weddings, the lovers of the earth who should see an uptick in sales of electric cars after today's events, the women and the others who are sick of the whole systemic mess - those are the key members of the new world being born before your very eyes. - At least they are the efficient causes."

"And I suppose Ana is part of your gang of 'efficient causes'?"

"What, you don't know? Far worse than her fatal insider knowledge was her addiction to the male-female binary, to that notion of romantic love that the poets of the new world will put an end to."

"Where's Ana? What have you done to her?"

"*Liebestod, E lucevan le stelle* - sorry, that all has to go. I say no more."

"You killed Lucas Meeth."

"Who? No, sorry, don't flatter me."

"What's the point of all this? - All this killing and destruction?"

"Well, you can't make a new systemic omelet without breaking a few eggs. That was Trotsky's view - piker that he was. But we are striking far deeper than economics and the class struggle. The coming change is so fundamental that you can't even see it - like sound and light outside the narrow band of human perception. 'What's the point?' you ask? What is the truth, Mr. Lagarius - *Quid est veritas?* Are truths 'metaphors, worn out and without sensuous power; coins rubbed smooth of their images, metal worth nothing of their stamped value'? Maybe so. But they remain the coin of the realm, and enforce the rule of the realm, even without their face value. Not only do the metaphors of language never attain the immediacy of the thing expressed, worse yet, they never escape the political bias of their coinage."

"So the laws of science offend your gender studies?"

"Mr. Lagarius, even Newton's laws of motion are valid only at the median scale of measurement, and only for a male-dominated culture that sees space as a surface for conquest."

"So nothing is fixed; there is no identity; everything's a shapeless blob."

"Exactly. Exactly so. And yet make no mistake: There are nevertheless those who shape the shapeless. We are overthrowing those who have shaped the current system based on false claims that there *is* a fixed nature. Their claims begin with the claim that gender is fixed: Male or female, nothing else, they say. Our god is the hermaphrodite Barbelo, mother of the Self-Generated One, not some 'God the Father.' We generate ourselves, our sex, our identities, just as we please. Our scientists will master AVPR1A gene clipping, to increase altruistic behavior; they will immunize the boys of the future world at six months and twelve years of age from excessive testosterone, the source of all the violence in the world."

"Good to know that murderers like yourself will be running the show."

"Mr. Lagarius, you haven't got a clue," Ricce sneered with contempt. "Let me show you the final cause, the Unmoved Mover of the world to come, and the reason your system has failed.

"What a stupid system you have built! Your paternalistic god seeks to reward good behavior with an afterlife; your capitalism seeks to reward achievement with riches; and the night watchman political systems of your founding enforced them both. But hear me now: *The enduring systems are not founded on male-based rewards for success, but on female-based rewards for failure.* God's intercessors are feminine figures who offer a way to overcome that greatest failure, death. Give a reasoned male refutation of socialism in economic tomes that would fill a library, yet the gnawing envy against thy neighbor's slightly better fortune will provide its confirmation; government will grow without ceasing because it is an Artemis at Ephesus – a goddess with countless swelling breasts to insure against all the failings of fortune, health, unemployment, inequality, and any imagined 'microaggression' or slight. You have built a system on masculine reason and will, and you have assumed that every voter can discern the outlines of its splendid architecture. But they can't. They rely on the emotional nudges and impressions of a handful of friends – not Dunbar's hundred and fifty, but probably six or seven, after removing the redundancies who echo the same media celebrity or pop wisdom: The same number that guides the flight of clouds of starlings in murmuration. This is the number that in the presence of noise and uncertainty 'optimizes the balance between group cohesiveness and individual effort.' The new system succeeds because it rewards failure with emotional, non-rational supports – the warm, honeyed milk of the feminine. Everyone knows that rewarding failure on the large scale means collapse, but they want it anyway. They want life without the Crucifixion, without suffering and tragedy; they want the unending legal exceptions for themselves, the unending cornucopia of state benefits, and the sweet kiss-and-make-it-better of an all-accepting church awash with love, love, love. Lecture all you like with your reasoned architecture built for the centuries, but we will collapse it in a generation.

"*Solve et coagula*, Mr. Lagarius! *Solve et coagula*: We will dissolve all the differences of sex, of race, of personality, of talent, and of wealth into one base metal, a common metal that we will re-fire into gold. We will create the golden coin of a New Being, a being of everlasting peace, love, and harmony. We have found the Philosophers' Stone! – And just in time to avert extinction."

Lagarius heard the soft click and dial tone in his ear. He put down the phone. In the four televisions above the glass wall he watched the flickering, silent images. There was Senator Beddoes, behind in yesterday's polls, but interviewed on two screens with the label "Comeback Kid." There was Koyles Popoff in another screen, and in another, Aimi Eguchi, the K-Pop computer simulation whose "life" had matured into that of a journalist, the chipper mindlessness of her delivery now mute.

The waiter placed a glass of water on the bar in front of him.

"Your order?" he asked.

"No, thank you. I must leave for an appointment."

Lagarius understood clearly now that Beddoes had spared him only for his value as a scapegoat for his false flag operation. The benign tracking would be over; agents would be searching in earnest to arrest him, possibly using his last phone call to find him, if the senator's two agents were conscientiously monitoring him. He removed the phone's battery and placed it inside the RF bag in his jacket with the phone itself. It dazed him to think that the senator had somehow enlisted Ricce in his operation – or had he known? And if Ricce truly did not know about Lucas' death, then were the senator's two agents responsible?

Lagarius had overheard the waiter speak the name of the woman seated at the last bar. He stood up and walked toward her. She was almost finished with her meal. On the collar of her white knit shirt was clipped an ID badge with "TCM" in large letters. Yes, below the letters was the name he had just heard: Arusha.

Arusha was zaftig, with a slight overbite accentuating the plump rosebud of her lips – much like Zareen Kahn, or *La Parisienne* from the Minoan fresco at Knossos.

"I'm Carmine Lagarius," he said, extending his hand to her. "I suppose we still have an appointment at eleven o'clock."

She gave a sharp laugh and covered her mouth with her left hand.

"Oh, my! Yes. Well, you have found me out - I wanted to sneak in a lunch before our meeting with the editors. I'm sure it will be a long one."

Lagarius stood there as if lost. In his ears rang the music of her perfect diction, the luscious fullness of the spoken vowels, the exaggerated labials. This woman, whose emailed message he had thought of as "punctilious," would be that wonderful person who spoke in paragraphs, he felt sure. He held his hand in the air between them - the right hand that had just received the blessing of her handshake, soft, and with the lingering faint scent of musk and sandalwood. He felt his face turn red, blushing like a schoolboy. And Arusha blushed as well. They laughed in embarrassment.

Lagarius was grateful that his burner phone then rang, which he answered without looking to see who it might be.

This is a terrorist alert! Beware of terrorists in your area posing as policemen!

"Oh, I think you might delete that," said Arusha. "According to the newscast, that's the robocalling, entirely bogus. The attackers have really been quite clever in spreading panic. Apparently each area code across the country gets a tailored message. Where it's raining the message is to beware of terrorists with weapons disguised as umbrellas."

She took a deep breath and put her nearly finished bowl of pho aside, then the saucer of fresh basil leaves and bean sprouts, and the tiny bowl of nuoc cham with julienned carrots.

"I must speak about Lucas Meeth," she said gravely. "Mr. Meeth died accidentally.

"I went to the meeting at his apartment in Hoboken well before the appointed time. He was unprepared, with his shirt unbuttoned and no shoes on his feet. He was a very nervous, highly-strung person, which I regret to say was not improved by my inability to use sign language. In any case, he was excited about having visited on the previous evening the Adam Perry Lang steakhouse, newly opened in Manhattan. Chef Lang, as you may know, is something of a craftsman who makes his own signature steak knives. Mr. Meeth had purchased one of those knives during that visit, and he was determined to show me this prize possession. Well...."

Here Arusha began crying. She took a tissue from her purse.

"- Excuse me. As Lucas ran from the kitchen with the knife, his socks gave way on the waxed wooden floor.... The knife pierced his heart. He was dead immediately."

She wept and shook her head. Lagarius waited for her to recover.

"From Lucas I knew of the likely involvement of the authorities, and of the likelihood that they would want to suppress the information you had uncovered, at least until they had verified its authenticity. So I dialed 911 on Lucas' phone, which was still open to take a photo of the steak knife, and I deleted the call history between us. As I told you in our last email, I took his laptop, since I knew it would be impounded by the police and held just when we needed it most. I ran from the building before you arrived."

"You deleted the phone history and ran from the building because you would have been held for Lucas' murder."

"Yes, of course. That is the most terrible part. I had to be deceitful, and run. But Lucas was dead, and the information had to be saved. I feel guilty, although I would have done exactly the same thing, had I to do it over again. I'm sorry."

Lagarius looked up at the stamped tin ceiling and breathed a sigh of spent perplexity, shaking his head. Lucas falling on a damned steak knife, he thought - what kind of world is this? He looked out the storefront into the cold November light where the screaming mob was rushing past, this time in the opposite direction. He looked at Arusha, her eyes bright with tears, waiting for him to speak. He shook his head in bewilderment.

"What *is* the truth?" he said.

"'What is the truth?'" Arusha chuckled. "You're asking me what is the truth?"

"Yes."

"Family is the enduring truth," she said. "Our very identity springs from family."

"Families die. Sons, daughters, fathers, mothers, and all those before them: They fall, like starlings dropping from the sky. All those people rushing past the window there - whether they die today or a dice toss of years from now - every one of them will fall."

"Yes, of course. But they aren't forgotten."

"Then memory is the truth."

"No, I say *family*."

"But what is that? - Nothing but 'a procession of phantoms, going from nothingness to nothingness,' as someone said."

"Maybe not," said Arusha. "Those who deny that there is something eternal in those souls have no more proof than those who say they live forever."

"The evidence is against it."

"The evidence *of this world* is against it, to be sure."

"Ha ha! Now you have another world, where you can make up evidence as you please."

"Carmine, really! - May I call you 'Carmine'? Of course you get yourself into mischief should you try to apply your hopeful conjectures to this world."

"But," said Lagarius, "if those conjectures have no application to this world, then what's the point? Either they have an effect on this world, or they don't."

"It is indeed dangerous to make too much of those conjectures. Confucius said exactly this. Better than extracting philosophies or moral systems from them, it is better to simply perform the rites - the gestures that express our hopes."

"Ah ha," said Lagarius softly. "Gestures without content, empty religious rites, like a Japanese tea ceremony."

"You can put it that way if you must," said Arusha, laughing. "I'm sure you might say the same thing about prayer, that it is a useless exercise. And yet millions of people are quite benefitted by meditation, which might well be called 'prayer without content.' I would argue similarly for the rites of religion: That its expression of our hopes for what may come after death not only comforts us, but also inspires us to lift the honor of our family, whose remembrance is the very intent of these rites. You have this benefit, even if these fallen ones should be nothing better than a heap of dead starlings. But the bonus remains: Perhaps our loving family is somehow conscious of our remembrance, and somehow has life when we think of them."

Arusha looked at her wristwatch and stood up.

"We have our appointment soon," she said.

Lagarius absently took a step toward the door, thinking of what Arusha had said.

"Not that way," she said with a smile. "This restaurant is such a favorite spot with the journalists that we have a passage in back to reach it." She chuckled. "My paternal uncle Advaith runs it - you just met him."

"'Paternal' uncle?"

"Ah, sorry," Arusha winced at her own offer of the needless detail. "Dad's Indian; mom's Russian. It's complicated, as they say."

Lagarius paused, looking from the bright November outside with its insane society, to the black corridor behind Arusha, suddenly thinking of his escape from drowning on the surreal beach in Miami. He thought of Lucas and his bizarre death. He shook his head in stupefaction.

"So all of this has been just a matter of chance?"

"Not chance, but lack of intention - there's a world of difference. The motives for killing Mr. Meeth were perfectly real, even if no one held those motives."

Arusha appeared before him as a bright phosphorescence before the black passage that lay before them, looking at him with confident, intelligent eyes that seemed to say that the fatal threat awaiting them was almost an adventure. She extended her hand to him.

"Come," she said.

The word shaped by the sweet slight overbite and red lips seemed to his ears like an incantation. He felt strangely bewildered yet exultant. Carmine took Arusha's hand and they went into the darkness.

Other works by T.L. Hulsey:

Field Guide to Texas Secession
(forthcoming)

A Birdless Silence
(forthcoming)

Amid a Crowd of Stars
(forthcoming)

25 Texas Heroes
(2020, ISBN 978-1-883853-06-8)

The Art of Dying
(2013, ISBN 978-1-883853-04-4)

Twelve Delusions of Our Time
(2011, ISBN 1-883853-03-6)

Heroic Tales and Treasures of the Lonely Heart
(1993, ISBN 978-1-883853-00-6)